the right play anthology

Clean Sports Romance

taylor jade   **donna elaine**

natalie cross   **t. thomas**

To all the lovers of sports romance.

blindsided

Taylor Jade

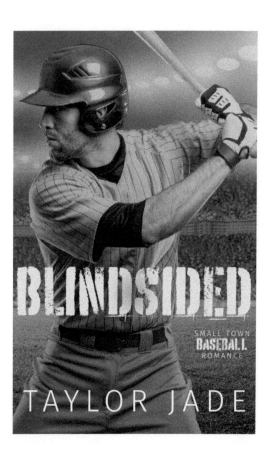

BLINDSIDED

SMALL TOWN
BASEBALL
ROMANCE

TAYLOR JADE

one

. . .

Tatum

FOUR YEARS AGO

MY SNEAKERS SQUEAKED against the dirty, worn linoleum tiles as I made my way down the narrow, school hallway to our lockers. My best friend was talking my ear off about her weekend, her mouth running a mile a minute. People milled around, laughter bouncing off the walls before first period.

Fear skated down my spine at the group of boys leaning against our green lockers. Ice filled my veins when gray eyes swept over my body. Millie, oblivious to my reaction, kept talking about the guy she had been crushing on for the last four years.

"He knew my name, Tate. He said, 'Millie, will you pass me a beer?' And girl, I froze like a complete idiot. Are you even listening to me?" She was talking about Friday night's bonfire, the one I had avoided despite Mille's insistent begging that I go with her.

I was barely listening to her, my gaze focused on the seniors of our baseball team lounging on our locker doors like they owned them. Zane Silver, Hunter Jackson, and Graham Jackson were heavily debating some game, shoving each other when they didn't agree, but huge smiles curled their lips.

Hunter and Graham were identical twins, their thick, brown hair brushing the collar of their t-shirts. Brown eyes similar to those of my dog at home flicked to me and Millie before focusing back on Zane.

"Oh, my God! You totally aren't listening to me, Tate!" she whined, yanking my arm back, making me jerk backward, my neck whipping painfully to look at her. "Tatum! What the hell is more impor-tant right now?" Anger sparked in her green eyes as they flicked to mine and then back to our lockers.

Tugging my arm from her grasp, I fixed my backpack, smoothed a hand down my now rumpled t-shirt, and glared at her. "They're on our lockers again," I whispered, and she rolled her eyes.

"Just like every morning, Tate. Don't let him get to you. He's just a stupid boy." If only it was that easy.

Zane Silver was, in fact, not just a stupid boy. In my head he was, but my heart felt differently. He was River High's star athlete and notorious bad boy. The girls loved him; the boys wanted to be him.

But before he was Zane Silver, the school's star ace, he was Zane Silver, the boy next door. The boy I used to walk home from school with. The one who used to save me from spiders and hold me when I cried about my daddy leaving me. He was the boy who knew all my secrets and the one I gave my heart to.

But then, his popularity grew, and mine became near nonexistent. Mom and I had to move to a smaller house, and we no longer walked home from school together.

Zane stopped asking about my dad, and the remaining pieces of my already fragile heart shattered, leaving me broken until Millie found me.

"Don't let him get to you, Tate. You are stronger than this. He doesn't always have to win." She linked our arms together at the elbows and tugged me along, straight into the lion's den.

Sucking in a strangled breath, I held my head up high despite the shake in my hands and reached for my lock, praying I'd get it open on the first try all while his gray eyes locked on me.

Twisting the mechanism, I tugged it after a minute, and, low and behold, nothing happened. "Still can't get it right, huh? It's only been four years, Grace," he *tsk*ed, my last name falling so easily from his lips. I cringed when he brushed my trembling hands away, fiddled with the lock for a moment before he easily popped it open.

I reached for it, my thanks just on the tip of my tongue as he snapped it right back shut. I gritted my teeth, willing myself to keep it together. "Better luck next time, right?" He laughed, Hunter and Graham joining him as I blinked back the tears already pooling in my eyes, praying they wouldn't fall over.

Did he know what today was? Did he remember? Did he care?

"Seriously, Zane? It's not funny!" Millie slapped his shoulder and shoved him out of the way when he erupted into another fit of laughter.

Glaring at the lock through blurry eyes, I tried again, willing the shake in my fingers to leave, and eventually, the lock fell open.

"Wasn't so hard, huh?" he taunted, and the first tear rolled down my cheek. I hated myself so much right then. For falling apart. For even shedding *one* tear with him near.

"Leave me alone, Zane." I clenched my teeth, nearly biting my damn tongue on his name.

"Why? Can't handle a little morning teasing? Lighten up, Grace." After grabbing my chemistry book from my locker, I clutched the heavy text to my chest like it was a bulletproof vest against his taunting and careless words. Slamming the metal door shut, I closed the lock and turned to Millie, waiting for her to grab her things so we could get out of there.

He nudged my shoulder, causing me to stumble forward, tripping over my own feet. Millie glared at him over my shoulder and hurried to get her things out so we could get a move on.

"Quit it. It's not funny." She pushed her glasses up the bridge of her nose.

I didn't have to be looking at Zane to know there was a smirk tugging at his beautiful lips. "Not my fault she can't take a joke, Millie."

Whirling around, I jabbed my finger straight into his toned, hard chest. I hated that pain radiated up the digit while he appeared completely unaffected. "Leave me alone, Zane!" He grabbed my wrist, his long, thick fingers sending sparks of electricity through my whole body. I wished every day I didn't still respond to him like this. I hated what he could make me feel.

"Now, now, no need to get your grandma panties in a bunch." Hunter and Graham chuckled behind him. Heat crept up my chest and into my cheeks at his crass comment.

Blinking back tears, my vision blurred, his haunting, gray eyes no longer hypnotizing.

"Did you forget?" I whispered, loud enough so only he could hear me. "Did you forget what today was?" His fingers tightened their hold around my wrist.

"That it's Monday?" For the briefest moment, I thought maybe—just maybe—the boy I had loved wasn't gone. But I was just a foolish, naive girl wishing for something that would never be again.

Another stab to my battered heart shouldn't hurt this bad, but it did.

"It's been ten years, Zane." My voice broke on his name. Regret flashed in his eyes as I yanked my hand back and turned away from him before I completely fell apart in the hallway. He would *not* get to witness that today.

He wasn't supposed to forget. He wasn't supposed to make my life miserable. Not today. Not on the ten-year anniversary of my dad leaving and never looking back.

But then again...Zane was supposed to be my rock. And he certainly wasn't that anymore.

Now...

Zane was just my enemy. My tormenter.

He stopped caring about me long ago.

two

. . .

Zane

PRESENT DAY

DROPS OF SWEAT rolled down the back of my neck, sinking into the thick fabric of my uniform. I wiped a hand down my face, squinting through the bright rays of the spring sun beating down on the field, which made it near impossible to see clearly.

The first game of the season always brought on a special kind of unease and excitement. The crowd sat on the edge of the metal bleachers as Hunter rounded the bases. A cloud of dust was left in his wake as he skidded to a halt on the last base, scoring the first home run of the game. Cheers erupted around the field as the crowd roared.

Once he made it to the dugout, he fist-bumped his twin brother, Graham, and then made his way over to me. "Congrats, man!" I clapped him on the back, and he nodded his gratitude before slumping down on the bench. A water boy handed him a green Gatorade bottle, and he greedily inhaled the cold water.

"Feels good to be up there. It's everything I dreamed it would be." He bent forward on his knees, his dark eyes surveying the crowd. "Almost feels too good to be true." His gaze settled on me, and I shook my head.

He always worried I pulled strings to get him and Graham on the team, but in reality, we had worked hard and gotten what we deserved. He just needed to believe it.

"We deserve to be here—all of us do."

"You're sure your dad didn't throw some money at them?" He glanced around to make sure we were still alone. God forbid anyone overheard this conversation and began to question if I'd really earned my position on this team.

I'd spent hours on the field, pushing myself to become better. No one was perfect, and there was always room for improvement in this game. A new technique to employ.

The work never ended, and because I knew that—understood that—was the reason I was able to stand here today.

This wasn't the life my dad had wanted for me. He had been my biggest fan as a kid, always in the front row of every game, wore those obnoxious baseball dad shirts, and even held up the signs that had my name and number on them, but as I got older, he wanted more for me. Wanted me to have a life off this field. Outside of baseball.

He wanted his only son to follow in his footsteps at the law firm he'd started in his early twenties, and being a lawyer was the last thing on my mind. Being stuck in an office all day or inside of a courtroom… Just the mere thought made my skin crawl and itch.

I lived and breathed baseball, and when I chose it over him and the promising career he wanted for me, things between us changed drastically. No longer did he support my dream. Instead, he stayed at the office or went home to my mother when I was playing. He stopped showing up in the bleachers, and he got rid of all his baseball support clothing and items.

He made it clear where he stood, but I still wasn't changing my mind. My happiness mattered, and this field, this sport, made me happy.

Shaking my head, I looked at Hunter, his dark brown eyes assessing my features. "He wants nothing to do with this life. I chose my path. He doesn't support it."

Hunter and Graham found it hard to believe my dad, the one who had been at every game and knew everything about my favorite sport, could just turn his back on me. But when I chose the college that offered the best baseball team and not the best law program, my fate was sealed. A tear ripped through our relationship, and I was beginning to believe it was irreparable.

"He'll come around," Hunter tried assuring me. I didn't say anything because I didn't believe him. "I still remember your first big pitch. He screamed louder than any dad on the bleachers that day, and he spoke about it for months to anyone willing to listen."

That was a good day. It was when I decided I wanted to play this sport for the rest of my life. The adrenaline that coursed through my veins after the loud clap of that bat against the ball I had thrown with everything I had still echoed in my ears.

If only he had shared the same dream, maybe he'd be on the bleachers today instead of hiding away in an office, ruled by the demands of clients. Never truly happy.

"I'll believe it when I see it," I grunted.

———

We won the first game of the season, and as per season ritual, the party was held at the rookie's house. Which meant Graham, Hunter, and I were scrambling to prepare our three-bedroom house for a long night of drinking, pizza, and video games.

Sometimes, being the rookies sucked. Other times, it was alright.

"Alright, don't shoot me." Graham dragged a hand down his face, wincing as he looked at me and Hunter as we attempted to organize the messy kitchen and living area that was about to be crowded with our teammates. Sure, our place would probably get trashed, but at least while everyone was sober, they wouldn't think we lived like animals.

"What did you forget?" Hunter glanced up from wiping the stove we hadn't bothered to clean in the last two weeks. Grunting, his brows furrowed in concentration—and probably a bit of frustration—he scrubbed the black surface, his jaw clenched.

"Well, I didn't forget… I just thought I had bought something." Graham scratched his head sheepishly.

The twins had been my best friends since elementary school. They were more like my brothers than friends, and despite their similar looks, they both had strikingly different personalities. Graham was the softer brother, super forgetful, kind, and never on board with confrontation.

Hunter, on the other hand, was ready to fight anyone and everyone at the drop of a bat. He was loyal, extremely defensive of his family, and most of the time, easy to anger. And usually, he was mad at his twin.

Hunter stopped scrubbing to look up at Graham, who was smiling at his brother like his innocence was gold and he could do no wrong.

"Please don't tell me you forgot to order the pizza," Hunter grumbled.

"Oh, no." His twin scoffed. "That'll be here in ten minutes." Graham chuckled nervously, and I grimaced. His job was to get the food and drinks. Order enough pizza for the team and buy enough beer to keep the boys entertained.

"You forgot the beer?" I guessed, and he nodded.

"Seriously, Graham?! You forget something every time we have to host! You had one job, you idiot!" Hunter threw down the rag he was using on the stove and turned to his brother, clenching his fists.

And...here we go.

"Don't worry! I'll run out and get it. I need to grab a few other things anyway. I've been meaning to go." I announced. Graham visibly deflated, shooting me a thankful look, while steam still blew from Hunter's ears. Graham—always the people pleaser. And Hunter—always ready to blow the world apart.

"You have to stop cleaning up for him. He'll never learn. He's a grown adult, Z." Dismissing him with a shrug, I grabbed my keys from the bowl on the kitchen island and left the house. Graham remained quiet, but I could feel his gratitude despite him never saying a word.

I hated entertaining the team anyway. Any excuse to get out of there was a good one. Hunter and Graham were social butterflies; they thrived around others. Me? I preferred peace and quiet. To be on my own.

I'd rather celebrate my win alone, with just Hunter and Graham, or with the girl I planned to spend the rest of my life with—not a bunch of guys who only wanted to get drunk.

But the girl I planned to spend the rest of my life with wasn't an attainable dream.

I managed to ruin that in high school.

three

. . .

Tatum

IT WAS Saturday night and instead of joining my best friend at some bar, I was picking up fruits from the local grocery store.

I'd recently started a new health-cleanse, a new diet that was strictly fruits and vegetables, and in the last week, I'd lost nearly three pounds. The diet didn't include alcohol, so joining Millie at a bar where we would drink our weight in tequila was not an option.

Buying fresh strawberries for my dinner seemed like a better idea and got me out of the house, too. Glancing at the twenty different strawberry cartons, I analyzed each one, looking for the biggest, juiciest strawberries.

"Can you hurry up?" a teenage girl asked from my right, rolling her eyes as she looked down at a list in her hand and then at me.

Good Lord. Rude much?

"I'm not stopping you," I retorted. The thought of smacking her crossed my mind. Man, if I was only just a few years younger...

She sighed and reached around me to grab a carton and then hurried off. I rolled my eyes and focused back on the strawberries in front of me, hoping my peace wouldn't be disturbed again by some bratty girl with no manners.

Finally choosing what I deemed the best, I put it in my shopping cart and then focused on the honey crisp apples.

Twenty minutes later, I was browsing the rest of the aisles, my cart full with more fruits than I intended to buy and some protein yogurt to add to my smoothie mix.

Just as I was exiting the frozen aisle, a loud commotion at the front of the store caught my attention. I quickly looked that way, my heart stopping and lurching into my throat at the sight.

"Don't move!" a gruff voice yelled. Panic seized my body, leaving me frozen, as I took in the three men running into the store, faces hidden behind black masks, guns pointed in front of them. My hands shook, growing clammy. I couldn't bring myself to look away, to move—anything. Something in my mind was screaming at me to get down, hide behind something, but I just continued standing there, making myself an easy target.

My body was disconnected from my brain.

Everything and everyone around me came to a halt. A child cried. Someone whispered prayers. And I froze as the three men walked briskly and confidentially towards the cashiers, guns raised at the clerks.

"Open the drawers now," one of the men demanded, his gun pointed at the male clerk. Even from here, I could see his pulse beating wildly at the base of his throat, his eyes wide with fear. His face was so pale, it looked like he'd faint at any moment.

"I-I can't without a transaction," he whispered, voice quaking with fear.

Move, Tatum!

My body still refused to unlock and obey my brain.

The robber looked up, his dark eyes immediately landing on me. I squeaked—the first my body unlocked enough for me to do anything. He lifted his hand and crooked his finger at me.

I was going to vomit. Pretty sure I was about to throw up everywhere. "You! Come here now."

Breathe, Tate. Breathe. Just breathe.

I looked around, seeing nothing but fear and panic in the eyes of every shopper around me as the man's voice echoed in the eerily silent store. Even the obnoxious music wasn't playing anymore.

"Did you hear me? Make your transaction!" He shifted the gun to me, and I willed my feet to move. My knees knocked together, adrenaline making my body tremble. "Don't make me pull the trigger. I didn't come here to hurt anyone, but I will if I have to."

Move. Breathe. Inhale. Exhale. Move your feet, Tate! I screamed at myself, sliding my heavy feet against the floor, my cart bouncing into a metal bin of discounted items, knocking it over in my panic. I couldn't breathe. Why couldn't I breathe?

The man walked over, his strides long and purposeful. His gloved hand wrapped around the end of my cart, and he yanked it forward, pulling me along with a gasp. My fingers wouldn't unlock from around the handle of the cart.

This isn't happening. I should have gone for drinks with Mille. I'm going to die in a grocery store. Buying fruit for a stupid diet.

"Hurry up!" he growled his dark eyes glaring at me as I shakily lifted the items out of my cart and onto the conveyer belt. "Scan the items!" he yelled at the clerk, who shook his head, refusing. I rolled my lips into my mouth, trying not to plead with him to just cooperate. This man may shoot someone. Was a few hundred dollars in a drawer really worth a human life?

The robber then pressed the cold metal of the gun to my temple, and I froze. Pinching my eyes shut for a moment, I willed myself not to scream. To not open my mouth. I feared it would only make the situation worse.

What had I done to deserve this?

"Scan them, or I'll blow her brains out!"

I was going to die. All because of a stupid diet. Because I so desperately wanted to be thin to get a man. To find someone to share my life with. A life that was about to end.

"The cops will be here any minute," the clerk whispered, just making the situation worse. I glared at him, fear gripping every cell in my body as this man held my life in his hands. Why couldn't he just scan the stupid strawberries?

"For your sake, I hope she's still alive, or you'll have to live with her death on your hands." In seconds, I was suddenly yanked backward behind a strong wall of muscle. My hands automatically curled into the fabric of the random man's shirt, and I held onto the stranger like my life depended on it all while fighting to keep my balance from the sudden movement.

"Shoot me instead." The man's deep voice, almost strikingly familiar, washed over me as I clung to him.

"How sweet," the gunman cooed. "I always love a pathetic hero. How about I just shoot you both?"

No. No. No.

Pulling the man back, a cry escaped my lips at the glimpse of red and blue lights flashing from the front entrance. *They had to hurry. Or we would die.*

"Time to go!" one of the other robbers yelled, already making a run for it. Fear, panic, and relief crippled me as I started to sink to the dirty floor, my knees officially giving out on me.

The man turned, his strong arms wrapping around me before I could collapse, holding me up as the tears flowed freely from my eyes. Sobs wracked my chest so strongly, it hurt.

I almost died.

A stranger came to my rescue.

I almost died.

I almost died.

Opening my eyes, blinking past the tears, I looked up into familiar gray eyes, my heart squeezing with a different type of fear. Oh, God. Zane Silver.

"I've got you. You're okay now. You're okay, Tate," his deep voice soothed, washing over me like expensive whiskey, his strong arms still holding me up. Those gray eyes scanned my face and then my body, looking for wounds that didn't exist.

"Zane?" I whispered, voice cracking with emotion.

He nodded and drew me fully into his arms. I sank into his embrace, crying harder now. Holding me firmly to his hard body, he absorbed my tears and trembles of fear. "Everything is okay. You're okay."

"We almost died. There was a gun. A gun. Pointed at me. At you. A gun," I rambled through my tears, my mind struggling to process and make sense of the last five minutes.

Cops surged into the grocery store, guns drawn, scanning the crowd for the robbers that were long gone. The crackling of police radios filled the air. People began sobbing and crying. Others were yelling. The officers immediately tried to contain the situation.

"You're safe. You're alive," Zane whispered, his gray eyes holding all of my attention despite the chaos around us. His hands ran over my hair before he cradled my face, his thumbs brushing the tears off my damp cheeks.

"Because of you," I croaked.

I was only alive because Zane Silver, the man I loved but hated me, had placed his body in front of mine.

Because he decided my life was more valuable than his.

four

. . .

Zane

THE SUPERMARKET WAS EMPTY, considering it was a Saturday night, and most people were either partying, at bars and restaurants, or chilling at home on their couches.

I filled a shopping cart with enough beer to sate a rowdy group of guys and skimmed the other aisles, looking for anything else I might need. I really didn't want to go home. I would have to at some point because the guys were waiting on me to bring the beer, but I was postponing it for as long as I could.

I'd rather be at a dingy supermarket, pretending that I needed groceries, than partying with my teammates. How sad was that?

My phone buzzed with a text, my apple watch vibrating with the notification from Graham asking for chips. Naturally, he'd forgotten the snacks, too. If his head wasn't attached to his body, he'd lose it. I chuckled and shook my head, heading for the chip aisle to grab his favorite kind.

With all snacks loaded into the cart, I pushed my cart to the check-out counter, but I paused at the commotion before me. Standing there, her chocolate-brown hair longer than I remembered from high school, body toned to perfection in a pair of tight black leggings and a soft-looking sweater, was none other than Tatum Grace. The girl I had crushed on for most of my youth stood a few feet away from me, her body stiff, eyes locked on a man dressed in all black, pointing a gun straight at her chest.

"You! Come here now." He crooked a finger at her, beckoning her forward, and she visibly shook, turning her head side to side, looking for help but receiving none. My hands tightened around the handle of my cart, rage pulsing through me. Just who did he think he was, putting *my* girl in danger? Pointing a gun at her like her life wasn't valuable? Like it meant less than a few dollars?

"Did you hear me? Make your transaction!" His body shook with rage, the gun trembling in his fist as he pointed it at her.

My heart sank, and adrenaline coursed through my veins as I ditched my cart and edged closer. Needing to save her. I couldn't let her go out like this. As it was, this would haunt me for the rest of my life.

I wouldn't have her lifeless eyes staring back at me, too.

I had spent so many years torturing her, trying to hide my feelings in the most pathetic way. All for it to come down to this. To this moment. I would have to throw away all the years I spent painting a completely different picture of who I was in her eyes. Everything I'd tried hiding from her would now come to the light.

But none of that mattered. It couldn't end like this. *She* couldn't end like this.

"Don't make me pull the trigger. I didn't come here to hurt anyone, but I will if I have to." *That's what they all say,* I bitterly thought. He couldn't even try to be original. And the way that gun was trembling in his hand—he was new at this. Didn't really know what he was doing. And he was just as scared as the girl he was threatening to kill.

She pushed her cart forward, her feet sticking to the ground as she moved, forcing her to drag them. She walked straight into a bin of discount items, sending it to the floor, the noise loud in the eerily quiet store.

I focused on the man's face mostly hidden by a black ski-mask, doing my best to make note of important facial features; the police would be here soon. They would need characteristics.

Blue eyes like the clear sky on a sunny, Summer day. Scar just under his right eye before it disappeared beneath his ski mask. A hint of a tribal tattoo peaked out from beneath his mask before disappearing into the hoodie he wore.

He rushed forward and yanked impatiently on Tatum's cart, pulling her along, her gasp of shock loud and painful. I barely bit back a snarl at the way he was handling her.

"Hurry up!" he sneered at her, his dark eyes drilling a hole into her pretty head. I wanted to strangle him with my bare hands for looking at her, for speaking to her, for making her scared. She was an innocent woman just trying to buy fruits. She didn't deserve this.

Her trembling hands latched onto the fruit in her cart, and she raised it slowly, putting it down on the conveyor belt. My heart beat heavily against my chest, every beat thrumming loudly in my ears. But my focus was honed in on them all while I kept check on my surroundings, making sure no one important was paying attention to me—like the other robbers he'd come in with.

"Scan the items!" the robber barked at him, his voice echoing around us. The clerk merely shook his head in refusal, and I clenched my fists, waiting for the robber's next move.

If that clerk survived this, he'd be lucky if I didn't break his jaw. The money in that register was *not* worth Tatum's life.

The gunman didn't hesitate to press the gun to Tatum's temple, and her body turned to stone. Lava flowed through my veins, tinting my vision red.

"Scan them, or I'll blow her brains out!"

The clerk blinked slowly at the robber while I inched closer, swallowing past the lump in my throat. She wasn't going to die. I wouldn't let that happen. Not a chance. Her fate rested in my hands, and I wouldn't be the one to fail her.

"The cops will be here any minute," the clerk whispered like an idiot. I gritted my teeth, narrowing my eyes at him for a moment before I focused back on who was important—Tatum. But it took a lot of restraint to bite back the urge to strangle the dumb man.

"For your sake, I hope she's still alive, or you'll have to live with her death on your hands." I didn't hesitate to move when I saw his finger slip over the trigger. He was willing to kill her over a few bills, and I wasn't allowing that to happen.

Wrapping my hands around Tatum's wrist, I yanked her backward with all my strength and immediately took up position in front of her. Small hands instantly curled into the fabric of my shirt, her fear seeping into my skin as she shook behind me.

"Shoot me instead." I looked the robber straight in the face, daring him. But I could see the wariness in his eyes. I was lean, but I had bulk on my side. Strength. Determination. I wasn't shaking and afraid.

I was an opponent he didn't want, and his baser instincts recognized me as a predator. But that didn't mean he didn't open his mouth and say something stupid.

"How sweet," he crooned. "I always love a pathetic hero. How about I just shoot you both?" Tatum whimpered and tried to pull me back, but I remained steady, glaring the coward down. In this moment, I was an unmovable mountain.

And I also knew he wasn't going to shoot. He might've shot Tatum, but not me.

"Time to go!" another voice yelled, and the man turned, seeing the red and blue lights flickering in the distance. He glared at me one last time before fleeing the scene like the coward he truly was.

They'd left empty-handed, and no blood had been spilled.

Tatum's blood hadn't been spilled.

I turned just as the woman in question started to crumple to the ground. I quickly settled my hands on her slim waist, holding her up as she sobbed, breaking my heart.

The cries tearing from her plump, pink lips tore my soul apart. Pain sliced through my chest as I did my best to console her through her fear. Blinking slowly, she opened her beautiful, vibrant green eyes.

God, I could look into them forever. Her dark lashes were wet from her tears, and her cheeks were red from fear and crying, those lovely, green eyes glassy. Even in such a fragile state, she was the definition of raw beauty.

"I've got you. You're okay now. You're okay, Tate." I looked over her face, then her body, checking even though I knew she was okay. My adrenaline faded, and I began to shake as I went over the last five minutes in my head.

"Zane?" she cried, her angelic voice breaking on my name.

"Everything is okay. You're okay." I need to reassure her and myself because I could have lost her. The girl I wanted for as long as I could remember was standing in my arms, but she was nearly shot right in front of me. I was given a second chance—a second chance to win her over the right way. To right the wrongs of the past and prove to her I could be the man she needed me to be this time.

I was no longer a kid. I was a man who knew what he wanted. And I was going to go after it.

I wasn't going to mess it up this time. I was going to fight. I was going to show her the man I had become in the last four years. I wasn't a kid afraid of loving a girl anymore.

I was a man looking for the woman I wanted to spend the rest of my life with.

"We almost died. There was a gun. A gun. Pointed at me. At you. A gun," she cried, her words incoherent as the police raided the supermarket, coming to our rescue almost too late. I barely heard the sounds of everyone beginning to panic, crying and yelling, and the police officers trying to contain the situation.

"You're safe. You're alive," I whispered, pressing a kiss to her forehead. I ran my hands over her hair before bringing them to her sweet face, cradling her damp cheeks in my hands. Using my thumbs, I brushed some of her tears away, but more only fell to replace the ones I stole.

"Because of you," she whispered back, her voice shaky and trembling.

Before I could say a word, two police officers strode up to us, wanting our statements. They wanted to question us in private, but I wasn't allowing that to happen. Tatum was a mess, her words almost incoherent through her tears and sobs. I did my best to console her while I gave my statement and whatever characteristics I remembered from the robber who'd held Tatum at gunpoint.

"Tate," I murmured as I led her to her sedan. She wasn't in any state to drive. She was still shaky, and I could see exhaustion weighing down her shoulders. Tiredness lingered in her green eyes as she looked up.

"Thank you. Thank you, Zane." She looked away before she finished speaking, focusing her green eyes on her car.

"What are you doing tonight?" I blurted before I could stop myself. But I didn't regret my question.

For me, there was no more waiting around. I wanted her as mine. I was done wasting time. I just needed to convince her of how I truly felt.

She snapped her head in my direction, and I smirked despite the situation we'd just left and the crazy, nightmarish night we'd just experienced together. A night that bonded us in a way we could never ignore.

"Me? Going home and thanking God that I am alive," she said softly, not an ounce of teasing in her words. She truly meant what she said. My heart clenched in my chest for her and everything she'd gone through tonight.

"How about some pizza and we thank Him together?" She bit her lip and started to shake her head. A lump formed in my throat, and I roughly cleared it. I wasn't letting her walk away tonight. "My treat," I coaxed, and she sighed before looking back at her sedan for a moment.

She was going to deny me. I was sure of it. I couldn't expect this night and our trauma bond to suddenly make her want to be around me.

So, I was surprised when she quietly said, "Come to my place and we can order something."

five

· · ·

Tatum

COME *to my place and we can order something.*

What had I been *thinking* inviting Zane to my apartment?

Clearly, I hadn't been thinking at all. Zane was the *enemy*. He'd turned his back on me years ago. Chose his popularity over our friendship and everything we'd shared together.

Yet, here I was, inviting him to my place like we were just long lost friends.

Clenching the steering wheel in a death grip, I checked my rearview mirror for the tenth time.

Zane's black Jeep Gladiator was still tailing me, and if I stared long enough, I thought I could make out his cocky grin. But I had to be crazy, right? Because who could smile at all after the night we'd just had?

Did I clean the kitchen before I left?

Did I make my bed?

God, were my floors a mess? Did they need to be vacuumed?

I hated this side of me. The side that obsessed over every little thing. The anxiety that riddled my day-to-day life and activities. Why should I care what Zane thought of my apartment? I didn't know, but I cared all the same.

Pulling into the small apartment community I lived in, I parked in my designated spot and watched through the back window as Zane easily found the guest parking.

Drumming my shaking fingers against the wheel, I forced myself to suck in some deep breaths and get my racing heart under control. Once my trembling had eased, I turned the car off and exited the vehicle. *It's just Zane Silver, a guy who used to bully you in high school.* He's not that person. He could be. But a bully wouldn't try to save me, would he?

What on Earth was I thinking inviting him of all people to my tiny apartment for pizza? It was official. It was no longer a question. I'd officially lost my mind tonight during that attempted robbery.

Zane exited his truck with the same confidence he used to waltz around high school with, and my nervous heart fluttered against my breastbone. I so wasn't prepared for this. I crossed my shaking arms over my chest, trying to exude a little confidence that I definitely wasn't feeling.

Why did he have to be there today? I wasn't ungrateful, but his presence combined with the night I'd had was leading me to make some screwy decisions.

"You've got that look on your face." His lips tilted in the smallest smirk, and my heart stopped in my chest. Why did he still get to me like this? "The same one from high school—you pinch your brows, bite your bottom lip, and your eyes glow with hatred."

He stopped at my trunk and waited for me to make my way to him. "I don't know what you're talking about," I grumbled as I *slowly* made my way closer. "This is my face. If you don't like it, then don't look at it." He chuckled and shook his head at me, amusement lingering in his eyes. But I could see the lingering exhaustion there that came with the crash of an adrenaline rush.

"Alright—no need to be so defensive, Tate," he said as I led him toward my apartment building. "Not trying to make fun of you, kitten. Put the claws away." I stopped and whirled around, causing him to bump into me.

"I knew it was too good to be true." I jabbed my finger against his hard, toned chest. "You haven't changed at all, have you?" I waited for his cocky response, all while my brain short-circuited from our proximity.

"Oh, I've changed, baby. Might want to get me inside your apartment before I show the whole parking lot." He wiggled his brows, and I scowled. *Men.*

"Shut up! Stop that, Zane. Don't be a jerk." I stormed the rest of the way to my apartment building and stomped down the hall to the glass door where I buzzed us in, then walked as fast my short legs could carry me down the carpeted hallway.

Elton John was blaring from my neighbor's door, and the heavy stench of marijuana floated into the hallway. Katie's on-and-off boyfriend must have ended things again. It was a vicious, rough cycle she continued to put herself through when she could just find someone better.

I didn't glance behind me at Zane as I stuck my key in the lock and fidgeted with it until the lock turned. I jiggled the doorknob until it opened. "Looks like you need some maintenance," he mumbled behind me.

At least he didn't make a stupid joke about how I'd always struggled with locks. He loved to get on my nerves about my locker when we were in high school.

"It's fine."

"Have you always been this feisty, Tate, or is it the new you? I don't remember you having claws in high school." He followed me into the small apartment, kicking off his sneakers at the door where my runners were neatly tucked into the corner.

He noticed.

He turned to where I was still standing at the door, holding it open like a damn idiot. clenching my jaw, I quickly closed it so I wouldn't look stupider than I already was.

"I learned to stand up for myself. No one was going to do it for me," I muttered as I kicked off my own shoes. Double checking that I threaded the deadbolt, I headed into the kitchen and went straight for the fridge, praying for a cold beer or two.

I had quit drinking a month ago, part of the new diet I started with Millie. I had at least lasted longer than her, but tonight, I needed something to numb my nerves. I didn't want stupid fruit and veggies. I didn't want water. I wanted beer and greasy pizza.

Finding two beers in the fridge, I offered one to Zane, who took both from me and popped the caps effortlessly. He handed one of the bottles back to me wordlessly. Bringing the cold lip of the bottle to my lips, I took a long pull, the cold liquid racing down my throat.

Yep. This was exactly what I needed.

I could get through tonight. Zane and I weren't in high school anymore. We weren't enemies. We were just old classmates who nearly died in a shooting.

I nearly died tonight.

Taking a shaky step back, I leaned against the counter, letting it take my weight. I suddenly felt weak, the exhaustion really making itself known.

"You're looking a little pale there, Tate," Zane noticed, his gray eyes studying me. Concern washed over his features, and the fingers of his free hand twitched at his side.

"I nearly died tonight," I muttered, reaching up to rub at my forehead.

"But you didn't."

"I had a gun held up to my head," I whispered, tears blurring my vision. I sniffled. "I just wanted to get some fruit. I didn't do anything wrong." The first hot tear rolled down my cheek. "Why did they pick me? Why couldn't I just move? Why did I have to stand there like an idiot?

Zane placed his bottle down on the counter with a loud clank and closed the space between us. Taking my bottle from my shaking hand, he set it down behind me. His scent crowded me, his gray eyes sweeping over my features, his big body over-whelming. My lips trembled as I tried to hold back my tears. I was so tired. I didn't want to cry again.

"I'm out of my league a little here, Tate. Tell me if this is okay?" His large, tan hands settled on my waist, his heat sinking through the thin layer of my leggings. I nodded, swallowing past the lump in my throat. At that moment, I didn't care about our past. I didn't care about all of my unanswered questions. I just needed comfort. To be held. To know that everything would be okay.

"You weren't picked," Zane rasped, his thumbs brushing under my shirt to rub the skin of my waist. I shivered. "He didn't know you. You were just in the wrong place at the wrong time, but it's okay because I was there." He ducked his head, forcing our gazes to lock. "I was there, kitten. And I know we had a rocky past, but I wasn't going to let anything happen to you, Tatum. I couldn't stand back and watch you get hurt."

Dropping my forehead to his hard chest, I let the tears fall as the night's events crashed into me. His strong, lean arms wrapped around me, one hand holding the back of my head, his other arm banded tight around me. Our bodies were flush, and I clung to him, seeking out his heat and his comfort and his security.

"Why?" I croaked.

Zane drew in a deep breath, and raggedly, he whispered, "I don't want to have any more regrets with you."

six

. . .

Zane

TATUM YAWNED, her green eyes shutting for a moment as she leaned her head against the comfy, back cushion of the couch. Concerned, I quickly finished putting in our order for pizza at the closest pizza spot to her house before turning to give her my attention again. I needed to think of a way to distract her. Otherwise, in pure Tatum style, she'd dwell on what happened tonight. And after what she'd just gone through, it was the last thing she needed.

"Still prefer ham with tomatoes, onion, and bell pepper, right?" I asked her. I mean, I guessed it was a little too late to ask her in case her tastes had changed considering I'd already put the order in, but I could always quickly cancel it and put another one in.

There wasn't much I wouldn't do for this woman.

She opened her tired eyes, her gaze roaming over my face, something akin to nostalgia lingering in them. "You remember?"

I roughly cleared my throat, suddenly overcome with sadness. I didn't want her to see it though. She didn't need my feelings right now on top of everything else. "Tatum, kitten, I may have been a world-class jerk, but I never forgot a single thing about you."

Her throat bobbed as she swallowed—like she didn't know what to do with what I'd just told her. And I couldn't really expect her to believe me. I mean, I *had* turned my back on her because I couldn't hide what I felt for her anymore. If I'd continued being her friend, I would have screwed everything up, and we would have lost each other anyway. Every single day I'd spent in her presence had pushed me closer and closer to blurting my feelings for her.

And she didn't reciprocate them. She'd made that clear.

It was easier to pretend I hated her. That I couldn't stand being in her presence. It was easier to taunt her for the things I actually adored about her. Always struggling with locks? How in tune to her emotions she was? I *loved* those things. They made her unique.

They made her Tatum. *My* Tatum.

She roughly cleared her throat and grabbed the TV remote, pressing play on the movie like she needed *something* to distract her from the turn our conversation had taken. I didn't say another word, not wanting to push her too much, too soon. She needed time to cope. Not only with my reappearance in her life tonight and my 180-degree change from who she knew me as, but she'd been held at gunpoint tonight. A mere couple of hours ago, she'd thought she was going to die.

The movie was just beginning to get good when a knock sounded on her apartment door. She moved to get up, but I waved at her to remain sitting as I stood to my feet. "I've got it, kitten," I told her as I strode to the door.

When I opened it, a young girl was standing there, probably around eighteen or nineteen. She was holding the pizza and breadsticks I'd ordered. She beamed at me, her eyes lighting up. "Oh, my God! You're Zane Silver!" she squealed.

I grunted. I hated this about being pro. It'd been bad in college, but now that I was in the leagues, it was all the time. "Pizza?" I asked.

She flushed. "Oh. Right." She quickly handed the boxes to me. "Can I get an autograph?" she asked, batting her fake eyelashes at me.

"Another time," I told her evasively, my voice sounding bored to my own ears. Her smile fell, but I couldn't bring myself to care. Tonight had been absolutely insane; I wasn't in the mood for baseball bunnies. And the only woman I wanted to smile at me was lost inside her head and treading on eggshells around me.

I closed the door and headed back to the living room, setting the pizza box and the breadsticks on the coffee table. "Plates?" I asked Tate when she sat up straighter, her rumbling stomach audible to my own ears, even from where I was standing on the opposite side of the coffee table. That pretty blush I loved stained her pale cheeks right after, finally giving her some color. She'd been pale all evening, and I was growing increasingly worried about her.

"Cabinet above the Keurig," she told me as she opened the pizza box. "Thank you for ordering food," she said as I headed into the kitchen.

I smiled at her over my shoulder, enjoying the way her pupils dilated the tiniest bit and her sweet mouth parted. God, I couldn't wait to kiss her. To taste her.

I bet she was as sweet as her personality.

My tastebuds tingled at the mere thought of claiming her mouth.

I grabbed two plates from the cabinet she directed me to before stopping at the fridge. "What do you want to drink?" I called as I opened the fridge, grabbing a beer for myself.

"Water," she called back. "Thanks."

I headed into the living room with two plates, a beer, and a bottle of water. After unscrewing her lid —because God knew she struggled with opening anything—I set her water in front of her before placing two slices of pizza on her plate as well as a breadstick and her own dipping sauce. If she still had the same tendencies that she did when we were kids, she'd need a whole cup of marinara sauce to herself.

I used to tease her about it all the time. A fond smile touched my lips at the memory.

"What are you smiling about?" she asked after she chewed her first bite of pizza.

I chuckled. "How much marinara sauce you used to eat," I told her honestly.

She shrugged. "I like marinara sauce." Surprising me, she stuck her tongue out at me. I barked out a laugh. I'd missed this side of her so much. "Don't judge my eating habits."

I flashed her a smirk. "Never, kitten."

———

I was dozing off, the second movie Tate put on boring me half to death, when Tatum's scream echoed throughout the apartment. I bolted to my feet at the same moment she jerked awake, sobs tearing from her throat, tears streaking down her cheeks as they poured from her haunted, green eyes.

The look in them left my soul feeling vacant. Tonight would haunt her for a long time to come.

"Kitten, I'm here," I rasped as I settled back down on the couch. Immediately, I drew her into my arms and gently rocked her side to side, peppering kisses to her damp cheeks and her forehead. "Breathe, kitten. It's going to be okay. You're safe now. I won't ever let anything happen to you."

Her fingers were twisted into my shirt, stretching the material, but I didn't care. Turning her head, she burrowed her face in the curve of my neck and continued to cry, her body trembling in my arms. I tightened my hold on her, wishing I could wipe the grocery store part of the night from her mind, but I couldn't.

I couldn't, and I hated it.

So, I did what I knew I *could* do, which was keep rocking her, whispering soothing words to her, and keeping my hold on her tight to keep her grounded. Her tears eventually slowed, and before long, her breathing regulated. She slumped in my arms, relying on me to support her weight, which I certainly didn't mind.

Easing to the edge of the couch, I slowly stood to my feet with her cradled against my chest. She tightened her hold on my shirt. I brushed my lips to her hair. "I've got you," I whispered.

She made a small noise in response.

Her bedroom was easy to find. It was just so... Tatum—warm colors, lights strung around the ceiling, plush pillows all over her bed, and a fuzzy, shag rug on the floor.

Gently, I set her on her mattress, and she shook her head, her eyes still not opening. "Stay," she mumbled, though her sleep slur was so heavy and thick, I barely understood her—barely. "No go."

"Okay, kitten," I said quietly, running my hand over her hair. "I'll stay. But you have to let me go so I can get in bed, too."

She slowly—very slowly—uncurled her fingers from my shirt, and I peeled it over my head before sliding into bed on the other side. She curled up against my side, her head resting on my chest.

Nothing could have prepared me for how good it felt to hold her like this. To cuddle with her as she slept. To be the person she sought out when she was spiraling.

My phone vibrated for the umpteenth time tonight. Sighing, I pulled the device from my pocket.

I grimaced at the insane number of messages I had from Hunter, Graham, and even some of my teammates. Ignoring our teammates' messages, I opened my group thread with Hunter and Graham, not even bothering to go through their previous messages. More than likely, they were both yelling at me about the snacks, the beer, and going MIA.

> Zane: Something came up. Was involved in a grocery store robbery. Tatum was held at gunpoint.

> Hunter: Hold on, WHAT?! A grocery store robbery? Tatum? GUNPOINT?

> Graham: Dude, are you okay? Is Tatum okay? Was anyone hurt?

> Hunter: I'm still stuck on Tatum, to be honest.

> Zane: I could've died tonight, and you're stuck on Tatum?

> Hunter: If you're texting me, you're okay. Tatum lives near here?

Hunter and Graham both knew how I felt about Tatum. They both also knew she was the only girl for me. Every woman I tried to date didn't work out because I just compared them to Tate.

Graham: Don't be insensitive, Hunter. Are you okay, Zane?

Zane: I'm okay. Probably need a couple of mental health days after this, but I'm okay. Tatum...not so much. I'm here at her place. She's not handling it well.

Graham: Can't really blame her, man. Being held at gunpoint and thinking your life might end wouldn't be easy for anyone to navigate and move past. She needs time.

Hunter: She needs some of that Zane alkjdjhdghjjg

Zane: Did you spasm or something?

Graham: I stopped him from sending something very inappropriate.

I snickered. I loved my best friends. Just texting them made this night a little more bearable. They were silly, but they also didn't dwell on things. If I said I was okay, they left it be, trusting me to know myself and what I was capable of handling on my own.

> Zane: I need to get some sleep. But I wanted to check in and let you guys know what was going on. It'll probably be all over the news tomorrow. You can fill the team in or let Coach know. I'll call him in the morning so the PR team can get on top of this.

> Hunter: Sounds good, man. Take care of yourself, alright? We'll hold down the fort. And tell Tatum we said hi.

I scoffed but sent back a thumbs up before locking my phone and setting it on Tatum's nightstand. Yeah, I wasn't telling her they said hi yet. She really didn't like them after they joined in on my teasing of her in high school. But maybe soon, I could get her to give them a second chance.

Because like me, they'd grown up, too. None of us were the same stupid kids we'd been in high school, and if I was going to be with Tate, I really needed her to like my best friends again.

After all, they may be the only family I had left.

seven

. . .

Tatum

I SLOWLY CRACKED open my eyes. Sunlight washed over my bed, warming my body through the sheer curtains over my floor-to-ceiling bedroom windows. My eyes were puffy, swollen, and a bit tender when I rubbed the sleep from them.

Groaning, I shut my eyes again, pulling the blankets tighter around me, partially wishing last night had never happened. But I couldn't bring myself to wish it all away, even if I really tried. Because Zane had been there.

Zane had been kind.

Zane had taken care of me. Soothed my fears.

He'd been the guy I remembered instead of the cold-hearted monster he'd turned into when we started high school.

The smell of frying bacon and coffee infiltrated my nostrils under the blankets, and I pushed them down, blinking blearily into the room. Groaning, I rolled onto my back and sat up. Had Zane stayed the entire night? I *vaguely* remembered pleading with him to stay—which made my cheeks turn the shade of a ripe tomato—but I hadn't actually expected him to still be here this morning.

And it *had* to be him. Because Millie had zero cooking skills.

I slid out of bed and quickly made my way to my attached bathroom, taking the time to wash my face and brush my teeth. After pulling my messy hair, which was in need of a wash, into a bun on the top of my head, I wrapped my robe around myself and shoved my feet into my slippers before heading out of my room and into the kitchen.

"Good morning, kitten," Zane called without turning around. My heart skipped a beat in my chest. Did he sense me that easily? I was even being quiet. How was it possible that he'd known I was there so easily?

Like he used to when we were kids... That was slightly painful to think about.

When we were younger, before high school, he used to turn and face me whenever I entered a room. He had always instinctively known I was right there. It used to make me feel so safe and warm inside.

"Morning," I said softly as I made my way to the Keurig. I started myself a cup of coffee and leaned against the counter, my arms wrapped around my chest as I watched him flip the bacon in the pan. Scrambled eggs were already made, and he had a stack of pancakes waiting to be devoured. My stomach rumbled at it all. It looked delicious.

"I put your phone on the charger," he said, jerking his chin in the direction of my phone where it was laying on the bar.

Silently, I walked over to it and unlocked the screen, only seeing one message from Millie letting me know she was safe and staying over with a guy she met at the bar. I shook my head at her message with a heavy sigh. She was so reckless, and no matter how much I warned her that she was doing something dangerous, she never listened. Just turned a deaf ear to everything that came out of my mouth.

"Trouble?" Zane asked, eyeing me when I set my phone back down and walked back over to the Keurig to doctor up my coffee.

I shrugged as I spooned sugar into the mug. "Just Millie. Out being reckless again. Nothing new."

He hummed. "She was always a character in high school. Surprises me you two are still friends, honestly," he told me.

I frowned at him, not liking what was implied by that declaration. "Why? She actually stuck around, Zane."

He visibly flinched but didn't say a word. I sighed, forcing myself to backpedal. I didn't have the energy to fight with him this morning. "Sorry," I mumbled.

He shook his head. "Don't be sorry, Tatum. You're just saying what's on your mind. And you're suspicious. You have every right to be." He smiled at me, even though I could tell it was forced. Still, it meant a lot that he was trying. "I promise I'll explain everything. But first, you need food. We can talk about our lives. Where we are with our careers—or jobs," he hastily added, making me snicker. I missed witnessing him trip over his words when he thought he said something he shouldn't have. He flashed me a grin that was real this time. "We'll ease into the bigger, deeper conversation."

I smiled at him and grabbed the plate he held out to me. "Okay. That sounds good, Zane."

He pressed a kiss to my forehead, which made my heart skip a beat, before stepping aside to let me pass. I headed to the breakfast table in the corner of the kitchen and sat down, pouring syrup onto my pancakes. He took the seat next to me.

"So, what's been going on with you since we graduated?" he asked, seeming genuinely interested.

"I went to college and got my degree in social work," I told him. "I work with kids in the system —give them a voice in court so no one walks all over them or puts them in situations they don't need to be in."

He swallowed his food, staring at me in awe. "That's...that's brilliant, kitten. It's amazing, really." My cheeks darkened, and I ducked my head, focusing on my plate. He reached over and tipped my chin up, forcing our eyes to connect. "You..."

He shook his head. "You've always had a big heart, kitten."

"Those kids have no one," I said softly. "They *need* someone on their side, and I'm that person."

He brushed the pad of his thumb over my cheek. "I'm in awe of you," he whispered.

A soft smile tilted my lips all while something shifted between us. The air was electrified, though neither of us acted on it. Looking like he really didn't want to, he dropped his hand and rested it on the table beside his plate.

"You chased baseball, didn't you?" I asked him, changing the subject. I already knew the answer to my question. I was apparently a glutton for punishment and had followed his entire career from high school to college to pro. And I still watched every game he had.

So, I also knew they won their first game last night. Hunter had scored the first home run of the season.

He chuckled. "Yeah, I chased baseball. From the moment I held a bat in my hand for the first time, I knew it was my life goal. And then pitching? It's everything." I could see the love for the sport shining in his eyes. "It's not easy. The training. The drills. Some days, it's downright exhausting. But it's one hundred percent worth it."

I cleared my throat. "I knew you followed your dream," I said quietly. He looked at me in surprise. I shyly looked down at my plate, my face, neck, and ears on fire. "I followed you through college and when you went pro. Great game last night."

He chuckled. "Look at me, kitten."

Swallowing thickly, I forced my head up so I could look into his beautiful, gray eyes. "What?" I whispered.

A soft smile tilted his lips as he gazed at me with something in his eyes I couldn't quite place—or rather, didn't want to. Wasn't sure I wanted to believe it.

"You've got to be the most selfless person I've ever known," he said. "You're unmatched, kitten. And I've been in love with you since we were kids."

My fork clattered to my plate.

eight

. . .

Zane

I WATCHED as a range of emotions passed over Tate's face—disbelief, anger, fear, confusion, a glimmer of happiness.

She finally settled on confusion. A deep frown pulled at her sweet lips, and a crease appeared between her brows as she studied me, her breakfast forgotten for the time being.

"What did you just say?" she finally asked, her voice quiet and small. I hated how small it was. Hated the lack of trust. But it was all my fault.

I coughed into my fist and reached for my coffee, needing to wet my suddenly parched throat. She waited, but in a way, it was like she was daring me to repeat what I'd just said to her.

And I was nothing if not a risk taker.

"I've been in love with you since we were kids, kitten. I'm *still* in love with you. Not seeing you for years didn't change any of that."

She reached up and shoved her fingers through her dark hair before she dropped them to her lap with a smack. "Are you *kidding* me, Zane?"

"What? No," I rushed out. I reached for her hands, but she tugged them back. Swallowing thickly, I jerked up from my seat. It was my turn to jab my fingers through my short, black strands. Spinning around, I faced her again. "I screwed up, Tate. God, I know I did. But I just—I need a chance to explain. Please."

She twisted her robe in her fingers as she watched me begin to pace. I was trying to figure out a way to say what I needed to. To put into words why I'd made the decisions I did. They were selfish; I knew that. And there was a chance she'd never forgive me.

But there was also a chance we could move past this. And I was clinging to that chance with both hands.

"Alright..." she quietly spoke. I jerked around to face her, coming to a halt so abruptly, I stumbled. "Explain."

I swallowed thickly. I hadn't been one hundred percent sure I'd even get to this point with her, but I certainly wasn't going to waste it.

Looked like I was winging this.

"One day, we were chilling at the park on the swings. It was near the end of eighth grade. It was cloudy and windy. A little bit chilly. Hunter teased you about liking me, and you said, 'Eww! I would never! Being with Zane is just...disgusting!' Do you remember that?" I quietly asked her.

She flushed, properly embarrassed. Reaching up, she tucked her hair behind her ear. I continued before she could speak. Now that I was going, I couldn't stop. If I did, I'd never get this all off my chest. I'd been bottling it up for years, and now that the top was off, it was overflowing like a shaken-up soda bottle.

"I was hurt. So badly, Tatum. Cut to my core. I may as well have been bleeding out on that playground." Tears swam in her eyes. I forced myself to look away because if I didn't, I would stop speaking. Because I couldn't bear to hurt her another second.

I drew in a ragged breath and scrubbed my hand over my day-old scruff. "I made the choice to focus on my popularity and baseball more than you. I let us drift apart on purpose. I took to teasing you because I knew it annoyed you and you hated it. I did everything I could to put distance between us because I thought it might hurt less. And it might keep me from blurting how I feel about you."

When I looked at her, she was crying, silent tears sliding down her cheeks. Quickly, I ate the distance between us and crouched in front of her. Cupping her face in my hands, I frantically brushed her tears away with my thumbs. "Please don't cry, kitten," I pleaded. I couldn't stand the sight of her tears when I knew they were because she was hurting. I hated them.

She sniffled, her watery, green eyes running over my face. "I hurt you." Her voice cracked on the word hurt, breaking my heart. "I'm so sorry, Zane."

I shook my head. "Don't, kitten. Don't go there in your head, you hear me?" I pressed a kiss to the tip of her nose. "Stay in this moment with me. Please. The past is the past. All that matters is right here. Right now. And hopefully building a future with you. I want that more than anything."

"I lied to Hunter that day." Her words hit me out of left field—like a baseball smacking me in the face. I blinked at her in surprise. I didn't understand. She swiped a tear away. "I was in love with you, too, and I was terrified you would find out and ruin our friendship. You meant too much to me. I'd rather have you as my friend than nothing at all."

I sank onto the chair I'd vacated at the beginning of our conversation, my heart throbbing painfully in my chest. We'd both lost so much time out of fear. If we'd just forced ourselves to move past our fears back then, where would we be now?

"I'm sor—"

"No," I growled, placing a finger over her lips. "We're not doing that, you hear me?" I grabbed her hands in mine. "Just tell me you still feel the same way, kitten. Just tell me that, and we can figure everything else out from there."

A wobbly smile tilted her lips. "Of course, I do, Zane. Those feelings never went away. Every guy I've dated, I just compared him to you—"

I kissed her. I couldn't stop myself. It was nothing more than a peck, but it rocked my entire world, nonetheless.

"Say you'll be mine. Say you'll give me a chance," I pleaded.

She nodded, a breathtaking smile tilting her lips. Her eyes were a bit hazy but still so beautiful as she met my eyes.

"Yes, Zane." I grinned at her and lifted her hands to my lips to kiss each of her palms. "I'll give you a chance."

Those were the best words I'd heard in my life. They even trumped me finding out I'd made it onto a pro-ball team.

———

The place was surprisingly clean when I walked through the door of the house I shared with Graham and Hunter, which was probably mostly Graham's doing. Hunter was a slob.

As I shut the front door behind me, I could hear the TV playing one of Graham's favorite shows. Hunter poked his head out of the kitchen, arching an eyebrow at me. "Well?"

I frowned at him as I toed my shoes off by the front door. "Well, what?" I didn't know what he was asking me about.

"Tatum," he snapped at me, growing impatient. I rolled my eyes. "What's the deal?"

I smiled. Couldn't help it. Just thinking about holding her in my arms all night, making her breakfast, kissing her, cuddling her all morning…

The kiss…

"She's giving me a chance," I told him. "We still have a lot to work out with me being pro and needing to travel, but I'm confident we'll get it together and find a common ground."

"Bout time!" Graham hollered from the living room. I snickered.

"Yeah—we're tired of seeing you comparing every woman you meet to her," Hunter griped. I narrowed my eyes at him. He was treading on thin ice. "But all jokes aside, I'm happy for you, man. And it'll be good to finally welcome Tatum back into our circle again. Nothing's ever been right without her."

He wasn't wrong. Hunter and Graham were my best friends, but they'd been really good friends with Tate, too. She was the person able to calm Hunter down with a scolding look, and she was the perfect comforter when Graham was lost in his head.

My phone rang in my hand before I could say anything. Looking down at my screen, my mood immediately plummeted.

Dad was calling me.

Sighing, I held up my phone to show Hunter. He muttered a curse before disappearing back into the kitchen. I answered the phone on the way to my room.

"Hey," I grunted, not particularly pleased to hear from him. Even now, my hands were already shaking, adrenaline coursing through my veins. Our phone calls only continued to get more and more negative, and I wasn't sure how much more of it I could take.

"I need you to come home this weekend. There's a charity event—"

I sighed, cutting him off. "Dad, I have a game this weekend. You know that. I can't miss the game. This is my career—my job. I'm bound by a contract," I reminded him, hoping the word contract would spark something inside his little lawyer-y brain. But, of course, like usual, everything I said about my baseball career went in one ear and out the other.

"It's at seven—"

"Dad!" I barked. He finally went completely silent. I drew in a deep breath and pinched the bridge of my nose. "I'm not coming." My voice was firm. I was not backing down on this.

"This isn't up for negotiation," he snapped.

"You're right. It's not. Because I'm grown, Dad. I pay my own bills. I own my own car. I have already paid you back every cent you spent on my college tuition. You don't get to tell me what I can and can't do anymore. I'll be at my ball game this weekend, fulfilling my duties as the pitcher."

"If you don't come this weekend, I will cut you off, Zane." His voice held a silk-edged warning, but I no longer cared. I was done with these stressful conversations. Done with his constant tugging. Done with him always trying to make me feel bad for not being his perfect son and following in his footsteps.

I barked out a laugh, but it lacked any real humor. "You know what, Dad? Cut me off. I don't care. I'm done. Don't call me again."

With that, I ended the call. No doubt, I'd just lost Mom, too. She would never stand up to him. She loved me; I knew she did. But I also knew she loved her husband more.

Maybe one day, we could work things out and be a family again. Maybe one day, Dad would move past his anger. But I knew that day wouldn't be any day soon.

Blowing out a soft breath, I leaned forward, bracing my elbows on my knees. I closed my eyes and hung my head, the pain in my chest stabbing. No matter how long Dad and I had been fighting— which was years—cutting him off didn't hurt any less.

But my boundaries and my mental health had to take precedence at some point. And that point was today.

nine

. . .

Tatum

MOM'S FACE appeared on my screen, and I quickly answered her video call, a wide smile pulling at my lips. "Hi!" I exclaimed. I loved phone calls with my mom. She was my best friend, and I could come to her about anything.

She and my stepdad had worked hard to give me a normal childhood. I spent all of my holidays with them and my older brother, Bryan. And we also tried to do a family vacation at least once a year, even if it was just for a weekend. Family was important to all of us, and I loved how close we all were.

"Hey, baby. You're glowing. I was a little worried after I saw the news article about that shooting. You were named, Tatum. Are you okay?"

I blew out a soft breath, my light dimming. Her brows were pulled low over her eyes, and I could hear Dad and Bryan murmuring in the background, no doubt eavesdropping.

"I don't really want to talk about it," I told her honestly. "If I do, I'll cry and freak out, and I just… I'm tired of crying, Mom." She nodded understandingly. "I'm sure the news article covered everything. But I'm okay—as much as I can be right now. Zane was here, and he…he helped."

"Zane?" she asked, her brows arching onto her forehead. "I saw his name in the article—that he saved you. But he was there? With you? At your apartment?"

I flushed and nodded just as the front door opened. Millie walked in with sunglasses over her eyes, no doubt suffering from a hangover. She threw up a wave in my direction before heading straight to her bedroom. I focused back on my phone.

"Yes, he was here," I said, answering my mom's question. I grabbed a bottle of water and headed out onto the balcony so I could talk to her in private without my nosy best friend butting in. "We, um…might be together now?"

Mom squealed. I laughed. Bryan poked his head into the picture, frowning at me. "If he hurts you again, he's got me to answer to," he said. I loved this about my brother. He was overprotective, but he also knew how to step back and let me make my own decisions, my own mistakes, and my own choices.

I couldn't learn and grow if he was constantly hovering.

I snorted. "I can handle myself, Bryan."

He grinned at me. "Never have to with me having your back, little sis."

Mom shoved him away before beaming at me. "All my dreams for my baby girl are coming true," she gushed. "Now…" She settled on her recliner. "Tell me everything."

———

Millie was ranting. Raving. Throwing her arms around. Pacing. She was out of sorts, tears in her eyes as she apologized for not being there with me last night.

"I just…" She sniffled, swiping at her cheeks. "You could have *died* last night, Tate. I could've lost my best friend in the whole entire world." She sank onto the couch beside me. I quickly drew her into a hug.

"I was okay," I told her quietly, not really wanting to talk about this. But Millie had found out through social media before I could even figure out how to broach the subject with her. "Zane was there, and he…he saved me, Millie."

She swiped at her eyes and frowned at me. "Zane? Zane Silver?"

A blush stole over my cheeks as I nodded. And then, I began to recount to my best friend everything that happened. When I finally had it all out in the open, she squealed and launched herself at me, almost knocking us to the floor. I burst into laughter, hugging her back.

"My best friend is going to get her happily ever after!" she screamed, almost bursting my ear drum.

———

> Zane: Hey...I know we just saw each other this morning, but I'm having a bad day. Can we do dinner?

I frowned at Zane's message, worried about him. What could have happened since he left my place? Did he get into a fight with one of the twins? Did something happen with his team?

> Tatum: Of course. But I'm not in the mood to go out anywhere.

> Zane: Can you come here then? I'll have food delivered. Whatever you feel like eating, kitten. Just need you.

My heart skipped a beat in my chest at his last sentence. *Just need you.* But despite his sweet words, I could also feel the rawness behind his words. He was hurting, and he needed me.

> Tatum: Surprise me. I'll be there soon. Just shoot me your address.

The house they lived in was a small, two-story home in a quiet, family-oriented neighborhood. A jeep, an SUV, and Zane's truck were parked in the driveway. I parked by the curb and slid out of my car just as Zane stepped onto the porch, a tight smile pulling at his lips. The sight of it had me worrying even more than I already was.

"Hey, you okay?" I asked, immediately making my way to him.

He tugged me into his arms as soon as I was within reaching distance and burrowed his face into the crook of my neck, drawing in a deep breath as he squeezed me to him. I quickly wrapped my arms around his torso, wishing I could do something more to ease whatever was going on inside of him.

"Thank you for coming," he said softly.

"Stop hogging her!" I heard Hunter shout from inside.

I laughed softly as Zane pulled back from me, shooting a scowl over his shoulder. He shut the front door behind him and led me over to the porch steps. We took a seat beside each other, and he grabbed my hand in his, linking our fingers together.

"My dad and I have been on the outs since senior year of high school," Zane began. He stared out over the yard, not looking at me. His jaw was tight, his muscles bunched in his arms. I moved closer to him, pressing our sides together. He relaxed a little.

"He wanted me to follow in his footsteps, and I wanted to play baseball."

I rubbed my thumb along his knuckles, staying quiet, giving him the chance to get this off his chest. "Today, he called me expecting me to just turn my back on my team, on my career, to come to some charity event he's hosting. You know, for his stupid image because he never does it for the actual grater good. I refused. We fought." He swallowed thickly. "I cut him out of my life, which means I probably lost my mom, too."

"Oh, Zane," I whispered, leaning against his side. His pain was like a pulsing throb inside my own chest.

His Adam's apple bobbed as he shut his eyes, drawing in a ragged breath after. "I just...I needed your comfort. You make things...easier."

I cupped his cheek and turned his head to face me. Leaning up, I pressed my lips softly to his. "I'm always here if you need me," I told him quietly.

He dragged me closer and kissed me deeper, his fingers lacing in my hair. I moaned, opening my mouth beneath his. When his tongue touched mine, fireworks sparked along my veins. My brain emptied of everything but this man and the way he made me feel.

"Guys—Seriously?" Hunter groaned. "On the *porch*?"

Zane slowly pulled back from me. My cheeks flamed red, and I ducked my head against his chest. He cradled me close. "Screw off, Hunter," he growled.

Hunter snickered, not the slightest bit fazed by his best friend's grumpiness at being interrupted. "Food is getting cold. You two comin' in or what?"

Zane looked down at me, ducking his head so our eyes would meet. "You hungry?"

I shrugged. "What'd you order?"

He chuckled, seeming a bit lighter now. I didn't know if it was the talk or the kiss, but I was giddy it was because of me regardless. "Your favorite— Chinese." I quickly stood to my feet, and he barked out a laugh, standing as well. "I'll take that as a yes. Come on."

Hunter walked in ahead of us, and once we were crowded around the coffee table in the living room with trays of food in front of each of us, Hunter smirked at me.

"Good to see you again, Tate. Still struggling to open locks?"

I scowled at him, wishing I had something to throw in his direction. "Screw you, Hunter."

He threw his head back, laughter ringing around the room. And Zane joined him, making me elbow him roughly in the ribs. He snickered and leaned over, softly kissing me again, easily wiping away my irritation.

"Love you," he mumbled.

My soul righted itself at those words, and some of my irritation slipped away.

"Love you, too," I said quietly.

A twinkle lit up his gray eyes, and my heart soared.

about the author

Taylor Jade is the queen of hopeless romantics. You can find her in front of her computer, creating a new, beautiful world for her readers to get lost in or with her nose stuck in a romance book.

Living in Florida since the day she was born, Taylor hates the intense heat but loves chilly Florida winters. Often, Florida finds its way into her books, giving her readers a taste of what her home feels like.

Besides writing and reading, Taylor also loves jet skiing and water skiing. Somehow, she manages to juggle her hobbies, her writing career, a full-time job, and college all at once like a master.

also by taylor jade

kick start of the heart

Donna Elaine

DONNA ELAINE

Kick Start
OF THE
HEART

one

. . .

Grace

"MUM! Come on! Sir said if I'm late again I'll have to do fifty sit-ups!"

I roll my eyes as I continue pulling my long brown hair into a high ponytail whilst jogging down the stairs.

"You're not going to be late. Stop nagging." I grab the keys from the side cabinet and hold open the front door. Tyler picks up his large bag which contains his sparring kit and rushes towards the car. He throws his bag into the back seat before slamming the door and climbing into the front.

"It's my turn to sit there!" his little sister shouts as she rushes past me and to the car. I let out a deep sigh and pull the door closed, pushing it quickly to make sure it is secure.

"Lucy, you can sit there on the way back." I open the back car door for her to climb in before strapping her into her seat.

"It's my turn though," she sulks crossing her arms over her chest whilst pouting. I lean over and press a kiss on her forehead.

"Stop sulking and you can have a cookie whilst Tyler is training, okay?" I smile as her face lights up. It's her favourite part of waiting for her brother to finish his Tae kwon do sessions. She sits in the leisure centre café drinking a hot chocolate or milkshake and eating one of their giant cookies.

I close her door and take a deep breath before climbing into the driver's seat. I start the car and head away from the house and to the leisure centre, wishing for once I could just sit in my pyjamas and not have to rush around after the kids. I just wish I had some time to myself instead of having to be a Mum or Nurse all the time.

I quickly push the selfish feelings away; I wouldn't give up all my kids do for love or money. I'm so proud of what my son has achieved with his Tae Kwon Do. At nearly ten years of age, he is less than one year away from hopefully gaining his black belt. It's a great accomplishment and he has been working so hard, not only in class which he goes to three or four times a week but at home too.

"Don't forget I need a new theory booklet after Lucy ruined mine," Tyler reminds me.

"I did not!" his sister protests loudly behind me.

Tyler turns in his seat to look back at her. With four years between them, they continuously argue. It's as if one is always trying to push the other's buttons. They have a great knack for pushing mine at the same time.

"You dropped a milkshake all over it!" Tyler points out.

"But if you had put it away as I asked you to, she wouldn't have been able to *accidentally* spill her drink on it, Tyler," I point out as I try and pay attention to the road and not the way the kids are now bickering across the car.

I swear for the whole ten-minute drive to the centre the two of them argue about the theory booklet, and then the way Tyler wouldn't play with her. How she embarrassed him in front of his friends and finished with the fact Tyler wouldn't let her join in at Tae Kwon Do. I let out a sigh of relief as I pull into the car park knowing that for the next hour, the two of them will be separated and I may get a coffee in peace. Okay, there isn't much chance of that, but a tired mum can wish, right?

We all pile out of the car and Tyler grabs his bag from the back before rushing towards the building ahead of us.

"I'll come and meet you after class and get the booklet!" I call out as Tyler holds up a hand to show he heard me before joining a couple of his friends he has seen and heading inside.

I help Lucy out of the car and head for the soft play area she plays in when her brother is training. As soon as we are inside, she runs off and I stand at the café counter to order the usual coffee for me and a milkshake for her. I grab two cookies, knowing her brother will be tired and hungry when he finishes. Finding a table, I sit down and take a long soothing breath, taking a couple of moments to calm my racing mind. When I open them again, I try and push the constant worry of doubt and failure to the back of my mind as I look around from my seat.

I watch all the kids and adults walking up to the Tae Kwon Do class in their doboks (training suits) and belts worn proudly around their waists, their kit bags hanging over their shoulders. As always that prang of jealousy hits as I think of all they are achieving and how much fun they have in class. For an hour they get to forget all their day-to-day jobs and responsibilities. A few spot me and wave as they head up the stairs to the dojang (training hall) Master Owens has on the top floor. I remember when I was one of them smiling on the way up for an hour of training, getting my butt kicks regularly until I got so good even the grown men struggled to take me down.

I started my Tae Kwon Do journey when I was a little younger than Tyler. When I was eight, I had been bullied so bad I didn't want to go to school. My best friend, Jenson Crawford, begged me to go to class with him hoping it would give me the courage to stand up for myself. It worked and within a month of starting at the academy, I was no longer afraid of the bullies and loved every minute I was training. I went from the timid little girl who would keep her head down, avoid anyone and everything and never say boo to a goose, to the girl who walked into every room with her head held high, not afraid of anyone. That feeling stayed with me as I achieved every belt through the years, and entered more competitions than I could count, usually placing in the top three in every event I entered. I not only gained my black belt but my second and third dan, which is the same as a third black belt. I loved my whole journey.

But unfortunately, life started to get in the way when my husband of ten years left me which meant I had no one to watch Lucy whilst I trained. I tried to continue in the sport I loved, but eventually, my patience started to wear thin and I realised I couldn't be a single mum and train like I used to. The final straw came when I competed and got my pride handed to me on a silver platter. I was knocked out in the first fight because I was distracted and nowhere near my usual standard. I decided to step back, give up what I loved, and put my kids first. Whenever I miss the thrill of the mats, I remind myself that Lucy and Tyler are happy, and I don't have to worry about who will watch them. Even if that means I step back from the one thing I had for myself.

two

. . .

Jenson

"THANKS ALL FOR A GREAT CLASS, I will see you next time!"

I start clapping my hands and the thirty-three students I have just put through the wringer join in as I hear a chorus of "Thank you, sir". They all head to the far end of the room to gather their things and put their socks and shoes on. I head to the opposite end, grab my water bottle and take a deep drink from it.

It feels so good to be back here in my old training hall after nearly twenty years, fifteen of which were spent serving in the army. I had only been back in the area a few days when I bumped into my old Tae Kwon Do instructor. He asked if I would like to teach a couple of his classes. I jumped at the chance as there isn't much else I can do with my time now.

I moved back to the area to help my dad as he hasn't been looking after himself properly since he retired a few years ago. My sister and I don't want him to go into a home, and he hates the idea of strangers coming into his space. So, I moved in with him to try and make sure he's eating, showering, and keeping the house clean. It's been going well, but it's early days. I'm sure we will end up arguing at some point, which would be nothing new. But we always end it with a couple of fingers worth of whiskey and a laugh.

I wipe my face with my towel and throw it in my bag as I head back to the front of the room to see how many people will be training in the next class.

"Sir, my mum needs to pay for a new handbook."

I look at the blonde kid in front of me and smile.

"Sure thing mate, will give me a chance to tell her how well you did today." I watch as his face lights up and he pushes his chest out with pride.

"Thanks, Sir, I'll go and get her," he yells rushing towards the door where the students and their parents are all trying to pile out of one side as the next class try and come in the other. I shake my head smiling as I remember how eager I used to be to get into training every day. I watch the kid run out the door and soon reappear dragging a woman with a child on her hip. My jaw drops as she looks up and I see the amber eyes of my childhood best friend. She stops and stares at me for a moment, obviously trying to decide if I look familiar or not. I walk towards her with a wide grin and chuckle out loud.

"Gracie? Is that really you?" I stop in front of her and cross my arms over my broad chest to stop myself from throwing my arms around her. Excitement crashes through me as I come face to face with the one person, I have missed above all.

"Oh my goodness, Jenson!" she laughs as her whole face lights up. "I didn't recognise you! You look amazing, I mean good, I mean …"

"Not like the skinny rake, I was last time you saw me?" I offer up a wink when she looks nervous, hoping to put her at ease.

"Well yeah, how are you? Last I heard you were in the Army," she asks lifting the girl a little higher on her hip.

"I'm good, finished my service and came home a week or two ago to look after Dad," I answer eagerly. "Is this your son?" I ask looking down at the student standing beside her.

"Yeah, this is Tyler," she says putting her hand on his shoulder proudly. "Ty this is Jenson Crawford," she adds. Tyler's face lights up as I laugh.

"You're the one who got Mum to join the academy!" Tyler says excitedly. "Grant told me all about you and how you broke his nose in the middle of a competition." Grace and I burst out laughing as I nod.

"Yeah I did, I can't believe he told you about that."

"He's my godfather, he tells me loads of stories about him and Mum when they were growing up. Your name comes up a lot."

I look at Grace who is obviously trying not to laugh.

"Yeah, I bet it does." I laugh. "Guess that explains why you are so good; you have a three times world champion as a Mum and Grant as a godfather!" I can't miss the pride on his face as he looks at his mum and nods. He obviously looks up to her. "So, what nights do you train, Gracie? Master Owen has me helping most nights now," I ask, eager to see her at training again.

"Oh, I don't train anymore. I don't have time between the kids and work. But Tyler is here three times a week and Lucy wants to join the little ninjas class in a couple of months," Grace beams as she looks at the girl on her hip who is looking at me with a deep, intrigued look on her little round face.

"That's a shame, I never thought you would give it up." I look at her daughter as I nod in Grace's direction. "Your Mummy used to beat me up all the time in class. No one could win against her." The little girl laughs as she looks at her mum who shrugs.

"That was a long time ago, Mummy's nowhere near good enough now."

"Sir! Do you want me to start the warm-up?"

I turn to see one of the older black belts as he points to the mats where about forty adults are jogging around the perimeter.

"Yeah please, I'll be there now," I call back whilst holding up my thumb. I quickly turn back to Grace and smile.

"I don't know where the booklets are right now, but I will make a note to have one ready for Tyler's next class." I turn my attention to Tyler who looks a little disappointed. "I will make sure you have it at the beginning of the class I promise." Tyler nods and forces a smile.

"Okay Sir," he replies.

"Good lad, when are you next here?" I ask him.

"Friday and Sunday," he answers. I look to his mum who nods.

"Great so I will have one ready for tomorrow as it's Friday and Mum can pay then," I tell him as he nods and bows to me.

"Thank you, sir."

I quickly bow back. "It's my pleasure. I will see you tomorrow." I look ahead at Grace and smile at her. "It was great to see you."

"It was good to see you too. See you later," she replies abruptly and turns to walk away, but not without flashing me a nervous smile.

"I'm going to make it my mission to get you back to training, Grace," I call out to her before I can stop myself. She laughs as she looks over her shoulder at me.

"Yeah, good luck with that one."

I watch her walk from the room and decide right there and then I will get her back on the mats. Talent like that should not be wasted. I turn back to the room and head over to the black belt who is barking out warm-up instructions.

"Ten burpees. Go!" he shouts before looking at me with a smile. "You remember Grace then?" he asks chuckling. I cross my arms over my chest as I look around the room.

"Who doesn't remember being thrown on the floor a hundred times a week by her? She was something else! Why the hell did she quit?" I ask leaning against the wall behind me.

"No one really knows. Her husband left her for another woman around the same time as Lucy was born. She tried to continue but the kids would sit at the back of the class and she would be distracted by them the whole time. We tried to offer her help, but she wouldn't accept it. had a tough time at a comp one day which seemed like the last straw. She threw in the towel and never came back to class. She supports Tyler no end, but she refuses to come back."

I nod as I understand it must be hard as a single mum to train when there is no one to watch the kids. But surely there must be a way for her to get back to what she loves. The passion and skill level that she had should not be wasted.

"Everyone, please thank Mr Williams for taking the warm-up," I yell as everyone stops and bows to Gareth next to me. "Line up in rows of six! Go!" I call out and watch as the students all rush to line up in belt order. The black belts at the front of the class all the way back to the white belts. I yell out the first pattern they are taught and watch as all execute it perfectly.

As I call out patterns and they all perform to the best of their ability my mind sneaks back to Grace and how well she looked. I always knew she would grow up to be a beautiful woman, but seeing her today just proves that she looks better than I ever imagined. I'd love to see her build on her confidence and show her son just how amazing she used to be. But first I need to get her to open up to me and see if there is anything I can personally do to aid with that. An idea takes bloom and I find myself smiling as I realise, I may be able to help her in the best possible way.

three

. . .

Grace

"WHAT DO you mean you can't have the kids this weekend? You know I have work!"

I hear my ex-husband sigh on the other end of the phone, causing my jaw to clench as my anger rises.

"There is nothing I can do Grace. Michelle is ill and it wouldn't be fair for her to deal with the kids whilst she is feeling like this."

I feel my blood boiling as I listen to his sorry excuse. If it was the first time this had happened maybe I would have a little more consideration for them. But I've lost count of how many times in the last five years he has put his mistress over the kids.

"It really is about time you started taking your responsibility to your kids over that of the woman you left them for," I growl through gritted teeth.

"There is no need to be like that Grace, I always put my kids first. You just don't like the fact that I have moved on and you are still alone."

I pull the phone away from my ear for a second and stare at it open-mouthed. Did he just go there?

"Do you know what Robert, go to hell." I hang up and slam my phone down on the table a little too hard whilst holding in a scream. I place my head in my hands and close my eyes before quietly counting to ten in an attempt to calm down.

What kind of parent puts their own kids behind everything else? I swear he cancels more than he has them, and he was the one that demanded that he had them every other weekend, to ensure "he had quality time with them". I quickly pull up my rota on my phone and look the who I am on with this weekend and if there is another nurse to swap with me. I notice two of my friends are off and quickly send a message to one of them to see if they can help or even watch the kids for me for a few hours each day. Lorraine is the first to get back to me.

> Lorraine: Hey, sorry but we are all away on a family holiday this weekend, it's why me and Rosie are off together. Take it the waste of space isn't having the kids again?

> Me: Oh gosh, I can't believe I forgot, I'm so sorry! Yeah, I'll tell you more when I see you once you get back!

I put my phone back on the table and press the palms of my hands to my eyes as I try my hardest not to cry. The last thing I need to do right now is humiliate myself in front of everyone sitting in the leisure centre café.

"Rough day?"

I look around at the voice behind me to find Jenson smiling at me softly.

"Rough life," I sigh as I go back to leaning against the table with my elbows as I massage my temples, hoping to stop the stress headache that's building.

"Want to talk about it?" he asks gently taking a seat on the other side of the table. I notice he's in his Tae Kwon Do training gear, and looks as amazing as he did yesterday. I realise I'm staring and quickly shake my head.

"You don't want to know."

"Try me," he answers as he sits back in the chair and crosses his arms over his chest.

"My waste of space ex is meant to have the kids this weekend, but apparently his new wife is ill, and it wouldn't possibly be fair for her to have the kids around when she feels so poorly," I explain in a tone that I know makes me sound petty, but at the moment I don't care.

"But you have to have the kids when you are ill?" Jenson frowns, making me feel a little less unreasonable.

"Exactly! He would never change his days to have them to help me out. But I'm expected to drop everything for the woman he left me for? How is that even acceptable to ask of me? It's not like I have a job where I can just leave them short-staffed. I have to find cover for my shifts this weekend and no one is free. My parents would normally help out but they are out of town for the next week seeing my brother. I don't know what to do." Damn, I hadn't meant to unload all that in one frail swoop.

I'm about to apologise for my outburst when I spot Lucy out of the corner of my eye rushing towards me and quickly force a smile onto my face, ignoring the soft reassuring one on Jenson's as he realises what I'm doing.

"You okay, Lucy Lou?" I ask as she comes to a stop at the table with a big grin on her face.

"Mummy, can I have a cookie now please?" she asks cheerfully as she bounces on the balls of her feet. I nod before grabbing my bag to find my purse.

"Of course, let me," I stop as my phone rings. I look at the screen and see George from work calling me. An idea quickly runs through my head as I answer the phone. "Hang on George two secs," I say before looking to Lucy. "Let me just get this work call and then I will take you I promise."

"I'll take her for the cookie," Jenson says smiling before standing up and holding out his hand for Lucy. "Do you want to come with me sweetheart and we can let mummy speak in peace?"

"You don't have to do that?" I protest but Jenson shakes his head with that reassuring smile again, instantly putting me at ease.

"Do what you need to do, I won't take her out of your sight, I promise."

"I didn't mean!" I protest, realising what he thought I was implying, which I wasn't.

"I get it, please just do what you need to do." Jenson looks at me and I nod.

"Thank you," I sigh as I look to Lucy who is watching the whole exchange, knowing she isn't allowed to go off with anyone without my permission. "It's okay, you can go with Jenson and pick out a cookie," I reassure her and hand her my purse. I watch as she looks back to Jenson and smiles before taking his hand which is still held out and head off towards the café counter. I watch them for a moment grateful that Jenson was willing to distract her for a short time for me.

"Gracie? You still there?"

I quickly turn my attention back to the call.

"Sorry, I was sorting Lucy. I'm glad you called I need your help."

———

Jenson

As I stand in the queue with Lucy to get her the cookie and a milkshake, I watch Grace as she sits deep in conversation with whoever is on the phone. Her shoulders are hunched forward as she leans her head against her hand which is rubbing her forehead. Her whole body screams exhaustion and defeat. I look down at Lucy who is scanning the goodies in front of her.

"How often does Mummy work, sweetheart?" I ask, knowing I shouldn't but I need to know.

"She works when we are in school, or with Daddy and Mummy Michelle." I feel my brows lift in surprise. No wonder she doesn't train anymore. How can one woman work so much whilst being a single mum? I look back over to her as she shakes her head still deep in conversation on the phone. As I watch her, she wipes her cheek as if brushing away a tear and my heart breaks. I look back down to the little girl beside me who is a spitting image of her mother when we were her age, the only difference being she is blonde where Gracie's a brunette.

"Do you want to pick one out for Mummy and Tyler too?"

Lucy looks up at me with her big amber eyes, just like a mum's and nods eagerly.

"Go on then, my treat. Which one is Mummy's favourite?"

We get our treats as well as something for the others and head back to our seats just in time for Grace to finish her call looking even more defeated than when we left.

"Mummy this is for you," Lucy announces with a big grin on her face as she pushes a piece of chocolate cake in front of her mother. "Jenson got us all something," she adds climbing into her seat as I place the milkshake in front of her and her cookie. Grace looks from the cake to me, and I see I was right about her being close to crying. Her eyes are sparkling with the tears in them which she keeps blinking back.

"Any luck?" I ask quietly, hoping Lucy is too caught up in her treats to listen in. Grace shrugs as she closes her eyes for a moment, takes a deep breath and lets it out to calm herself.

"George offered to cover my nights I'm on call if I do his days. I'm going to try and see if my sister-in-law is free to have the kids. If she isn't then I don't know what I'm going to do."

Grace reaches over and runs her hand over her daughter's head lovingly, as she tucks into her cookie.

"I'll watch them for you."

Grace's wide eyes snap to mine.

"What?" a nervous laugh bursts from her full lips.

"I'm free. I'm not working at the moment and have nothing planned. I'm more than happy to help out," I reply hoping she will say accept my offer to help.

"You do realise I work twelve-hour shifts and will be out of the house for thirteen," she laughs. "I could never ask you to watch my kids for that long," she adds shaking her head and smiling.

"You didn't ask, I offered. I'm more than happy and willing to watch them as long as you need me to. I watch my nieces all the time for my sister. My body clock is still very much in the army. I wake up at five every morning, so it doesn't matter what time you need me, I can be there. I even know how to cook so can feed them as well," I add grinning hoping to put her at ease.

I watch as Graces face softens and she looks to her daughter again as she considers taking me up on my offer. I reach across the table and place my hand on hers. She looks at me and I offer her what I hope is a reassuring smile.

"I wouldn't offer if I didn't want to. I'm more than happy to watch them this weekend if it helps you."

"But you have classes to teach here," she starts to argue, but I shake my head.

"There are more than enough black belts to help out. I can bring Tyler to his class and sit down here with Lucy just as you do." I squeeze her hand softly. "I know it's been nearly twenty years and you have no reason to trust me. But, I'm still the kid who made you pinkie promise to us always having each other's backs." A laugh bursts from Grace's lips as she smiles at me. "Let me help you, if only for this weekend."

As I watch Grace, I see the moment she relaxes and accepts my help.

"As long as you are sure you can handle my two," she starts. I chuckle as I nod.

"If I can handle twenty guys on tour in Afghan, or worse thirty kids upstairs, I can handle your two." I grin as a smile creeps onto her lips and she looks back to Lucy.

"Do you mind spending the day with Jenson Saturday and Sunday?" Lucy looks at me and smiles.

"Will you bring cookies?" she asks causing me to laugh out loud.

"How about I bring the stuff to make them?" I offer which earns me a big grin. She looks back at her mum.

"He can come, I'll be good." She grins at her mum who watches her for a moment before letting out a deep breath and turning her attention back to me.

"Okay then. Looks like you are watching the kids for me this weekend," she replies as I see some of the tension leave her shoulders. I smile knowing that I was able to ease some of the stress she carries around.

"I'm glad I can help." I glance at my watch and sigh. "I need to get up to class, but ..." I pull out my bag and dig out my pen and notepad. I quickly scribble down my number and hand it to her. "Message me your address and what time you need me. No time is too early. I can be there whenever you need me to be." I stand up and smile at Lucy. "I will see you tomorrow little miss. Think about what you want to do, and we can do it, okay?" Lucy grins at me as she nods. I look to her mother who seems to have relaxed a little more.

"Message me," I reinforce before placing my hand on her shoulder as I stand beside her.

"Thank you," she says as she places her hand over mine. I smile at her touch.

"Anytime," I reply. I turn and head off towards the training hall, feeling hopeful that the weekend will go without any issues and that I haven't bitten off more than I can chew. There again I don't think there is anything I am not willing to do to help out my old friend, no matter how much time has passed. Gracie is still someone who means the world to me, time will never change how I truly feel about her.

four

. . .

Grace

I CLIMB into my car and pull out my phone for the hundredth time today. The last time I checked, five minutes ago, there was still no word from Jenson or the kids. The last message I received was at two this afternoon when Jenson messaged to tell me to stop checking in on them, they would call me if there were any issues. I hadn't messaged that many times. Okay, maybe it was a handful of texts. I look back through the messages and see that between eight this morning and two this afternoon, I had sent ten messages and made one phone call. Okay, yes, I had been a little persistent, but I feel so bad for letting him give up his weekend to watch the kids.

I pull out of the staff car park and start the short fifteen-minute drive home. I check the time on the screen and see it's just after eight in the evening. My feet are aching, my back hurts and my shoulders are tense to the point I can hardly move them. I had been looking forward to being on call this weekend as it's the only time I get to relax a little. Instead, I have been rushed off my feet driving around here, there and everywhere.

I come to a stop at a red light and roll my head to try and loosen the aching muscles. I'm sure there's nothing to worry about at home. Tyler and Lucy had been so excited about Jenson coming around. The poor guy probably hasn't had a moment's peace all day.

I still can't believe he offered to help me out like this. I haven't seen the guy in years, but he jumped straight back into being the best friend he was.

When we were kids we hung out every single day, we played out until it was dark and our parents shouted for us to come back inside. As we grew up, we stayed just as close, always training together, practising our patterns in the garden, or sparring together. We supported each other at every competition and celebrated each other's wins like they were our own. I had cried for days when he told me he was moving away as his parents were getting a divorce and his mum was insisting he moved to Scotland with her. Living down in Cornwall, Scotland couldn't be any further away and he broke my heart when he left.

We tried to stay in touch for a while, but it was long before the time of social media and eventually, we lost touch. I always wondered what happened to him. Was he happy with his life? Was he married with kids? I tried to find him on Facebook and Instagram a few times over the years but was unsuccessful. When his sister moved back I hoped I would it meant he was coming back too, but he never did. That was when I found out he was in the Army and stationed up north. His sister offered to pass on my details to him, but I told her not to bother. He wouldn't have wanted to hear from me anyway. But even after all these years seeing him brought out that little cluster of butterflies in my stomach I used to get when we were kids. I shake my head as I pull up outside my house, parking on the drive as Jenson's is parked on the street in front of the house.

I climb out of the car and head for the door, listening for any noise coming from within. But there's nothing. Worry tightens in my gut and I quickly let myself in. As I open the door, I'm greeted by the unmissable smell of Spaghetti Bolognese and can hear the TV. I head into the lounge to find Jenson and Tyler sitting on the sofa transfixed by the film on the TV.

"Transformers, again?"

Both heads spin around grinning at me.

"Of course, it's the best!" Tyler exclaims rolling his eyes as Jenson chuckles. He's sat back on the sofa with his arm across the back, looking relaxed and at home.

"Where's Lucy?" I ask looking around.

"Fast asleep, she crashed about half an hour ago, so I put her to bed."

I stare at Jenson and then at my watch checking the time.

"She's in bed already?" I ask amazed. I watch as the smile on Jenson's face slips.

"Yeah, sorry. Should I have kept her up?"

"No! Not at all! I'm just surprised. She can be a nightmare at bedtime," I explain, shrugging off my jacket and hanging it over my arm.

"She's been a nightmare all day," Tyler sighs not taking his eyes off the screen. I look back to Jenson who shakes his head.

"She's been as good as gold. Very busy, but not a bother at all." Jenson stands from the sofa and walks up to me. "How was work?"

"Good thanks, busy and I need a long hot bath. But a shower will have to do until tomorrow night. I just want to eat and sleep before I have to do it all again in the morning." I grin trying to hide how tired I am. Jenson watches me for a moment, making me wonder if he can still read me as well as he did when we were kids. He shakes his head and places his hand on the top of my arm and squeezes gently.

"I'm going to shoot and let you rest." He reaches over the back of the sofa and ruffles Tyler's hair. "Be good and help your mum."

Tyler turns around and rolls his eyes.

"I'm always good."

"That's debatable," I laugh as I walk towards the front door with Jenson. I hang my coat on the banister as he opens the door.

"Thank you for today, you have no idea how grateful I am."

Jenson turns and looks at me with a cocked brow.

"I think I do. You have told me about twenty times today alone."

I smile nervously, realising I had nothing to worry about.

"I promise to lay off the messages tomorrow. It's just hard leaving them with people who haven't had them before."

"Well, I have had them now and all three of us survived. Tomorrow, I don't want you to worry okay?"

I find myself nodding as I smile at him. "Good. Your dinner is in the microwave, and everything has been cleaned up. I'll be back at the same time tomorrow. Eat, put your feet up and relax." Jenson leans in and places a kiss on my cheek before turning around and walking out of the door. "See you in the morning," he calls as he rushes towards his car leaving me staring at his back, as the cheek he just kissed heats up. I manage to wave as he drives off and close the door, before leaning against it and finally exhaling the breath I was holding.

"I like Jenson, he's fun. He can look after us more often," Tyler calls as he walks past me and up the stairs more than likely to play on his PlayStation. I push myself away from the door and head into the kitchen, desperately hoping I am right about the Bolognese.

The first thing I see walking into the kitchen is a vase full of flowers in the middle of the table as well as a placemat and cutlery set out. There is also an empty glass on the table as if waiting to be filled. I walk over to the microwave and spot a bottle of red wine open next to it. As I open the door of the microwave, I find a plate of Spaghetti Bolognese inside.

As I heat it, I pour myself a glass of wine and take a small sip to taste it. I let out an involuntary moan as the smooth liquid flows down my throat. The man has good taste in wine, I'll give him that. The aroma coming from the microwave has my mouth watering. I hadn't realised how hungry I was until now. As soon as the microwave pings I carefully take the plate from it and sit at the table. One mouth full of the food has me moaning again. I pick up my phone and open the messaging app. I type out a text, read it and quickly delete it. I can't just text him, can I? I mean, I know I've been texting him about him having the kids, but does he really want to know that I think he's a great cook? I rewrite the message, determined to tell him anyway but my finger hovers over the button before finally pressing send.

> Me: Thank you for the food, you didn't have to feed us. It tastes amazing like the wine. Thank you.

I place the phone on the table and tuck into my dinner trying desperately not to check it for a reply, but my eyes keep darting for the phone just in case.

I finish the lovely meal and start to clean up when I hear my phone signal a message.

Jenson: You are more than welcome. I'm so glad you enjoyed it. Eat and unwind before you get some rest. I'll see you in the morning. X

I smile as I take my phone and re-filled wine glass into the lounge where I plan on catching up with a little TV and unwinding before bed, as I have been told to do.

five

. . .

Jenson

"DID you see my pattern at the end of class, Jenson?" Tyler asks excitedly as soon as he sees me standing by the entrance of the Dojang.

"You nailed it, dude! Every move was spot on! Keep it up and you will get your black stripe no problem!" I call as I watch him grab his training bag and push his feet into his sliders before heading over to me. I try to keep hold of Lucy's hand, but so many people are trying to get in and out of the training hall that she keeps getting knocked around.

"Watch it guys, one at a time!" I yell out picking her up and placing her on my hip.

"Sorry, Sir!" a few people call back as they part out of our way so we can head for the stairs.

"Tyler! My man!"

I look to my left and see Tyler grinning as he jumps up and high-fives his godfather. Grant looks at me with Lucy on my hip and grins.

"You've been back five minutes and she already has you babysitting. You are just as wrapped around her little finger as you were when you left," he teases. I shake my head as I look at the two kids. "Or are you two finally…" he wiggles his eyebrows at me as my eyes widen.

"Pack it in! I'm helping a friend that's all," I warn.

"It's meant to be Dad's weekend, but as usual he cancelled."

I look to Tyler whose face has dropped. Grant looks down at him and sighs before squatting down. The six-foot-eight giant towers above Tyler, even after going as low as can.

"Hey, at least you get to hang out with Jenson. He was always the life of the party when we were younger. You will have fun with him. I'm sure your dad had his reasons for cancelling." Grant says as he gets Tyler to look him in the eye.

"Don't forget we are going to the beach Ty!" Lucy exclaims excitedly on my hip. I lower her back to her feet now the area is less crowded. Ty looks at us and nods before looking back to Grant.

"See you next week?"

Grant nods as he stands back up and ruffles Tyler's hair. We all say goodbye before heading to the car.

"So what do you reckon? Beach for ice cream then home to cook dinner?" I ask once everyone is strapped in and we are on the road. "What do you fancy eating?"

"Can we make a roast for Mum; she always misses out on Granny's roasts."

I look at Tyler through the rearview mirror and smile.

"Absolutely, let me know her favourite and we will pick everything up on the way home." I see the look on his face and can see how happy that has made him.

"You do a great job at looking after your mum, Ty," I point out glancing at him again.

"Someone has to. She spends all day and night looking after other people, she needs someone to look after her."

I glance at him in the mirror again, surprised by how mature he sounds for a kid that's not even ten yet. The thought of no one but a nine-year-old boy looking out for my Gracie hits me hard. She has always had the biggest heart and would do anything for anyone. The thought that she never had someone look after her back makes me realise that things need to change. Grace deserves to be treated the way she has always treated everyone else and I think I have just the idea to make sure that happens.

"Do you two fancy helping me to take care of Mummy tonight?" I ask. The two kids share a quick look before nodding at me with big grins on their faces. "Great I have just the plan," I add as I come to a stop at the beach car park. It wasn't the beach I originally planned to take the kids to, but this way we will have time to have ice cream then go to the shops and pick up everything for a roast dinner and treat for Grace.

I watch as Tyler takes his sister's hand and they both head onto the sand together. Pulling out my phone I send a quick message to Grace.

> Me: Hey, Tyler smashed his patterns this morning. He is a great kid, they both are. X

I'm not surprised when my phone vibrates in my hand, signalling a text message.

> Grace: He really is. I couldn't be prouder of him if I tried. I am extremely biased though. Hope they are both behaving. X

I look back at the beach and smile as the two kids talk to each other excitedly. I quickly fire off a message, telling her all is fine before following after the two monsters as they wait to spend my money on some yummy ice cream.

six

. . .

Grace

I WALK UP to the front door smiling as I hear Lucy laughing through the open window of her room. I should have known her being in bed early last night was a one-off. That little lady hates going to bed. I open the door and head up the stairs where I hear a deep growl followed by high-pitched laughter. I stand outside her room for a moment watching the scene inside. Lucy's lying in bed and Jenson is reading her favourite book to her. He is doing different voices for each character and she looks mesmerised.

I find myself laughing when Jenson roars again making Lucy jump and squeal laughing with her hand on her chest. Both turn to look in my direction with broad grins on their faces, looking happy and content.

"Mummy your home!" she cries as she rushes out of the bed and towards me. I grab her as she jumps into my arms so I can squeeze her like I do every time I come home from work.

"Looks like I was just in time to save you," I laugh as Jenson climbs to his feet and I walk over to Lucy's bed to place her back in it.

"Jenson does the best voices!" she exclaims excitedly, her amber eyes sparkling with excitement. I look at him laughing remembering how he loved doing impressions when we were kids. He sucked at them, but they were funny, nevertheless. Jenson looks back at me proudly as he puffs out his chest.

"At least someone appreciates my amazing vocal talents!"

I pat his chest playfully whilst smiling at him. "She's five, give her time." I bend down and kiss Lucy on the head as she yawns. "Get some sleep, I'll finish the story for you tomorrow."

"But I want Jenson to read it to me!" she argues. I open my mouth to say Jenson will want to go home, but he stops me.

"I don't mind finishing it, as long as you don't want to get rid of me." I notice he looks nervous which is just ridiculous. I don't want him to go yet. I don't feel like we have had a chance to catch up.

"Of course not, I just thought you would be sick of the sight of us by now," I laugh stepping away from the bed. "You finish the story I'll go make myself something to eat," I add as I start to head out of the bedroom.

"Your dinner is in the microwave," Jenson calls back. I turn to look at him feeling even more grateful for this wonderful man. I was dreading having to cook tonight.

"Thank you," I say meaning each word. I wonder if he notices that some of the tension from my body disappears.

He gives me a knowing wink and sits back on the floor next to Lucy's bed before continuing with the story. I walk out of the room and down the stairs listening to the two of them, giggling happily.

I find Tyler in the lounge his nose in his Tae Kwon Do theory book.

"Hey, dude," I call as I walk past. I get a wave in return as he continues to read. I shake my head smiling as I head into the kitchen and over to the microwave. I open the door to see a roast chicken dinner in there waiting for me. I sigh contently as I haven't had a homemade roast in so long. I quickly heat it, and look at the table where there is a place set for me again. I have to remind myself that this isn't something to get used to. Come tomorrow it will be back to eating the kids leftovers and fending for myself, as it's always been.

Robert never thought to cook extra food for me, in fact, he never cooked. I would have to make his and the kids tea before going to work and eat what was left over. I shake my head trying to ignore the thoughts that have started to creep in. Even after five years my ex-husband still manages to make me angry over the way he treated me, I couldn't see how little he respected me until it was too late and he was gone and had replaced me with his younger girlfriend.

The microwave beeps giving me something to focus on other than my growing rage. I take my now hot food and place it on the table. The aromas from it make my mouth water and I dig in like a starved woman.

"Hungry?"

I look up to see Jenson leaning against the arch between the lounge and the dining room.

"I didn't get a break," I mumble behind my hand, attempting to hide how much food I've managed to shove in my mouth. Jenson laughs as he heads into the kitchen, squeezing my shoulder as he passes.

"Then by all means, don't let something small like manners or me stop you," he calls as I hear the fridge being opened. I chuckle to myself as I go back to devouring my food.

I don't notice him walk back in until he places a glass in front of me and starts pouring some wine into it. I notice there isn't a glass for him and quickly finish chewing what's in my mouth.

"Join me for one, if you have time that is."

Jenson smiles at me for a moment and nods before heading back into the kitchen and retrieving another glass. By the time he has sat down and poured himself a drink, I've finished my food. Sitting back I relax into my seat and let out a content sigh.

"Where did you learn to cook like that?" I ask picking up my glass and taking a sip of the cool white wine. I moan as it comes alive on my tongue.

"And learn about wine? Because this is perfect!" I add picking up the bottle to see what it is.

Jenson chuckles as he takes a sip of his.

"One thing about being in the army is that you learn to appreciate good cooking and decent alcohol. Everything tastes like sand when you are stationed abroad."

"How old were you when you joined? Your sister said you were young," I ask taking another sip of the cool wine. Jenson smiles as he looks to the side vacantly.

"I was eighteen. I sat a couple of A Levels in engineering and maths and one of the teachers suggested I join so I did. I wanted to get away from Mum and wasn't sure where to go. The army offered me a way to escape and grow, so I took it."

I remember his sister saying life with his mum was tough. Jenson and his mum never really got along; she used him as a way to hurt his father. She stopped him from coming back during school holidays and made it difficult for them to have any type of relationship.

"Do you miss it?" I ask looking at him. He shrugs his shoulders.

"I never thought I would be in for so long. It was only ever meant to be temporary, but things changed, and I just continued as I was. I miss the rest of the team I was usually stationed with. I was lucky enough to fight alongside some of the best men and women I have ever met. But I'm also glad to have gotten out in one piece, I know plenty who didn't." A sad look crosses over his face and I can see there is a pain there he hides away. I'm about to ask about it when he shakes his head and looks back at me.

"What about you?" he asks, obviously not wanting to discuss the army anymore.

"What about me? I haven't served," I laugh taking another sip of my drink.

"You might as well have, you are a nurse, that can't have been easy at times."

"It wasn't, or isn't I should say," I admit taking another sip of my drink. "But I can't imagine doing anything else. I love that I work out in the community, I get to see new faces all the time as well as some old ones. People are getting to stay at home for longer with us going to them. I was in the wards of the hospital until Robert left. He didn't give me any warning I just came home one day and his bags were packed."

"That must have been a real shock for you."

I nod as I look into the lounge and see the sofa is empty. Knowing Tyler is upstairs I finally admit everything out loud.

"It was, I knew we were far from perfect, but I never thought he would leave as he did. I was devastated at first. Tyler was four and didn't understand why all of a sudden his dad wasn't here. I was pregnant with Lucy, it was the last shift before starting maternity leave when he left. I didn't know what to do. I tried to carry on as normal as possible, but I was heartbroken. He didn't even come to the hospital for Lucy's birth. He came once she was born."

I look around the room and all the pictures on the wall of when Lucy was born and when the kids were little and although I'm smiling and holding my babies I was dying inside.

"But by the time Lucy was six months old I realised that I wasn't devastated about the end of my marriage, it was never about that. Everything I had been feeling was the loss of a father figure for the kids. Yes, Robert still saw them every other weekend and once during the week, but they deserved so much more. They deserved a parent that was always present and there for them. That's why I gave up Tae Kwon Do. I couldn't do it and be there for my kids. My last competition showed that when I was so tired, and stressed I lost in the first round of sparring. I never went back to class after that."

"Do you miss training? The competitions? taekwondo in general? I know people miss you."

I let out a sigh and look to the far wall where all our trophies and medals are displayed. I know there are even more in the loft, but I have moved mine away to make room for Tylers. I would have put them all away if he had let me, they are a reminder of what used to be.

"I do, but I'm not going back. I will always choose my kids happiness over my own. Lucy gets bored easily and Tyler hates being left to entertain her, so there is no way I could train anyway."

"I could help? I could watch Lucy whilst you train," Jenson starts but I shake my head.

"I don't even remember the patterns that well and the step sparring has changed so much. I don't know I guess I just feel too old to be starting all over again." Jenson looks at me, his blue eyes watching as I feel them seeing through the excuses. I take a deep drink before blurting out the truth. "It's not that I haven't thought about going back, I have so many times. But the thought of being in that dojang with everyone expecting the three times world champion to be amazing and instead I fall flat on my face. I'm better off leaving things as they are."

Jenson continues to watch me as I wait to hear what words of wisdom he will come out with in the hope of getting me back on the mats. I know that if anyone can get me back there, it's the guy in front of me. We had the best chemistry when training and competing, no matter how badly I thought I was doing he would be there cheering me on with Grant, it's not been the same since he left. He takes another sip of his drink and sighs.

"So what about you? What do you do for yourself?" he asks. I shrug as I pick up the empty plate and carry it into the kitchen. Needing a second to think before I give him an answer because I know he won't give up until he gets one. I hear the chair scrap across the floor and know he is walking in here behind me.

"Stop stalling. I might have been gone for a long time, but I can still read you like a book. What do you do for you?"

"Plenty. I read or watch TV," I start, but when I turn and see him leaning against the door frame with his arms crossed over his chest I know it's not enough.

"You deserve to do something that is for you Gracie."

"I'm a mum I don't." I start but Jenson cuts me off.

"Don't give me that. Yes, you're a mum, an amazing one. Tyler trains three or four times a week, he goes to football, Lucy goes to dance classes, and I know she will go train just as hard as Tyler when she starts at the academy. But whilst you are running around after them or work, what are you doing for your own well-being? I've had them for two days and I'm exhausted."

I open my mouth to apologise but Jenson holds up his hand to stop me.

"That wasn't me complaining, I have loved watching them for you. They are great kids, I'm exhausted but very happy I got to spend time with them. But I don't know how you do this day in and day out as well as work on top of it. You must need a break from it all, even if just an hour a couple of times a week."

I turn back to the sink and start washing up the plate. I know he's right, but I just can't go back to training. I'm not good enough anymore and I will never be as good as I was again. I don't know how to be just average there. I feel two hands on the tops of my arms and I turn to see Jenson standing behind me.

"I'm sorry, I shouldn't have pushed. I guess I forget that it's been a long time and you don't want or need my advice like you used to. I don't have the right to act concerned when I didn't even check in with you over the years." He takes a step back and offers me a small smile.

"If you ever need a babysitter or a friend, you have my number. I don't want to lose touch again. The offer to train with you whether in the dojang or somewhere away from anyone else is there just shout. I've missed you, Gracie. Just remember I'm here if you need a hand with anything, okay?" He looks at me with arched brows and I enjoy the feeling of having my best friend back, there never has been anyone who has come close to replacing him. Yeah Grant has been around, but it was always Jenson and me against the world.

"Deal," I reply holding out my Pinky. Jenson looks at it for a moment and smiles before wrapping his little finger around it.

"Pinky promises still count even now we are closer to forty than fourteen," he winks as he steps back from me.

"I wouldn't dare break one," I reply grinning.

"Jenson it's done!" Tyler calls from the lounge. I frown as I see Jenson grinning from ear to ear.

"Thanks, dude," he calls back as he heads into the dining room and refills my wine glass. He hands it over before pushing me towards the lounge.

"What's done?" I ask trying to fight against him.

"Tyler just ran you a bath with some salts I picked up earlier. Now go upstairs, have a bath and relax." Jenson orders and he points up the stairs. I look between Tyler and Jenson and see them fist-bump smiling at each other.

"I can't I still need to iron the uniforms for tomorrow and make the lunches." I start but Jenson shakes his head and starts leading me to the stairs again.

"I've done all that. Tyler helped. All you need to do tonight is put your feet up and rest. If you need anything it can wait until tomorrow."

I see Jenson grab his jacket from the hook and shrug it on. He leans around the door frame and calls to Tyler that he will see him tomorrow at training and then back to me with a smile.

"I don't know how to thank you," I whisper holding my glass and feeling more relaxed than I have all day knowing that everything has been done for me, for the first time in forever. Jenson takes a step forward and smiles.

"You can thank me by taking it easy. Call me if you ever need a hand again, I'm more than happy to spend time with the monsters." He leans in and for the briefest moment, I wonder if he is going to kiss my lips. It's almost as if he stops for a moment and considers it before changing course and kissing my cheek instead. I watch Jenson open the front door, feeling a little disappointed and confused by the change in the way I see the man in front of me. He turns back to look at me one last time. "Think about what I said. Do something for you, you deserve it."

I nod once before he steps out and closes the door behind him, leaving me holding my wine and staring at the door, wondering what's happening to me. No one ever does things like this for me, ever.

I turn on the spot and head up the stairs with a million thoughts drifting around in my head. All focusing on Jenson and the feelings I am developing for him.

I get out of the bath half an hour later feeling relaxed and ready for bed. I pick my phone up from the side where I left it and see two missed calls from Robert and a text message from Jenson. I ignore the calls and open the message.

> Jenson: Hope you have a nice long soak and sleep. It has been great spending time with the kids.
> Although I might change your name from Gracie to Diane as you really are Wonder Woman doing it alone.
> Sleep well xx

I smile and am about to type out a reply when there is a knock on the bedroom door. I quickly check the towel's wrapped around me and call for Tyler to come in. He looks nervous as he holds out his phone.

"I told him you were in the bath, but he demanded to speak to you."

I force a soft smile and take the phone from him.

"Thank you, dude. You go brush your teeth, I'll bring it back to you when I'm done."

Tyler nods and walks out looking sheepish as I lift the phone to my ear.

"What is so important you had to call three times?" I demand as I close the bedroom door to ensure Tyler doesn't hear anything he shouldn't.

"How were you at work today?" Robert snaps down the phone.

"I had to swap shifts as you couldn't have the kids the last two nights," I point out.

"So who is this Jenson, who has been looking after my children? Did I say a strange man could look after them?" he barks down the line. Who does he think he is?

"Since when do I have to have your approval with who looks after OUR children? I have known Jenson my whole life for your information, he offered to watch the kids as you apparently couldn't."

"You should have taken the time off work. You didn't have to go in."

"Yes, I did. I am contracted to work every other weekend, the weekends you are meant to have the children. If you are that bothered by not having them then you shouldn't have cancelled!"

"Michelle was ill, I told you that."

"What about when I'm ill? Do I get to send them to you when it's not your day to have them? No, I have to soldier on as I always have. So no, I don't accept that as an excuse. You should have still had them."

"This Jackson isn't to have them again," Robert demands through gritted teeth sounding annoyed that I am answering him back. He has always hated it when I got a backbone and didn't do as he said. But we are no longer married, he has no control over me anymore.

"His name is Jenson and yes, he will. He has offered to help me whenever I am struggling,"

"Struggling? They are in school five days a week and here every other weekend. How can you be struggling? That's the way it's always been with you. You were forever looking for a reason to hand them over to someone else. That's why you went to those stupid classes and played on the mats. You said you were training but it was just a reason to step away from the responsibilities of being a parent."

At that moment it hits me why I really gave up the one thing I loved. Robert. He made me feel guilty for spending time away from the kids whilst I trained. He told me it made me a bad parent and that I was selfish.

"Do you know what? We are not married anymore, and I don't need to listen to a word you say. Unless it is to discuss you collecting or dropping off the kids, I do not need to talk to you." I hang up Tyler's phone and pick up my own. A new lease of purpose and determination rushes through me as I type out a message. By the time I press send my hands are shaking but I feel taller and prouder of myself.

> Me: I want to start training again. Will you help me before I go back to classes? x

seven

· · ·

Jenson

I CHECK my bag one last time before carrying it out of my room and down the stairs.

"Are you sure you are going to be okay Dad? I feel like all I have done this week is run out on you," I sigh as I walk into the sitting room where my dad is in his favourite recliner watching the TV with Bobby, his Yorkshire Terrier lying on his lap.

"I am perfectly capable of looking after myself, Jenson. I am a big boy." Even though I can't see his face I can almost hear the eye roll. I place my bag on the floor and head into the joined kitchen to make up a bottle of cold water to take with me.

"Where are you going anyway?" Dad calls. I tighten the lid and dry it off on the tea towel before walking back into the lounge. There's no point answering he won't hear me from in there. He hates to admit it, but the old man is going deaf. But at nearly seventy-five years of age, he is doing well for it.

"Gracie has asked me to meet her today to go over some Tae Kwon Do patterns." I place the bottle in my bag and look at my dad to find him looking at me with a big grin on his face. "What?"

He chuckles whilst shaking his head. "Even after all these years, you two are still inseparable." He turns back to the tv still laughing to himself. "I'll never understand how you two didn't end up together. That idiot she married never made her as happy as you did."

"Dad we were just kids, it wasn't like that," I sigh picking up my large bag and placing it over my shoulder. Dad turns back to me with his cocked brow.

"Wasn't it? You could have fooled me. She's in the slightest bit of trouble and you go running, tell me I'm wrong." As he turns back to the TV, I realise it's exactly what Grant said the other day when he saw me with the kids. Yes, she was my best friend and first real crush, but who doesn't fall in love with the girl they grew up with? But do I still feel that way about her? Probably to be fair. The idea of her struggling makes me want to be there for her and the kids. Do I want to be more than just a friend? I don't know. I can see how protective Grace is of the kids, which is only to be expected. Do I want to get my hopes up that we could be happy together as a family, only for her to turn me down? I don't think I could deal with that rejection, not from her of all people.

I say goodbye to Dad and head out of the house to the car. I chuck my bag into the back and jump behind the wheel to head over to her place where we're meeting. I can't wait to train with her again, to see her go back to being the martial artist I remember her being. I know Tyler would love to see her in class again. I don't think she realises just how much that kid looks up to her, not only on the mats but in general. He has so much love and respect for his mum, he wanted to be a part of everything Sunday when we were trying to get things done to make life a little easier for her.

As I drive towards her house I try and think about all she does for everyone else, and I know getting back on the mats will do her the world of good. It can help her to clear her mind and just get back to who she is.

I pull up outside Grace's house and head to the front door, leaving my bag in the car until I know what she wants to achieve today. Before my fist even touches the door, it opens and I see Grace standing in her gym wear. She looks amazing in her fitted vest top and running tights. Her hair is up in a high ponytail with a loose strand hanging down each side framing her beautiful face.

"Hey," I quickly say swallowing the lump that has formed in my throat at the sight of her.

"Hi, come on in." Grace replies stepping back. I walk into the house, for some reason feeling more nervous than when I came this weekend to look after the kids.

Grace walks ahead of me through the lounge and dining room and into the kitchen where there are two cups on the side and I can smell the coffee brewing in the pot. I try desperately not to stare at her, but I'm fighting a losing battle. What was that about trying to keep my cool and not falling for this woman?

"I need a cup of the good stuff before we begin," Grace says snapping me out of my thoughts as she goes about making her drink before turning to me and holding up a cup. "Want one? Milk? Sugar?"

"I never say no to freshly brewed coffee," I reply smiling at her. "Splash of milk no sugar," I add quickly. I watch her hands shake as she pours the milk causing it to splash over the side of the mug. I take the milk and hold her hand between mine.

"Sorry, I'm more nervous than I thought," she whispers avoiding eye contact. I let go of her hand and place a hooked finger under her chin before applying enough pressure to make her look at me.

"It's just you and me, like it used to be. You have nothing to prove or anyone to impress. You know I would never judge you." I look deep into her amber eyes for a moment and smile. "Anyway, even after a break, I'm sure you could still kick my backside, Wonder Woman." A smile slips onto her beautiful face as she relaxes, making her even more breathtaking than she was before.

"You're such a geek," she laughs turning to finish off the coffee.

"Hey, I've always been a geek, it's what makes me so appealing to the women. Can't you see them all queuing up to be with me!" I joke in the hope of helping her relax a little further.

A laugh bursts from her lips as she turns around to hand me a mug.

"However do you cope fighting them off all the time?" she sighs rolling her eyes at me.

I wink as I take the mug from her.

"It's a hard job but I somehow manage it," I tease.

We take our drinks into the lounge and sit on one of the sofas. I notice Tylers theory book on the coffee table and pick it up.

"I've been testing him. He wants to get his black stripe next month."

I flick through the book and see where he has highlighted things and written notes next to them.

"He's a natural," I comment. "His patterns are spotless and his floor work impressive. It's hard to find fault in anything he does when on the mats." I look up and see the pride in her eyes. "He must get it from his mum," I add smirking. Gracie rolls her eyes smiling.

"Maybe when she was younger. He could easily beat me now."

"Well, that's why I'm here to change that." I put the book back on the table and lean back in my seat. "I thought today we could do a little stretching and see how your flexibility has held up. Then, when warmed up, we can go through the first five patterns."

"Five? I don't remember the first five!" Grace exclaims, the panic evident in her eyes. Reaching across I place my hand on her knee.

"Don't panic, we will take our time with each pattern and see what you do and don't remember."

Grace nods as she takes a deep breath and tries to calm her nerves.

"Okay, I can do that. Just be patient with me."

I smile as I squeeze her knee. "I'll be whatever you need me to be, you've got this. I know you have."

Grace takes another deep breath and stands up pushing her shoulders back before rocking her head from side to side trying to gear herself up. I find myself smiling at her as I stand up and take her cup from her hand.

"let's get started then."

––––––––

Three hours later we are both a sweating mess, but Grace has a genuine excited smile on her face as she bounces on the balls of her feet. I grab the towel I've been using to dry off, and clean myself up before taking a long drink of ice water Grace has just given me.

"There was you saying you didn't know five patterns, you smashed six!" I chuckle as Gracie picks up the pads, we discarded an hour ago.

"I didn't think I did! It all came back to me. But I have a long way to go though."

"Not as far as you think. Give it a week or two and you will be ready to get back to class where you can beat me and Grant up just like when we were kids," I laugh as she grins.

"Or not," she laughs nervously. I roll my eyes as I start throwing stuff back into my bag.

"When do you want to train again?" I ask.

"Tomorrow?"

I look over my shoulder with an arched brow. "I thought you wanted to take it slow. That you didn't want to rush back to training nearly every day. Isn't that what you said?"

Grace shrugs as she wipes Tylers punching pads down and leaves them on the ground to dry.

"That was before I remembered how fun it was."

I laugh grabbing my bag and chucking it onto my shoulder.

"I have to take Dad to the Doctors tomorrow. He has a wound on his leg that keeps opening back up. I want them to look at it and dress it."

"Want me to do it?" she asks as she walks with me through the house. I turn to look at her frowning.

"Would you mind? He hates going to the Doctors as it is. He moans the whole time we are there."

"After everything you have done for me, it's no problem at all. I have stuff in my car so let me know what time and I will pop around."

"I appreciate that, thanks, Gracie." We stand at her door looking at each other for a moment, as if not knowing what to do or say next. I lean in and press a kiss to her cheek, as I have so many times, but this time it feels different. I can't help wondering what it would be like to kiss her full lips instead.

"Thanks for everything," she whispers as she presses a kiss to my cheek. I pull away from her slowly and smile as I reach out and tuck a stray section of hair behind her ear.

"I'm always here for anything you need from now on." I find myself saying, realising I mean it. I look into her amber eyes for a moment and force myself to take a step back when all I want to do is step forward and take her in my arms, to do what? Kiss her?

"I'll see you tomorrow," I say quickly forcing my feet to carry me to my car. "Say hi to the kids for me," I add as I throw my bag in the back. We both wave as I jump behind the wheel and drive off home, trying desperately to work out what I should do, because I know for certain that I am still completely in love with my childhood crush.

eight

. . .

Grace

"SO WHAT? He kissed you on the cheek and walked away?"

I roll my eyes at my phone as I drive towards Jenson's father's house.

"He always kissed me on the cheek when we were kids, it wasn't anything new," I sigh trying desperately to ignore the butterflies that come alive in my stomach every time I think of him and the afternoon we spent together yesterday.

"But you aren't kids anymore Gracie. You are both grown adults with adult feelings. Is he as hot as everyone is saying he is?" Lorraine asks unable to hide the excitement in her voice.

"Who told you he is hot?" I demand. I don't like the idea of others noting how good-looking he is. I mean he was always good-looking in a cute kind of way. But now that he has bulked up and gained a more manly look about him, there is something there I had never noticed before. He certainly suits his hair in the crew cut most army guys have.

"There are people from school talking. Plus, Dan said he had seen him down the pub one night and they had a drink or two," Lorraine explains.

Lorraine and her now ex-husband Daniel went to school with Jenson and me. We were all good friends, no one was surprised when Lorraine and Dans relationship carried on through college before they got married and had two kids. What did surprise us was that one day out of the blue they announced that they were separating.

"Well, they are right, he is very good-looking," I reply hoping to hide my irritation. I fail drastically as Lorraine bursts out laughing.

"Oh, come on just admit it, you want him."

"It doesn't matter if I want him or not. He wouldn't want a single mum with two kids," I point out trying to hide my disappointment.

"Bet he would if that single mum was you." Lorraine starts singing about me and Jenson sitting in a tree, and I burst out laughing.

"You are such a child, I'm hanging up." Before she has a chance to finish her song, I hang up still chuckling as I climb out of the car and walk around to the trunk. I retrieve my nurse's bag which holds all the things I may need for an open wound. Looking at the house I see the curtains in the window twitch as if someone had been looking through them. Was he watching for me? *don't be stupid*, I mutter to myself. I need to sort my head out and get over this ridiculous crush I have on him. There is no way he would be interested in me.

I walk up the path to the front door which opens before I reach it. Jenson is grinning at me in a pair of jeans and a casual yet fitted light blue shirt. He looks amazing. I realise my jaw has dropped open and quickly close it.

"Hey, thank you so much for coming," he says as he leans in and kisses my cheek. Something about it feels different and I can't stop the stupid smile that spreads across my face as his lips linger a little longer against my cheek than usual. When he stands back a little to let me in I find myself stopping in my tracks as our eyes meet and my jaw nearly drops again. I quickly blink away the *very* inappropriate thoughts that rush through my head. As I take in his outfit a thought very quickly dampens my mood.

"It's no problem at all. Am I holding you up? You look like you were heading out," I point out wondering where he could be going. I walk into the lounge where I see his father sitting in a recliner chair.

"He's dressed up for you, lass," he says as he grins at me.

"Dad!" Jenson snaps as I stop in my tracks and grin at his father.

"Afternoon Mr C. How are you doing?" I ask leaning in and pressing a kiss to his cheek. I always loved this man, no matter how much time passed between me seeing him, he always gave me the biggest hug and told me how much he missed me. He was like a second Dad to me for a long time.

"All the better for seeing you, lass. No wonder my son has such a thing for you. You are more beautiful every time I see you."

I hear Jenson warn his father to stop it as I giggle and pat his arm.

"Mr C, you've always been a charmer," I tease as I open my bag and pull out some gloves. "Now where is this cut that won't heal?"

———

Fifteen minutes later Mr Crawfords leg is cleaned and dressed. I place all the rubbish in a bag and seal it before Jenson takes it from me.

"So that's it now? I don't need to see a doctor?"

I look up at him and smile. "You will need the dressing changed regularly but I will put in a request for the district nurses to do it," I explain closing my bag.

"Can't you do it, lass? I don't get along with them district nurses. Plus, it gives you a reason to come around and see this one," he says pointing to his son. "He's in a much better mood when he knows he's going to see you."

"Dad it's not the nurses you will need if you don't pack it in," Jenson warns through gritted teeth as he looks at me and mouths "sorry" whilst shaking his head apologetically. I giggle at the two of them as they start bickering with each other. They have always had such a fun and happy relationship. It's good to see that they are just as close as they were when Jenson and I were kids. I was always worried that Jensons Mother was able to cause the wedge she wanted. But watching them now I can see she failed.

"Can I wash my hands somewhere?" I ask smiling at Mr Crawford.

"Yes of course. Boy, show the young lass to the kitchen."

Jenson waves for me to follow him as he stares at his old man with a clenched jaw. I start to laugh but quickly disguise it as a cough.

"Can I have a coffee now?" I hear his father call out as I approach the sink.

"No, 'cause you're a pain in my backside!" Jenson calls back before filling up the kettle, muttering under his breath, causing me to laugh out loud. "I'm so sorry about him. He thinks he's funny," Jenson sighs rubbing his face with embarrassment before holding out a tea towel for me.

"He's harmless, he always liked to tease you where I was concerned," I point out as I dry my hands and fold up the tea towel. "Lorraine was teasing me on the way over here as well, so I've been getting it from everyone," I add. Jenson looks at me with a grin on his face.

"I saw Dan last week. I couldn't believe that they had split up, let alone that he is having a kid with someone else!"

I laugh as I think of Dan's new woman.

"Did he tell you that Rosie is a nurse on Lorraine's ward and that they are really good friends?"

Jenson nods grinning as he goes about making his dad's coffee. He holds up a cup asking me if I want one and I quickly say yes.

"He seems happy."

I hum in agreement as I know how happy Rosie is with Daniel. She deserves it after everything she went through in her previous marriage. Lorraine and she are still really close, it's the perfect extended family and I couldn't be happier for them all.

I look at Jenson again and the way he's dressed, I take a deep breath before asking the question.

"So, did you get dressed up for me? Or are you going on a date?"

Jenson splutters into his coffee as he chokes on it.

"No, I don't have a date," Jenson chuckles as he grabs the tea towel I hold out for him and starts cleaning his shirt. He looks at me with a mischievous look in his eyes. "Unless you fancy letting me take you out for lunch?"

"Oh!" I gasp, I wasn't expecting that. "I wish I could," I add quickly as his smile slips. "But I have to go to work for a couple of hours for a meeting," I answer. But I don't miss the disappointment that remains in his eyes. I realise I'm equally disappointed. I force myself to remember that he wasn't asking me out on a *date*, just for lunch, as friends, I think. Why is this so confusing? I look at my watch and curse under my breath.

"I'm so sorry I need to go, I need to be there in half an hour." I down the rest of my drink and place my empty mug in the sink.

"No worries I'll see you out," Jenson replies quietly. I follow him through to the lounge and press a kiss to his dad's cheek.

"I'll see you later Mr C. Any issues with that leg, get Jenson to call me and I will pop round."

"Don't you worry about me, lass. But pop around whenever you want. I know we both like to see you," he says with a wink before looking at his son who looks ready to kill him.

"I'll bare that in mind," I laugh as I pick up my bag and head towards Jenson as he shows me to the front door.

"Thank you again for checking out his leg. Give the kids a big hug from me, I've been missing the buggers."

I can't miss the way his mood has shifted, I realise he thinks I'm rushing off after he asked me for lunch. Did he mean for it to be a date? I decide to show him I really would be interested if he was. What's the worst that could happen?

"Why don't you pop over later and hug them yourself? They have been asking for you to come around." I look into Jensons bright eyes and don't miss the way they expand as I smile at him.

"Are you sure I won't be in the way?" he asks as he places his hand on the frame behind me, leaning in so I have to tip my head up to look at him. Oh, my days, he looks hot when he looks down at me like this. Before I let any doubt sink in I press a quick kiss to his lips before ducking out of his way and heading down to my car.

"Dinner will be on the table for six, don't be late," I call out not daring to look behind me where I can feel Jenson's eyes burning into my back.

"I'll be there by five," I hear him call back as I get into my car and finally allow myself to look in his direction. He is standing in the doorway leaning against it casually grinning as his thumb strokes over his lips. I grin pulling away from the pavement and head towards work, feeling like I'm about to burst with excitement.

nine

. . .

Grace

MY STOMACH'S been in knots since I kissed Jenson. I still can't believe I actually kissed him. There were so many times when we were growing up that I thought about doing it, but I never had the guts to.

"Mum! He's here!"

My head snaps to the clock in the kitchen and see it's bang on five o'clock. He actually came at five! I thought he was just being funny. I can hear Lucy shouting that she wants to get the door and Tyler calling that she isn't tall enough. They are never this eager for anyone else who comes to the house.

They really must have had a good time this weekend with him.

I stand at the doorway to the kitchen and chuckle at the sight of Lucy dragging Jenson into the lounge talking at such a fast rate, I'm sure she will pass out soon if she doesn't take a breath. I can hear her telling him about a picture she drew in school. Our eyes meet and I nearly swoon at the teasing look he gives me.

When did this man get so sexy? I remember him being okay looking, but now with that devious lop-sided grin and heated look in his eyes … I'm in real trouble here. I swallow deeply when he winks at me before following Lucy to her little table in the corner of the dining room. I turn to head back into the kitchen to finish preparing dinner when I hear Jenson call out.

"Ty, can you give Mum that shopping bag please?"

Tyler walks in holding out a bag. I thank him as I take it and look inside. There is a bottle of the white wine he had left for me the other day, as well as a packet of Blackjack sweets. I chuckle as I pull them out and walk to the lounge. Jenson turns to me grinning as I hold up the sweets.

"How did you remember?" I laugh.

"Gracie, you made us stop every day on the way to school so you could pick up a packet. I spotted them by the till when I was paying for the wine and couldn't resist." Is there anything this guy doesn't remember about when we were younger? There again I still remember his favourite colour, the way he learnt the dance to "Tragedy" by Steps, so I had someone to dance with at Youth Club. The way his face puckered the first time he tried one of my aniseed balls; so many little things that make him, well him.

"Thank you," I reply trying to remember the last time someone did something for me just for the sake of it. When I look back at Jenson, I realise he knows how much that little gesture means to me.

"You are more than welcome, Wonder Woman," he winks before turning back to Lucy who is begging for his attention.

A few minutes later whilst I'm busy putting dinner together he walks up beside me. My heart skips a beat as he stands so close his arm brushes against mine.

"Anything I can help with?"

I turn and smile before shaking my head.

"You cooked for me twice this weekend. This is the least I can do."

"What if I like looking after you and want to help?" he reaches up and brushes some of my long brown hair over my shoulder. "I think it's been too long since someone truly helped you," he says softly. I look up into his eyes and know he sees the pain that I've kept hidden for a very long time.

There is so much I want to say to him, all my fears, my dreams, everything I have wished I could share with him over the years. But does he still really care as he did before? Has the time between us, changed who we are to the point we will never be as close as we once were? I swallow the panic rising inside of me, blocking my throat and making it hard to breathe.

"You could peel and grate them." I hand him a knife point to a pile of carrots.

"That I can do," he says with a smile as we get to work making the salad, chatting together and enjoying each others company.

———

I fall onto the sofa next to Jenson and let out a content sigh with a big grin on my face. We both sit with a glass of wine in hand and full bellies.

Dinner had been a success, not that you can ever go wrong with tacos. The four of us sat together at the table laughing and talking so much that dinner nearly went cold. The kids have been desperate for Jensons attention, and he's been more than happy to give it. When it was time to put Lucy to bed, she begged Jenson to read her another story, and wouldn't take no for an answer. I couldn't help sitting on the stairs for a moment, listening to the two of them laugh and make silly voices together. Lucy was so happy having him to herself for a bit.

Tyler also enjoyed some one-to-one time with him as they went through Ty's theory book and then Jenson helped him with his history homework. I forgot how much Jenson used to love history in school, he even managed to get Tyler to enjoy the work and had him asking all kinds of questions. It was great to see Tyler letting someone help him other than me. He shut himself off a little after his dad and I separated. Even Grant and his wife Philippa struggled to form a relationship with him, and it's taken a long time for Tyler to speak to him about stuff that's on his mind. But he seems to have taken to Jenson with ease.

I turn to say something to Jenson but find him watching me intently, with a small smile on his face.

"What?" I ask giggling nervously.

"Nothing, I was just thinking," Jenson replies with that smile still on his face.

"About what?"

"That I wish I had gotten in touch all the times I thought about it."

"You thought about reaching out?" I ask looking for any sign that he's lying. Jenson nods as he reaches out and brushes his knuckle down my cheek, leaving a trail of heat in its wake.

"You were the first person I looked for when I signed up to Facebook,"

"Why didn't you message me?" I ask frowning. Jenson lets out a deep sigh and sips his drink.

"Because I saw that you were married, I couldn't stand the idea of seeing you happy in someone else's arms. I closed the account and never reopened it." I stare at him in disbelief. "When my sister messaged to say she had seen you and you were pregnant I knew then I would never be able to return, not with you having a family without me."

"I didn't think you cared," I whisper as I turn to face him. "You never wrote back, I sent that last letter and waited for a reply, but it never came. I figured you had forgotten all about me." I feel my eyes fill with tears and try to blink them away.

"How could I ever forget about you?" Jenson asks cupping my cheek, forcing me to look at him. "You were my best friend. You knew me better than anyone. You probably still do because since you I haven't let anyone get as close." His thumb strokes over my cheek as a single tear escapes. "Every single letter that I received I replied to. I would wait for the postman each morning in the hope he would have a letter from you. When they stopped coming, I gave up waiting, but I never stopped caring. I couldn't face coming back here and you not wanting to be my Gracie anymore."

"I was always yours," I whisper as I try desperately not to cry. Jenson takes the glass from my hand and places it on the coffee table. He lifts my legs, so they were across my lap, as he moves close enough to take me into his arms and hold me against his chest.

"I messed up," I hear him say as he runs a hand over my head before kissing my hair. "I should have just told you how I felt, not hidden away like a coward."

"We were fifteen, maybe it all happened for a reason," I sigh as I lean against him.

"Like we were meant to come back into each other's lives whilst in our mid-thirties?" he asks as I nod. "Now that we are older and wiser?" Jenson teases making me giggle.

"I might be older, but I certainly don't feel wiser," I reply.

"So where do we go from here?" he asks into my hair. I lean back a little so I can look at his face.

"Where do you want it to go? Whatever you decide you need to be aware that I come with baggage, in the shape of two tiny humans."

A big smile spreads across his face. "Oh, I'm well aware of those tiny humans. Did you not hear? I am Princess Lucy's new BFF. It's a title I take very seriously."

"I'm being serious Jenson. I need to know if this is a bit of fun for you or if you are committed. I won't let those two get hurt, especially Tyler."

Jenson runs his knuckles down my cheek before cupping my face in his large hand.

"I'm deadly serious, I have lost you once and I have no intention of ever losing you again, Gracie."

"I don't want to lose you either, but I'm scared," I admit quietly.

"Of what?" he asks looking deep into my eyes. It's like he can see my inner turmoil. Just like he always could. It's why I could never lie to him, not even now twenty years later.

"Of being the one left on their own again," I answer honestly. Jenson closes his eyes for a moment and shakes his head.

"Gracie your ex-husband was an idiot. The only good thing he did for you was give you those two amazing kids upstairs." I open my mouth to disagree but Jenson places a finger over my lips. "Don't argue with me because you know I'm right. Tyler told me earlier about him demanding to speak to you after I left on Sunday. That he wouldn't take no for an answer, and that it was because Tyler had told him you had been to work. Let me guess he didn't like that I looked after the kids?" I let out a deep breath and nod.

"Please don't take it to heart, the kids loved spending time with you, and I am so grateful that you had them," I start but stop when he shakes his head.

"I don't care what he said about me having the kids. I didn't do it to please or upset him, I did it to help you. You three are my priority, not him and his new wife. All I care about is looking after you all if you will let me."

I smile as I nod my head because I know he will look after us, in a way that no one else ever could.

Jenson smiles back at me as the hand he has cupping my cheek slides up my head until his fingers are entwined into my hair and the look between us intensifies tenfold.

"Good, because I'm about to do something I always wished I had." In one move his lips press against mine and I instantly melt into the kiss. It starts slow and loving, but it doesn't take long before we are pulling each other closer desperately trying to claim back all the years we were apart.

ten

. . .

Grace

I WALK UP the stairs to the dojang, my training gear on and sparring kit on my shoulder. My whole body is shaking as I think of standing on those mats for the first time in four years. My heart races as I think of all those people expecting to see the confident, carefree Grace I used to be. The girl who smashed her third dan grading and was looking forward to going for her fourth as soon as she was able to. There was nothing that was going to stand in my way. But it all fell apart when Robert left, and I gave up all my dreams.

I lift my head to find Jenson standing at the top of the stairs in his training gear, which he wears when he is taking a class for the master. He has been working with me every couple of days for the last three weeks to get me here. We have trained in my large garden whilst the kids are in school, or even with them. He has helped me to get back some of my confidence, and even though there is still a lot to do with my technique, Jenson thinks I'm ready to face a class again. He wants me to step outside of my comfort zone and promises to be with me every step of the way.

When I reach him, I let out a deep sigh. Jenson takes my hand and gives it a reassuring squeeze. Before leaning in and placing a kiss on my cheek.

"Did the kids get off to their dads all right?"

I nod not trusting myself to reply. He threads his fingers into my hair and grins at me. "You've got this. You are more than ready to be back here. You looked amazing yesterday." Jenson leans in and whispers into my ear. "I'm not just me saying that because I think you look amazing, at any time of the day or night. Which by the way you do," he stands straight and winks playfully causing my cheeks to heat as my stomach flutters for a whole other reason. Jenson leans in and presses a kiss to my lips while pulling me against him.

"No kissing in the stairwell please!"

We both turn to see Grant grinning at us as he approaches in his training gear and bag over his shoulders.

"Well if anyone was going to manage it, it was you, Crawford," he laughs before zeroing in on me. "You finally coming back, Gracie?"

I take a deep breath as I nod. "Thought I better come back and remind you who's boss, Grant." Grant roars laughing as he walks past us and looks over his shoulder and waves a finger pointing to Jenson and me. "By the way, it's about time this became a thing, it's been too long." He bows as he walks into the dojang, as is tradition. "Drinks on me after training," I hear him call as he walks out of sight. We start laughing as we head to the door, bowing before entering. We walk over to where Grant is pulling off his shoes and get ready for the class to start. Just before I head over to the master to have a quick word and hand over my insurance money, Jenson places a hand on the bottom of my back and leans in to whisper in my ear.

"You got this Gracie, I'll be beside you the whole time, I promise."

———

"Here's to Grace, having taken a four-year break and is still able to kick all our backsides on the mats!" Grant calls holding up his pint. Jenson, Philippa and I all hold up our glasses in unison.

"It's so good to have you back Gracie. I've missed having someone to help me keep this one in check," Philippa says next to me pointing to Grant. I laugh and take a sip of my wine.

"Don't worry, I'm sure I'll be back beating him regularly soon enough," I wink at Grant who just shakes his head.

"I would argue with you, but we all know you could beat me now without even breaking a sweat," he laughs winking back. I shake my head whilst rolling my eyes and look to my right. Jenson's sitting back, relaxed in his seat, his left ankle resting on his right knee. His arm leaning on the back of my chair.

"You did well getting her back, Jenson," Grant says lifting his glass to him.

Jenson's eyes sparkle as a big smile appears on his face.

"All I did was give her the encouragement she needed. This woman is pure talent, a natural."

It's amazing how much of a difference it makes to have someone who believes in you and wants to see you succeed. For a long time, I have felt alone when it came to my successes, whether it was at work, at home with the kids or competing and sparring. Even my parents never really encouraged me to continue when I took the break. Grant and Philippa may have asked once or twice if I was ready to return, but they never pushed me, unlike Jenson.

Even after all these years, we have gone straight back to the way we were before he left. We never did anything without the other and he was my biggest cheerleader, and I was his. Every single time he stepped onto those mats I cheered him on. I missed having him ringside when he left. I think that was the moment I started to lose a little bit of interest in something that I love, because he wasn't there to enjoy it with me. I don't think there was a single competition that I didn't look out for him. I always held on to a little bit of hope that I would see him again. There was even a time or two I was sure I had seen him either in the crowds or on the mats competing himself, but I couldn't make myself go over. I was too scared of being rejected. If he was there and hadn't sought me out, then why should

I humiliate myself by looking for him? I wish I had now, I wish I had found him and told him how much I missed him and needed him in my life.

"You okay, Gracie?"

Jenson's voice pulls me out of my deep thoughts as he takes my hand in his. I look up at him and force a smile as I nod.

"I'm fine," I reassure him. he watches me for a moment as if making his mind up if I am or not. I roll my eyes before leaning in and pressing a soft kiss on his lips.

I turn to look at Grant who winks at me. "Just so you know there are no hard feelings. I know I was your number one choice and always have been, but it just wasn't meant to be sorry," Grant sighs dramatically placing a hand on his heart.

"It's all right dude, I know I will always be your number one guy," Jenson declares next to me Philippa and I burst out laughing as the guys play-fully blow kisses to each other.

"And on that note, I think it's time to go home," Philippa announces hitting her husband's arm.

We all quickly finish our drinks and head to the car park where all four of us are parked. Jenson and I wave to the others as they drive off.

Jenson turns his attention back to me. In one hot step, he's in front of me with his hands on my hips as he tugs me to him and presses his lips to mine, kissing me passionately. I wrap my arms around his neck and let him hold me close.

When he pulls away from me, he smiles as his eyes sparkle in the evening light.

"I am so proud of you; you were amazing in there tonight." He presses his lips to mine softly before grinning at me.

"I couldn't have done it without you," I point out honestly.

"Yeah, you could have, Gracie. You can do anything you set your stubborn mind to."

I look into his eyes and smile.

"The kids are at their dads all night," I point out. I watch as his eyes darken a little.

"Is that your way of asking me to come round for a bit and cook for you?" he teases as he presses soft kisses to my jaw and down my neck.

"I was thinking, I could cook for you," I reply as he takes my earlobe between his teeth. "And you could stay the night."

Jenson freezes with his lips against my neck. Slowly he lifts his head and me in the eye.

"Are you sure?" he asks. I smile at him nodding.

"Very."

Jenson grins and kisses my lips again. "Good, as there is nowhere else I'd rather be."

eleven

. . .

Jenson

Two months later

"MUM!" Tyler calls the moment he rushes through into the house, chucking his training bag on the floor as he runs off to find her. I roll my eyes and close the front door behind me. I'm just about to call for him to move the bag when an excited five-year-old comes rushing out of the lounge and trips over it.

"Gotcha." I chuckle as I manage to catch her before she face-plants the floor. I pick her up and she throws her arms around my neck hugging me tight. "You okay Lucy Lou? Did you hurt yourself?" I ask. She leans back in my arms shaking her head.

"Nope I'm fine!" she declares with a big smile. I place a kiss on her forehead and carry her to the kitchen, where Tyler is talking to Grace who is preparing dinner. I lean in and place a kiss on Grace's cheek before putting Lucy back on her feet.

"Please Mum, it would be my last one before I become a black belt and it becomes harder to place in the top three," Tyler pleads.

"You don't need to beg, I said it's fine. Of course, you can compete. I just need to find someone to have Lucy."

Tyler throws his arms around his mum with a big smile on his face.

"Thank you. Thank you. Thank you," he yells excitedly, jumping back from her and rushing out of the room.

"Pick your bag up!" I call after him laughing. I turn back to Grace and see her smiling as she goes back to chopping the veg. I walk up behind her so I can wrap my arms around her waist and plant a kiss on her cheek.

"Hey," she giggles as she leans against me.

"Hey yourself. Grant was asking after you. He wondered where you were."

"Yeah, he messaged after training to tell me all about the fifteen-year-old who bested you," she laughs. I sigh as I remove my arms and lean against the counter next to her so I can see her beautiful face.

"I let him beat me," I point out grinning.

"Sure you did, Crawford," she winks at me before going back to chopping the carrots on her board. I watch her for a moment and revel in the fact that she looks so happy. Even whilst standing in the kitchen cooking dinner she looks carefree and is smiling to herself.

The first couple of times I watched her like this when she was going about her daily life, I rarely saw her smiling. I wouldn't say she was sad, just surviving. It's hard to put into context but it was like she had no real purpose other than to be a mum and work. But since she started training again and spent time being Gracie, she seems happier overall. I wonder if she is ready to take the next big step in her return to the sport she loves.

"So I've been thinking," I say stealing a stick of carrot. Gracie looks up at me with that one cocked brow which the kids call "the Rock eyebrow" and I find myself grinning.

"Don't hurt yourself, that one brain cell is working overtime as it is," she sighs before slapping my hand as I try to steal another carrot stick.

I roll my eyes as she grins at me playfully.

"Yeah, yeah, you're hilarious," I sigh. "I'm trying to be serious here," I add.

"Okay, I'm sorry. What have you been thinking?" she asks placing the knife on the board and giving me her full attention.

"I was thinking with the comp."

"Nope!" she interrupts picking the knife back up and resuming her meal prep.

"Are you even going to let me finish?" I ask pushing myself away from the countertop. Grace puts the knife back down and turns back to face me.

"Of course, I'm sorry, go ahead."

I roll my eyes at her sarcasm but carry on regardless. "I was thinking you could enter."

"Nope."

I shake my head smiling she goes back to cooking.

"Are you not even going to consider it?"

Grace sighs and turns her head so she can look at me.

"I'm not ready to compete, I don't know if I ever will again. I'm not as good as I was, and I don't think I will ever be that confident again."

I take the knife from her hand and place it on the countertop before tugging her against me by her hips.

"I know it's a big step, but I really think you are ready for it. You used to love the buzz of competition day. Tyler says you still love taking him, and I know you miss the adrenaline rush of going up against someone you have never fought before. Not knowing whether you are going to be able to beat them or not. You have said so yourself. You even joked you had one comp left in you, so why don't you just do it?"

I can see her thinking about it, but I can also see the nerves are there too. Grace has been doing so well in classes. She now trains twice a week and with me in the garden at least once, if not more. Her patterns are near enough flawless, her step sparring perfected and watching her you would never believe she had taken a four-year break.

"Will you at least think about it, please?"

Grace lets out a sigh and nods as she drapes her arms over my shoulders.

"I will think about it," a smile creeps onto my face. "But!" she starts, and I give her my full attention. "*If* I say no, you don't keep bugging me about it. You respect my decision."

I hold up three fingers. "Scouts promise."

"You dropped out of the scouts after three weeks," she points out slowly shaking her head.

"Only because they wouldn't let you join," I tease smiling. It wasn't a lie. I'd asked if Grace could come too and was told no girls were allowed. I know it is no longer a rule as there are many girls in the scouts, but back in the 90's it was almost unheard of. Grace hums deep in her throat sceptically. I press a kiss to hers grinning. My smile slowly fades as I look deep into her amber eyes. One kiss is never enough when it comes to this woman. Her full luscious lips are like an addiction. I tug her against me and kiss her again, tightening my hold on her waist, needing as much bodily contact as possible as I kiss her, this time with more passion and need, which she quickly meets and returns.

"Can you read me this tonight please?"

Grace and I separate quickly and look down at the little moment killer standing with her favourite book in her hand. She steps towards me and holds it higher until I take it from her. I squat down smiling.

"You got it, Lucy Lou. Go get your nightie on, brush your teeth and I'll be right there." Lucy smiles as she turns and rushes up the stairs excitedly. This has quickly become a nightly thing. Whenever I'm here for dinner or staying the night, I put Lucy to bed and read her a story. I love doing it as it feels like one-to-one time with her, which is only fair as I also spend one-to-one time with Tyler helping with homework or testing him on his Korean for Tae Kwon Do. Last month he passed his black stripe grading which means in five months he can go for his black belt. I plan on encouraging Grace to go for her fourth dan as I know it would give her the boost to excel. She is ready, I know she is. But I just need to make her have the same amount of belief in herself I do in her. I stand up and press my lips to Grace's cheek.

"I'll be back in a minute, shout if I'm not down before dinner's ready." I quickly head up with Lucy's book in hand looking forward to hearing all about her day.

———

"Okay, I'll do it."

I pause, my fork halfway to my mouth as look at Grace frowning. "Do what?"

"The competition, I'll give it a go."

I place the fork on the dinner plate and take her hand which is resting on the table.

"Really?"

She nods nervously and takes a deep breath.

"You're right, I miss it. I usually watch Tyler when he's competing and wish I was down there with him. I know if I don't, I will regret it, so I'm going to do it."

I lift her hand and place a kiss on her knuckles.

"I am so proud of you Gracie. I know how scary the idea must be, but I also know you are going to smash it."

I watch as she takes a deep breath and looks down at her plate.

"I'm terrified I am going to make a complete fool of myself," she admits quietly. I take her chin between my thumb and forefinger and turn her head so I can look into her eyes.

"You will not make a fool of yourself. You are amazingly talented Gracie; you always have been."

"I'm so nervous. I feel sick just thinking about it."

I place my hand over her cheek and run my thumb over her silky-smooth skin.

"I will be there every step of the way. I'll be on the side of the mat, cheering you on."

"You will be umpiring," she points out. I shake my head.

"When Tyler said he wanted to enter I told Sir I couldn't do it as I would be supporting him. I told him I would only do the adults if you didn't compete." I look into her eyes and smile. "There was no way I could be there and not give you both my complete support. I have never felt as proud as I do watching you both in training. Tonight, I stopped what I was doing several times just to watch that kid in action. He gives everything a hundred per cent and leaves everything on the mats."

"He reminds me of you when we were younger," Grace says smiling. My chest swells with pride.

199

"That's because I was better than you and you hated it," I tease. Grace rolls her eyes again and goes back to her dinner.

"You wish," she mutters smiling to herself, looking beautiful with her cheeks flushed and a sparkle in her eye.

"I love you."

The words leave my mouth before they register in my brain. Gracie's smile slips as her head snaps around to look at me, her eyes bulging. I hadn't planned on saying it yet, I wasn't sure if she was ready to hear it. But I do love her, and the kids. They are my family and the thought of ever losing them terrifies me which is why I hadn't planned on telling her how I feel.

"I didn't mean to say that out loud," I admit nervously as I rub the back of my neck.

Gracie continues to stare at me, her eyes sparkling as they fill. *What have I done?* I should have never said it. I want to get up and leave, to give her time and wait to see if she is going to push me away. I place my hands on the table and push my chair back. I stand before leaning in and placing a kiss on her cheek as she continues to just stare at me.

"I'm going to give you space, I didn't mean to put any pressure on you." I let out a deep breath and rub my neck and I feel sick to my stomach. "I'll call you in the morning like I always do," I add hoping she sees I really am just giving her time. Grace continues to stare at me as I head for the door, wishing I had kept my stupid mouth shut. I walk into the cool night planning on heading to the car and probably to a pub for a drink or twenty. I can't believe I just blurted it out like that.

As I open the driver's side door I hear the front door open and turn to see Grace staring at me.

"So that's it. You are running away from me like you did when we were kids!"

She crosses her arms over her chest as she storms out of the house towards me.

"I'm not running, I'm giving you space," I reply tipping my head to the side.

"Looks like running to me. You didn't even give me time to process what you said before you darted for the door. So do you mean it or not!" she snaps coming to a stop in front of me.

"Of course, I mean it!" I snap back. "You and the kids are the most important people in my life. You are everything to me."

"Well, it doesn't look like it. It doesn't feel like it." Grace yells throwing her hands up in the air. "You don't tell someone you love them, apologise for telling them and run away!"

I stare at her for a moment before standing tall as I wrap an arm around her waist, pull her to me so I can thread my fingers into her hair, holding her in place as I kiss her and show her just how much I care about her. I feel her mould against me as her hands rest on my chest. I pull away, both of us gasp for breath as I rest my forehead against hers.

"I love you. I always have and always will. You were my first love, and I plan on being your last," I whisper holding her close to me.

"I love you too, you big dope."

I open my eyes and frown at her as a smile tugs at my lips.

"Dope?"

"It's better than some of the things I wanted to call you," she growls whilst slapping my chest, hard. "How could you think I didn't love you? It's

YOU!" she slaps me again for emphasis. "You make me and the kids happier than we have ever been. We all love you, dope!" As she goes to slap me a third time, I grab her hand to stop her and tighten my arm which is still wrapped around her waist.

"You've always been a violent little thing," I declare through gritted teeth. "It's one of the many reasons I love you so much." My lips meet hers again as I let go of her hand and pick her up so she can wrap her legs around me and I carry her back into the house, my lips not leaving hers for even a moment as I kick the door closed behind us.

twelve

. . .

Grace

"TOMORROW'S THE BIG DAY, isn't it?" Lorraine asks as I sit at the nurse's station on the ward. I popped up before signing out for the day knowing she and Rosie were both working.

"Yep. First competition in about six years," I reply trying desperately to ignore the panic building in my gut. "I keep trying to tell myself that I was always this nervous before a comp, that I'm not losing my touch."

Lorraine leans over the counter and picks up her water bottle.

"At least you will have lover boy there to cheer you on. How is the gorgeous Jenny?" she teases with a wink. I pick up a crisp from the packet I have on the side and throw it at her.

"Will you stop! He hated it in school, and he hates it now," I laugh as she sticks her tongue out at me.

"As mature as always, Lorraine," Rosie sighs from her seat shaking her head at our friend.

"Oh, shush you. Jenny knows I love him really. He got your heart pumping again anyway. OH!" A grin spreads across her face as her eyes widen.

"Oh no," Rosie and I mutter together as we both know what that face means.

"A kick start of the heart!" Lorraine yells excitedly before bursting out laughing. Rosie and I share a look before we start laughing *at* our weird but wonderful friend rather than *with* her.

"What is it with you and terrible one-liners?" Rosie asks as she rubs her swollen belly. Lorraine wipes her eyes as she continues to laugh, whilst walking away from us.

"I'm freaking hilarious, and you know it!" she calls before disappearing into a side room where I can hear an IV machine beeping.

I shake my head as I pull up some patient records on my phone to send over to the staff on call tonight. I see Rosie getting up and waddling over to the meds trolley. I honestly have no idea how she is still working. She only has a couple of months left until the baby comes. If I was her, I would be on maternity leave already.

"Rosie, want me to do something for you? Then you can put your feet up for a bit?" I ask pointing towards the chair she just left. She shakes her head as she heads into one of the single rooms.

"I'm fine!" she calls as she disappears from view. It might be fine for you but I feel guilty sitting here doing the easy work whilst she is on her feet. I quickly finish up and check the clock. With half an hour to go, I consider calling Jenson and seeing if he is at mine yet. I know he was hoping to get there early to relieve Mum as she doesn't like babysitting too late.

"Oh, thank goodness you are still here!"

I look up to see one of the A&E nurses in front of me.

"What are you doing up here, Ted?" I ask frowning.

"I needed to get out of there! There's a man refusing to see anyone but you. He's yelling at any nurse who goes near him."

I look up in a panic as my stomach drops.

"What's his name?" I ask climbing to my feet already knowing the answer. There's only one guy who would demand only I went anywhere near him.

"Crawford," Ted sighs as I see Lorraine walking out of her patient's room.

"Mr C is downstairs," I yell as I grab my bag and rush out from behind her desk.

"Keep me posted!" she yells as I leave the ward. I wave dismissively as the doors close behind me.

I see the elevator but know it'll be too slow so I take the stairs as quickly as I can, rushing past porters, doctors and patients alike, desperate to get down there as soon as possible. I can't believe I didn't think to ask Ted what he was here for. Has he had a fall? A heart attack? What if it was a stroke? He could be here for any number of reasons. The one thing I do know is that he hates hospitals and nurses and has been giving the district nurses such a hard time they asked me to do the dressing on his leg.

I manage to reach the A&E department in record time as I try to dig out my phone to see if Jenson had left a message for me. As soon as I enter the cubicle section of the ward, I hear that distinct voice louder than anything else.

"No, I won't stop shouting! I won't be seen by any of these so-called nurses. Get Grace in here now! She will tell you I'm fine!"

I rush to the cubicle and throw open the curtains. Two nurses turn to me, and I apologise as I rush into the cubical.

"Mr C I'm here," I splutter as I gasp for breath.

The first thing I notice is the amount of blood on his face and clothes. He's trying desperately to move about on the bed and looking like he has gone ten rounds with Olympic Tae Kwon Do gold medallist, Jade Jones. Jenson is beside his dad trying to stop him from moving about and covered in blood. He takes one look at me and I see the panic in his eyes. He doesn't know what to do to help.

"I've got this, Carol." I walk up to the nurse who has Mr Crawford's shoulders and take her place so he can see me. "I hear you are refusing to let anyone see to you?" I say pushing him back onto the bed. He groans in pain as he rolls onto his back.

"They tried to tell me I need to stay here, but I'm fine! It was just a fall!" he yells. I look to Jenson who is shaking his head in disbelief at his dad.

"Are you, okay?" I ask calmly. Jenson looks at me and nods but doesn't say a word. I know he's not, but his dad is my priority right now. I quickly place my hands over his which is still on Mr Crawford's shoulder and squeeze before looking at Carol.

"Can you give me a minute with them? See if the doctors are happy for me to take over for the time being?" I ask her, Carol throws her hands up.

"Trust me, Sister, you are more than welcome to this one," she mutters before leaving the cubicle followed by a student nurse, whom I hadn't noticed was beside her. I sit on the edge of the bed next to Mr Crawford and take his hand in mine.

"Want to tell me what you've been doing?" I ask him.

"I had a bit of a fall, I'm fine," He snaps pointing to his son. "This one saw a bit of blood and panicked. Demanded that I be brought into this cesspit! I'm fine just a little sore!" he goes to move again and curses loudly.

"Dad enough. You might have broken your hip. If it's not your hip it's your skull! Just stop already!" Jenson snaps. I let out a sigh and look at Mr Crawford.

"Will you let me clean you up and get you x-rayed at least? If they decide you need a canular I will put it in. Once they clear you to leave, we will take you to my place where I will look after you."

"Not happening, you have already worked twelve hours today, you need to go home to the kids."

I look to Jenson who is shaking his head at me.

"I'm fine, I'll get Mum to take the kids to hers and I'll get them in the morning."

"You and Tyler have the competition tomorrow," Jenson argues. I look at him with one arched brow.

"Your dad is more important," I point out.

"Not when it comes to *your* health. You told me you were shattered at lunchtime, you need to go home and rest."

I know he's right. I was only complaining an hour ago about how tired I was to a friend. But for now, the adrenaline is keeping me going. I look at his dad and know he has a broken hip just from looking at the way he's lying. I sigh as look at the trolley at the side where there is a dressing kit and gloves. I can see where the other nurses have tried to clean him up but he has fought against them. I take a deep breath and stand up from the bed and stick my head out of the curtains.

"Can I have a new wound pack please and a canular, has he been referred for an x-ray?" I ask Carol who looks at me and nods. "Thanks, let me know when they are ready for him, I'll go down with him and keep him calm." I close the curtain and look to the bed where Mr Crawford is watching me.

"Now, you are going to let me clean you up and get you some pain relief." He opens his mouth to argue, but I hold up a finger to stop him. "Don't you dare argue with me, ask your son, you will not win. Now do as you are told, let's get you sorted and then we can hopefully all go home."

Mr Crawford turns to his son who is watching me carefully. "Is she always this bossy?"

Jenson smiles and nods.

"Yep." He turns to look at his dad. "She can be violent too, so please do as you are told."

thirteen

. . .

Jenson

"IS HE STILL ASLEEP?"

I look at the nurse as she walks into the room. I nod before looking at my dad lying on the hospital bed.

"At least he's more settled now," she answers as she walks over to the IV pump and checks it. "Grace is good with him," she adds. I smile as I think of the amazing woman who took complete control of the situation last night and managed to get my dad to do everything, he was told for the first time in his life.

"I'm going to sneak out whilst he's sleeping to make a call and get a coffee. Any issues call me." The nurse nods as I sneak out of the room closing the door gently behind me. I look up at the clock as I walk past the nurse's station. Is nine in the morning, and it's been a long night.

Grace had managed to get Dad cleaned up and to have the canular placed in his hand. She stayed until he had the x-ray and we found out he had broken his hip. She had given him the bad news and got him to realise that he would need the surgery, whether he liked it or not. He finally agreed and she got him settled on the ward before finally heading home to get some rest.

She asked me to call her at nine when she would be getting up to prepare for the competition. I have left it as long as possible as I feel so guilty knowing she will be tired and nervous. I also feel terrible about letting her and Tyler down today. I walk out of the front door of the hospital and sit on a bench to pull out my phone.

She answers after two rings.

"Hey, how's he doing?" she sounds like she has been awake a while.

"He's sleeping. They are hoping to take him down to theatre in the next hour. How are you? Did you manage to get any sleep?"

"A bit, I woke up an hour ago and just got to Mum's to get Ty. Going to take him for breakfast before we head to the sports hall."

I rub my face as the guilt eats away at me. "Can you put him on?" I hear the phone being moved and the sound of Grace calling Tyler in the distance as she places a hand over the speaker. In moments I hear him taking the phone.

"Hey, Jenson."

"Hey, Dude. I am so sorry I won't be there today. I really wish I could be, but my dad needs me here."

"I know, Mum said. Is he going to be okay?" I hear the concern in his voice and find myself smiling.

"He will be after his operation. He'll need a lot of help afterwards," I admit with a sigh.

"I will help, and so will Mum. Lucy can sit with him too."

"He would like that, dude," I reply knowing my dad would be made up. We have started taking the kids to see him once or twice a week and he loves it. He has always been great with kids. He treats Graces two kids as if they were his own flesh and blood.

"Good luck today Ty. I know you are going to smash it. Tell Mum to keep me posted and cheer her on for me, will you?"

"Will do. See you later, Jenson!" he calls before handing the phone back to his mum.

"He sounds like he is raring to go," I chuckle as Grace hums in agreement.

"He is, he's been practising all morning."

"Take some pictures and videos for me to watch later, please. I wish I could be there for you both, I hate breaking my promise to you," I start, but Grace cuts me off.

"Hey, enough of that. This isn't your fault. He knows and understands that your dad is more important. So don't feel guilty. Is he behaving himself?" she asks, and I laugh remembering how she put him in his place a few times last night.

"He is. I think he is too scared of what you will do if he argues anymore."

"Well tell him I want to hear he has been on his best behaviour, and I will come and see him later tonight. I'm sure Tyler will want to show him any medals or trophies he wins."

"He will want to see yours too," I point out.

"We will see," she replies quietly, and I have a sneaky suspicion she is having doubts about entering.

"Gracie, I know it's daunting but…" There's a noise at the other end of the line, and I hear Grace call something.

"Sorry I need to go; Tyler won't stop bugging me. I'll call you later. Keep me posted on how your dad is please."

"Good luck Gracie," I call out before she hangs up. A sinking feeling hits me as I stand up to get a coffee and head back to the ward. I don't want her to give up and not compete today, she has trained so hard, and I believe she has a real chance of placing. I look at my phone and sigh. I don't know what to do to make sure she competes.

———

I look at the picture of Tyler holding two trophies with three medals hanging around his neck and feel so proud of him. He has placed in every section he entered.

Silver in patterns.

Gold in team patterns.

Silver in speed kicking.

Bronze in speed punching.

Gold in sparring.

I can't wait to see the videos Grace has taken. I know it will be a real joy to watch him competing and his mum and Grant were on the sidelines of every triumph. Where I should have been.

I look at my dad who is slowly waking up after his operation.

"What are you doing here?" he asks frowning. "Have you been here the whole time?"

"Where else would I be?" I ask shaking my head.

"The competition you dope."

I stare at him wide-eyed, why is everyone calling me a dope these days? I look at my phone where there is a photo of Grace and Tyler with his trophies, both smiling broadly. I quickly fill Dad in on all Tyler has achieved today.

"When does Grace start?" he asks. I check the time and sigh.

"In half an hour," I'm about to tell him more when my phone rings and I see Grant's name flash up.

"Hello?"

"Hey, Ty wants to talk to you," Grant says as he hands over the phone.

"Jenson did you get the pictures?" he asks eagerly. I chuckle as I look at my dad.

"I did! Well done, Dude! My dad says well done too," I add quickly as Dad gives me a thumbs up grinning from ear to ear. "Why are you calling me off Grant's phone?" I ask frowning.

"Because Mum's in the toilet for the hundredth time, and I can't remember her pin to unlock her phone." Worry tightens in my chest.

"Put Grant on, dude." I hear Tyler call Grant and the phone pass hands.

"Hey, the main man was amazing! You would have been so proud of him, mate," Grant exclaims and I can hear the pride in his voice.

"I am. He said Grace keeps going to the toilet is she all right? I want the truth," I warn knowing he will lie for her.

"No, she's not. I'm not sure if she's going to be able to do this, mate. She's shaking so hard and being sick. She is trying as she feels like she owes you and wants to show Tyler she's strong like him. But she is struggling."

"Keep an eye on her for me and give her all the encouragement she needs."

"I will mate, say hi to your dad for me." We say a quick goodbye and I hang up.

Leaning forward I place my head in my hands as I let out a long sigh. I look to my dad who I realise heard the conversation.

"Go."

I shake my head as I look at him.

"I can't you need me here," I start but he shakes his head.

"There's nothing else for you to do here. It's not like I can go anywhere, and I promise I'm not going to kick off again. Go and support her. Your Gracie needs you more than I do right now."

I look from him to the clock on the wall before jumping to my feet. I might not make it before her first category, but I need to try.

fourteen

. . .

Grace

I CAN'T DO THIS. My stomach's in knots, my hands are shaking so hard I know I will fail the pattern on presentation alone. My heart's racing it will only make it harder to keep a decent pace.

I look over to where Tyler is smiling and waving at me with Grant. The two of them give me a big thumbs up in the hope of encouraging me. I quickly look away not wanting them to see how scared I am. How did I use to do this so often? I don't remember ever being this nervous before.

There is a selfish part of me that wishes Jenson was here. He would help me calm down. He has kept me so calm in the lead-up to today, I don't know if I can do this without him. I know that's not fair; he would be here if he could. His dad is more important than this stupid competition.

"Grace Thomas!"

I look to the mats where an assistant is standing. It's a student from our class. I face her and bow before walking into the middle of the mats and facing the umpires and bowing again.

"What pattern will you be doing?"

I look at the woman trying to remember her name but can't.

"Uh .. Gae-Baek," I answer, hearing the stammer in my voice. She turns to the umpires and repeats my choice in pattern before signalling for me to get into the starting position.

"When you are ready, begin."

I get into the starting position and hear her giving me the go-ahead. I let out a deep breath and begin. But within five moves I know I have made a mistake. I do a completely different move than I should have. I stop and face the umpires.

"Sorry Sir, permission to start again?" They all look at me and nod. I quickly get into the starting position again. I glance to the side where the assistant is standing. I see her mouth "breathe" and I quickly take a deep breath to try and calm my nerves, but they are completely shot now. My eyes start to burn as I realise how much out of my depth I am.

"Are you ready?"

I look to the umpire and see them all watching me. I open my mouth to apologise and say yes, but my throat seizes, and I can't speak. They must see the panic in my eyes as one of them whispers into another's ear, they share a look and nod and I know I'm done.

"Grace, why don't you get a glass of water and attempt again in a bit when you have your nerves under control."

I stare at him for a moment, nod, force myself to bow and walk from the mats to where my stuff is. I pick up my bottle and take a deep drink.

"You okay?"

I turn to look at another black belt next to me and shake my head.

"First competition in six years. I don't know why I thought this was a good idea," I sigh rubbing my face. I feel her squeeze my arm before going back to watching the black belt on the mats now who is absolutely nailing her pattern. I can feel my son and friend watching me and know if I look at them I will cry. I should have known I wasn't ready for this. It's been too long and I'm not the same person I was six years ago. I look around me at the four other female black belts and know every single one of them will have been working for years to get here. They deserve the medals, not me.

I walk away from the mats with my bag in hand and throw my bottle inside.

"What are you doing, Mum?"

I see Tyler rushing towards me, Grant on his tail.

"I'm sorry sweetheart I can't do this."

"Grace, you know you can. If Jenson thought you weren't ready, he would have never pushed you to go for it."

"But he's not here, is he? He can't see what a complete mess I'm making of it!" I look Grant in the eye and fill mine filling with tears. "I don't belong here anymore Grant."

Grant looks at me for a moment before smiling. "Yes you do, and he will tell you so too," he says

223

pointing behind me. I turn to see Jenson rushing towards me.

"Am I too late? Did you compete already?" he gasps as he reaches us leaning against his legs to catch his breath.

"Mate, did you run here?" Grant laughs behind me. Jenson shakes his head as he stands up.

"No parking. I had to park down the street and run," he explains before looking at me. "Did you compete?" he asks again, and I shake my head. "Thank goodness I didn't miss it," he laughs as he looks around. He spots the mat on which I had just been standing, where a black belt is doing her pattern. He looks back at me frowning. "Why aren't you over there?"

I go to tell him, but a voice to the side of us interrupts.

"Grace? Are you coming back?"

Jenson looks between me and the assistant who was in my section. I see the moment he realises that I've walked away.

"Can you give us two minutes? Grace will let you know then," he asks. The woman looks back at me and I nod.

"Okay, I can buy you five minutes, but any longer and you will have to forfeit."

"She knows," Jenson answers giving her a nod. She holds up her hand showing five fingers before turning around and heading back to the mat and whispering to the umpires. I turn back to Jenson as he steps forward and places a hand on my cheek.

"Talk to me. What's going through your head?"

A tear slips down my face which he quickly swipes away. "I can't do this. I panicked and got the pattern wrong. I had to restart and."

"And now you don't feel like you can get back out there?" he finishes for me. I nod as another tear runs down my face. Jenson pulls me into his arms and holds me as I let out a sob into his chest. He runs a hand over my hair before pressing a kiss to my head.

"Tell me what scares you the most," he asks.

"Failing," I admit. Jenson pulls away and forces me to look into his eyes.

"No one here would ever think of you as a failure, Gracie. No one." He looks to the side of us and I follow his line of sight where Tyler and Grant are watching us.

"Even if you don't compete, I'm proud of you, Mum. You came back and tried your hardest. Just like you taught me to."

I look at my son and realise he's right. I always told him that no matter how he placed, I would always be proud of him because I know he did his best and left everything on the mats. Yet here I am walking away after one little slip. My Master's old saying runs through my head.

"A black belt is a white belt who never gave up."

When I came back to training, I pretty much started from scratch, I may not have been a complete newbie like white belts, but I had to learn everything again. I had to work hard, and I have. I've trained day in and day out to get to where I am. I may not be at the level I was at before, but that's okay, I am not the person I was before and that is thanks to the boy and man beside me now.

I look up at Jenson and see him smiling at me softly.

"Say the word and we will leave, it's up to you Gracie."

I look back to the mats and see the assistant glancing over at me. I take a deep breath and hand Jenson my bag before heading back over to the mat. I can hear the three guys cheering me on as I approach the assistant who is standing by the umpire.

"Do you wish to have another try, Mrs Thomas?" the umpire who let me take a break asks. I nod before bowing.

"Please, Sir."

He gives me a reassuring smile before holding a hand out towards the mat.

"Then please, take your position."

I walk onto the mat and stand on the starting spot. I close my eyes and take a deep breath, shutting out all the sounds around me. When I open my eyes again it's just me and no one else. The assistant gives the command and I take one last deep breath before starting the first move.

fifteen

. . .

Jenson

MY WOMAN IS A MACHINE.

From the moment she walked back onto the mats to the second she walked off it was like the old Grace had taken over. The one who never backed down from a challenge, who thrived under pressure and didn't let anything stop her. When Grace walked off the mats after her pattern all I wanted to do was grab her and swing her around I was so freaking proud of her. But Tyler got to her first and seeing the way her son looked up at her said everything I wanted to.

Tyler was in awe watching his mum perform and I don't think anything would have wiped the smile from his face. Even if she had scored nothing at all, he would still be the proudest kid here.

"You were amazing Mum! Your kick was so high and straight!" Tyler exclaims dragging poor Grace to the side as the umpires talk among themselves. I walk up to the pair of them and hand Grace her bag so she can retrieve her water bottle and towel. The sweat is pouring from her, and she has never looked more beautiful than she does at this moment. Red-faced and sweaty after giving it her all.

"Okay, I have the results here," the assistant announces as she walks onto the mats and everyone turns to face her. "First of all, I think you all deserve a round of applause for an amazing effort, you were all outstanding and showed amazing skill." Everyone around the mat starts to clap, with the occasional whistle or cheer sounding out loud. "It was a tight chase to the three places, but the umpires have scored fairly," the assistant continues as she looks around the room.

"In third place is 3rd Dan, Grace Thomas!"

I spin around to face her as Grace's jaw drops. Tyler starts jumping up and down on the spot cheering as he pushes his mum towards the assistant who's standing with the head umpire holding Grace's medal.

I watch as she bows to the pair of them, and they place the medal over her head before getting her to stand to the side.

I stand at the mats watching the silver and gold medals being presented to the winners, thankful that I managed to get here in time to watch her. As she chats with the other medallists and umpires, I can't take my eyes off her. She looks more like the old Gracie than she has since I came back.

She isn't even off the mats when Tyler runs up to her and throws himself into her arms, again. She laughs as she holds him tight.

"Knew you could do it Wonder Woman," I chuckle as I pull her into my arms and kiss her. "I'm so proud of you."

"I can't believe I placed!" she laughs as Grant pulls her out of my arms.

"I can, you are amazing!" he exclaims as he picks her up in a bear hug.

Grace laughs as he puts her back down on her feet.

"All Senior Female middle-weight black belts to mat four please for sparring." We hear being announced over the tanoid. Grace looks at me wide-eyed.

"Come on, let's get your kit on. You got this Wonder Woman." I throw in a cheeky wink to put a smile on her face. Grace looks around at Tyler and Grant, takes a deep breath and pushes her shoulders back.

"Okay let's do this."

————

"That's it Gracie, keep your hands up. Protect that right side." I yell from the side of the mats as I watch her sparring against some tough women.

"Three points to red," the umpire calls as Grace gets a kick to her opponent's head. Grace gets back into her starting position and waits for the go-ahead.

"Last push Gracie, you got this," I call out. She shows no signs of hearing me, but I know she can. She is in the zone now and on fire.

The next round starts and the women start circling each other, both looking for an opening. If Grace can get this round, then she is guaranteed at least silver. The next round will be against her and the other woman at the top of the board to see who wins the gold. Her hand starts to slip from her right again and I make a mental note to start focusing on that in training.

"Right arm, Gracie!" I call out and instantly it's there. Her opponent is trying desperately to get a punch in but Grace is blocking them over and over again. I can see the woman getting sloppy and know Grace will be waiting for the perfect moment for the counterattack.

"Two points to red!" the umpire calls out as Grace gets a kick to the woman's abdomen. Tyler jumps up and down with Grant shouting as Grace and her opponent bow to each other and the umpires.

"Five minutes then final fight!" he calls out before heading over to the assistance. I grab Graces water bottle and towel and hold it out to her as she approaches. Her face is covered in sweat as it's crammed into her protective helmet. She removes a glove to pull out her mouthguard.

"How often am I dropping that right arm?" she asks wiping her face with the towel.

"Too often, it's noticeable. You need to make sure you keep it up, the woman you are going up against has been watching you with her coach," I answer handing her the bottle. She looks over to the other side of the mat. I can see her sizing up her opponent and planning her game plan. Whenever she hasn't been fighting, Gracie has watched every single fight to work out their strengths and weaknesses. She has quickly become the fighter she used to be, and I know there is a real chance she could win this.

I hear Grant and Tyler both giving her advice and she listens whilst drinking her water. Occasionally nodding but I know she's only hearing half of what they are saying. When she looks back at me, I give her a wink and hold out my hand for her bottle.

"Win or lose, you place top two. Which is better than you expected. Go out there and do your best, listen to me but do what you need to do." I lean in and press a kiss to her nose, the only thing I can reach with her helmet in place. "You got this in the bag, Gracie."

She nods before turning around and walking back to the mat where her opponent is also waiting. They turn around for the umpire to attach the coloured tags to the back of their belts. Grace is once again red.

"Do you think she will win?"

I look down at Tyler and smile pulling him in against me.

"She has a real chance, dude. But win or lose she has been amazing." He looks at me and nods before we stand together and wait for the signal to be given for the fight to start.

———

The sound around the mat is something else. These two women have pulled in the biggest crowd of the day. They are matching each other point for point and the umpire is struggling to see who gets the punch or kick in first.

"Come on Grace!" Philippa shouts next to me. She has been umpiring over the other side of the hall all day, but she finished just in time to see Grace's fight.

"Attack Mum!" Tyler screams next to me. I place a hand on his shoulder but don't take my eyes off the women in front of me.

Grace has done amazing and kept her right arm up. I can't help wondering if she was doing it on purpose before, hoping to lead the opponent into a false sense of security.

"Oh, she nearly had her then!" Grant groans next to me. I nod as Grace narrowly missed kicking the woman in the head, only just blocking her counter-attack in time.

"Two points to blue!" the umpire shouts as Tyler groans. The two women quickly get into position and touch gloves, eager to get the fight over.

"Grace needs to get three points to win," Grant says next to me. I nod again not taking my eyes off her. She looks over to me quickly and I hold up three fingers. She nods as she turns back to the opponent.

The fight restarts and the women are not holding back. They are moving so fast it's hard to keep track of what's going on. Every attack is met with a defence and counterattack and they're fighting like machines. Both have sweat pouring down their faces and at one point the umpire stops the fight as neither can see. I quickly dry Grace's face and rush back off the mats knowing she will want it over and done with as quickly as possible.

"Come on, Mum!" Tyler screams. My heart is racing watching, I have never been as invested as I am in this fight. I watch as Graces right arm drops slightly, and the opponent notices the same time as I do. Before I get a chance to scream at her a foot goes flying towards her side. Just as I think it's all over Grace's arm snaps up and pushes the woman's leg away, causing her to momentarily lose her balance. Before she has a chance to steady herself Grace punches her in the side of the head.

"Three points to red!"

All hell breaks loose as Tyler, Grant, Philippa and others beside us start cheering loudly, jumping up and down on the spot. Grace and the woman she had just been fighting are both laughing and hugging each other, whilst getting out of the gloves and helmets. Neither of them pays any attention to us at the side of the ring as we continue to clap and cheer for not only Grace but her opponent as well. The umpire calls for us to stop and we wait for the final announcement.

He stands between Grace and her opponent and holds on to a wrist of each.

"Both women fought a tough fight and deserve their places on the leaderboard. But there can only be one winner!" he calls out before looking to the assistants and nodding. "The winner by one point … Red!" he yells holding up Grace's hand as she bursts into tears laughing.

There's no holding Tyler back, even if we wanted to. He runs onto the mats and jumps into his mum's arms wrapping his legs around her waist as she only just catches him in time. Both are laughing uncontrollably as she falls to her knees crying into her sons shoulder as they hug each other.

Everyone quickly follows suit and rushes onto the mats to congratulate both women on a fantastic fight. It feels like forever until I finally get in front of Grace. When I eventually get near her she is back on her feet with tears of joy running down her face. She looks at me and jumps into my arms, wrapping her legs around my waist as I kiss her.

"You're my lucky charm!" she sobs as she pulls away from me a little.

"That was all you Gracie, you didn't need me. You just needed to find yourself again," I point out.

"I couldn't have found myself without your encouragement," she adds grinning.

"Does that mean you will listen to me more often?" I ask teasing. Grace smiles as she shakes her head.

"Don't push your luck, Crawford."

I smile back at her as I lean in so my lips are by her ear.

"I'm going to see how far I can push you for many months, and years to come."

epilogue

. . .

Six Months Later

Grace

"LASS, you are wearing a hole in my carpet, will you sit down!"

I look to Mr Crawford and frown.

"Whose carpet? If I remember rightly this was my house!" I point out. Mr Crawford rolls his eyes dramatically.

He's been staying here since his accident. Jenson hired our friend Daniel to help build an extension on the back of the house for Mr Crawford to live in as he hasn't been as mobile since his accident. Janson and him moved in as soon as it was completed and to be honest it's been going well. Yes, there are times it's like I have three kids instead of two, but Jenson is great at keeping the peace and gets his dad to all his appointments and physio sessions. He even has him helping with dinner some nights.

"Am I late? Have you found out yet?"

I turn to see Jenson rushing into the lounge with his work boots still on his feet. He now works with Daniel doing anything he needs with wood.

"Get them off my carpet, Crawford!" I call pointing towards the entrance hall. He rolls his eyes looking just like his father for a moment. Turns out Jenson is a great carpenter and can make just about anything, which is fine by me as I now have extra shelves for all the medals the three of us bring home from competitions.

"No, they haven't called yet!" Tyler shouts towards the doorway where Jenson has disappeared. I look at my boy and smile.

"Mummy, Miss Sarah said you would both pass no problem!" Lucy calls as she walks out of the door, and I hear her and Jenson giggling together. I can't help but smile while listening to the two of them. I'm just about to go and see what they are up to when the phone rings. I look from it to Tyler for a moment and hear Jensons and Lucy re-enter the room. I take a deep breath and answer the call, quickly putting it on speaker.

"Hello."

"Is this Tyler and Grace Thomas?" the voice asks down the line. I take a deep breath before answering.

"Yes, it is, Sir."

"Excellent." Master Owens says as I hear papers being rustled in the background. "So, I have both of your results here from the grading yesterday. It was a privilege to watch you both as you are extremely talented. Obviously, something you have passed down to your boy. Who is officially now a black belt."

I turn around and grin at Tyler who looks like he is in shock. "He was also voted student of the grading but me and all other instructors. He was a privilege to watch and I cannot wait to see what he makes of himself in the future. He has a talent we know will only grow with the right amount of encouragement and guidance." I watch as Tyler stares at me his mouth still hanging open.

"He is in shock; sir as can be expected. Thank you so much for your comments and for rewarding him top grader, it is an honour he will never forget," I say looking to Jenson who is beaming with pride as he hugs Tyler.

"He works hard, and it shows as it does also with you."

My heart stops as I wait on tenterhooks.

"I am pleased to say you have also passed your grading and are now a fourth dan black belt. I look forward to seeing you both in training next week. We can discuss your places in the next world championships where I would like you to both represent England."

This time it's me who's left speechless. I can't speak as I stare from the phone to Tyler and then Jenson.

"I don't know what to say," I answer honestly.

"Well, you have until later this week to decide. Well done to the pair of you and I look forward to seeing what both achieve in the future." The line goes dead as he hangs up. I look at Tyler and burst out laughing as I pull him into my arms.

"You did it, dude, you are a black belt!" I exclaim as I cry with pride for my amazing son.

"So did you Mum! We both did!" he calls out as he hugs me back. I feel little arms wrap around my leg and look down to see Lucy smiling up at me.

"I knew you would both do it!"

"As did I."

I turn to see Jenson behind Tyler with a big grin on his face. He looks at our boy before pulling him back into his arms. "I never had a single doubt, dude. I am so proud of you," he looks up to me smiling. "Of both of you," he adds.

"We couldn't have done it without you believing in us," I point out.

"How could I not believe in you? You are both amazing. Not only have you passed your black belt gradings you have been chosen to represent England in the world championships!"

I look around my family and smile.

"Tyler will do amazing in them, but I won't be competing?"

Everyone stops and stares at me.

"Are you mad?" Mr Crawford calls from his seat. I shake my head at Jenson and smile.

"I wanted to prove that I could still do it and I have. Now it's time for Tyler to go as far as he can, whilst I watch from the sidelines and cheer him on."

"You're giving up again?" Tyler asks. I look at him and shake my head. Before looking at Jenson who is watching me.

"No, but taking it easy, followed by a short break," I answer. I watch as the penny drops and Jensons face goes from frowning to pure shock.

"You're not?"

I nod as I pull out the pregnancy test from my pocket and hand it to him. He stares down at it for a moment before grinning at me.

"Well, it's a good job I have this for you then," he exclaims as he reaches into his pocket and pulls out a ring box. It's my turn to stare at him as my jaw nearly hits the floor. Jenson just grins as he drops down to one knee.

"Oh, my goodness!" Mr Crawford gasps behind him, but I can't take my eyes off Jenson.

"Grace Charlotte Thomas, will you marry me?"

"Yes!" I scream throwing my arms around him and we both fall to the floor laughing.

"Thank you, for giving me everything I never realised I wanted or needed," Jenson whispers into my ear as he holds me tight.

"Thank you for accepting us," I answer grinning.

"Being without you three was never an option. I was born to be yours," Jenson replies as he kisses me whilst our family celebrates around us. Finally, the house is full of love and happiness, and it's all thanks to the man in my arms, and I could not be happier.

about the author

Donna Elaine is a fairly new author who writes short, sweet and clean romances. She has always been an avid reader and dreamt of one day writing her own books. She is so happy to finally be able to make her dreams a reality.

You can watch for more of Donna Elaine's works by following her on social media.

Facebook – https://www.facebook.com/Donnaelaineauthor

Instagram – https://www.instagram.com/author-donnaelaine

also by donna elaine

His Christmas Angel

A Fresh Dose Of Love (Dan and Rosies story)

ballroom spin

Natalie Cross

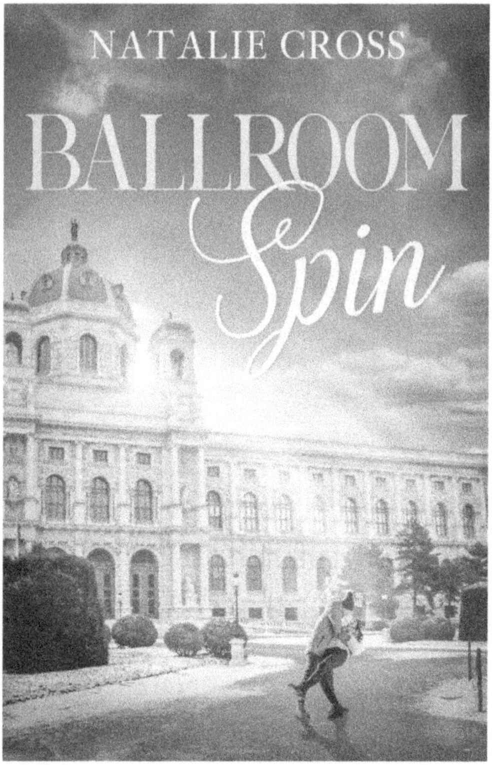
NATALIE CROSS
BALLROOM
Spin

one

. . .

Jackson

EVEN IN THE ragged throes of post-flight sleep, Jackson Alder couldn't help but make lists.

1. Ensure brother doesn't burn apartment down in his absence
2. Make DancesportTV a success, a lofty ambition that seems further and further away every single moment
3. Investigate infernal buzzing noise. Tinnitus? Brain tumor?
4. Seriously, investigate buzzing. Thousand wasps? Tsunami?

For the love of Baryshnikov, stop the buzzing!

Oh.

Jackson rolled over and swiped repeatedly at the alarm button on his phone until he knocked it off the bedside stand.

Jet lag was a beast.

His mind was all foggy and disheveled, much like his hair. He smoothed his errant brown curls down over his temples. So the overnight flight from Chicago to Vienna had been a mistake.

Coffee. He needed coffee.

Ugh, what was that smell? Okay, he needed to go to the bathroom and brush the funk off his teeth, and then he could find coffee.

As he emerged, breath minty-fresh and face splashed with water, his phone rang, and not the alarm this time. Jackson's stomach flip-flopped like a headless snake.

"Hey, buddy!" His voice was too high, too bright. It made him want to squint but that would no doubt drive his seven-year-old brother into a spiral. Like anyone needed that.

"When are you coming home, Jackson?" Topher's face was set in his traditional stink eye. Jackson had been on the receiving end of it more and more lately. He wished he could say it wasn't his fault, but he couldn't say no to work any longer. Topher got the short end of his attention.

"I'm so sorry, Jackson." Mrs. Carthage, the neighbor who had agreed to watch Topher this weekend, appeared behind the boy. She wore an off-the-shoulder paisley sweater. "He insisted on calling you. It's not too late there, is it?" The paisley caught his eye. Was it more brown or mauve?

He really was jet-lagged if he was delving into the colorwork of his neighbor's sweater. Or maybe it had just been a very, very long time since he had been in a relationship with anyone besides his Netflix subscription.

"It's fine, Mrs. Carthage. I'm happy to see you, Topher. I got in a couple of hours ago." He searched his brain for some benign thing to say that wouldn't sound like he was completely smashed. The ten hours of airplane captivity plus four hours of layover had made him a mushy mess. One that his list-filled dreams had not improved. "I'll be back Sunday night. Promise."

"Why did you have to go so far away?"

Why was it always so much worse to have a seven-year-old mad at him rather than his DancesportTV co-producer? Topher's stink eye was a thousand times worse than Noah's.

"Sorry. We need the footage." If he could get the video he needed at the Vienna Waltz Championship, maybe DancesportTV would finally take off and he could focus on only one job. Well, two, since he also had to parent his little brother. Okay, three, because he had the hourly pay as a bookkeeper for a local ballet studio, which he couldn't leave because they'd offered him a job when he most needed one. He forced pep into his voice. "Things are really getting moving in the Dancesport world. Evelyn Zhao is expected to make her big comeback at this competition."

Topher's frown deepened. "I don't think you'll get very far."

That interview would be the *get of all gets,* as Noah unnecessarily kept reminding him. In the three days prior to leaving for Vienna, he had done every spiritual thing short of trekking to a Buddhist mountaintop monastery to pray for that interview.

"Thanks for the vote of confidence." His phone buzzed in his hand with another incoming call. Noah. Perfect timing. Jackson's stomach churned with the desperate need for sleep and caffeine. "Look, Topher, I love you, bro. I'm sorry, but I really have to go. I've got Noah calling, and the waltz competition starts in"—he checked the time and winced—"just over an hour. I've got to get the video equipment set up." And eat. And shower. And drink approximately three gallons of coffee.

"Come home." Topher brooked no argument on that front, and hung up before Jackson could.

Jackson didn't even have time to sigh before the phone buzzed again. He swiped to accept it.

"We need that Evelyn Zhao interview," Noah said, not waiting for Jackson's greeting. At least Noah didn't believe in video calls.

"Yes, hello to you too, Noah. Yes, the flight was fine." Jackson sank onto the edge of the bed. It was so comfy, so cozy, so tempting to fall back into it and sleep for another three hours. "I am well aware of the need to speak to her."

"We've got a lot riding on this. You know views are down. Your last major interview with Patrick

O'Leary and Anita Goodman was over seven months ago."

As if he needed reminding. He rubbed a hand over his head before remembering that he had found six gray hairs nestled in his curls the other morning. He was only thirty-two years old.

"I'm aware. I've left her messages; she just hasn't called me back."

"Get on it."

Noah hung up on him too, because it was that kind of a day.

Jackson finally released the tension in his shoulders with a sigh. When he and Noah had started the online channel DancesportTV to showcase ballroom's brightest stars and bring the sport the attention it deserved, they'd known it wouldn't be easy. Hah. It was a Sisyphean task.

Especially since, if Jackson were ever able to do what he truly wanted, he would not mind talking to Evelyn Zhao on a one-to-one basis. He had followed her for years, ever since he had seen her dance at the Emerald Ball. She was so graceful, so clearly in love with dancing itself, and it struck a chord with him. Some people said she was standoffish or reclusive, but he had a feeling she hid a lot behind those dark brown eyes.

It also did not cure his infatuation that she was completely, entirely gorgeous.

His eyes drifted closed with him barely noticing it was happening.

Okay. Coffee. Coffee first, inner monologue second.

———

Evelyn

Evelyn Zhao's heart knocked incessantly against her ribcage, and she hadn't even started to practice yet.

"Right, so we do the natural turn to the reverse turn. How do you feel about the timing?" Her brand-new dance partner, Alexei Rostov, asked.

Terrible. If her heart rate were any indication, this competition was going to be a nuclear meltdown-level disaster. She should have waited longer after the accident.

"Evelyn?" Alexei stared at her like she wore *Creature from the Black Lagoon* mascara.

She pasted on a tight smile. "It's grand, really."

It was the waltz, that was all. Just the swift-footed, watch-out-for-other-couples whirlwind. It was the first dance she had learned, so in some ways, it seemed fitting for her great comeback.

It wouldn't be much of a comeback if she had a heart attack during practice.

Alexei stretched backward in a bend before straightening and cracking his neck. "Right. Let's do this." He extended his hand to her, his face creased with the professionally charming expression that had made him an International Standard ballroom star. "May I?"

This was her job. This was what she had wanted. All those weeks cooped up in a brace and then hours and hours of physical therapy. This was the goal.

She slipped her hand into his and let him draw her close, notching her body against his and leaning into the dance frame that after so many years felt a lot like home. At least Alexei went lighter on the cologne than her previous partner, Klaus. One fringe benefit of Klaus leaving her after her injury was that she no longer had to take twenty-five-minute showers to rid herself of his too-strong musk and patchouli.

Her heart raced, but she exhaled and focused instead on the sensations of the dance. If she closed her eyes, it would be easier. Then she could ignore her heart. She homed in on the feel of Alexei's hand on her shoulder, the tension in her body as she matched his rise and fall. Yes. This was better. This was soothing, familiar.

She maintained her dance frame as they spun around the practice floor, following where he led. That was his job here, if not elsewhere in her life. She didn't need extra encumbrances right now.

After the first set, her anxiety had cooled and exhilaration had taken over. Her muscles felt alive again, warm and supple. Her heart beat the way it was meant to do.

"How are you feeling? You look great." Alexei ran a towel over his artificially tanned forehead, then over his blond hair.

The thumping in her chest had lessened, making her buoyant. "Good. I feel good." She meant it. Thank heavens and the stars above, she meant it. She could do this. She could be a competitive athlete again.

"Great. Let's try again."

———

The time off made itself known after the fourth practice rotation. Sweat beaded along her forehead, dripping into her eyes. She hated when her palms moistened, much as she knew how her partners disliked it too. Too slippery. Too uncomfortable. She had to claw breath from her heavy lungs at every hesitation step.

She made it, though. She made it through the song and into the bow when Alexei turned her out. Barely. How was she going to do this in full makeup and costume in less than an hour?

"Are you sure you're okay?" Alexei asked.

She swigged from her bottle of water until she had drained it. "Fine. Just getting back into the swing. I'd better go and get ready."

"Sounds good. I'll meet you back here in a bit?"

"Grand. Grand."

Her heart pounded, knocking like it was playing the drum solo in an Aerosmith song. Not now. No, not now. Water. She needed more water, and she needed to be back in her hotel room where she could calm down. Then she could get her head into competition mindset.

Rubbing her chest, she beelined for the small café in the lobby of the hotel.

two

. . .

Jackson

WHY HADN'T he taken the time to learn German before coming to Austria?

Right.

Because one, his brother had gotten intensely interested in an elaborate Lego and magnet block behemoth that had swallowed their apartment, and therefore every spare moment he'd had was dedicated to cleaning because otherwise neither of them could move around said apartment.

And two, he barely had time to eat or shower anymore, much less learn a whole new language.

Still, as he perused the picture menu board of the café in the hotel lobby, he wished he had taken at least fifteen minutes to learn some basic words. "Bathroom" would be helpful. Or "coffee." At least the latter looked familiar in German, and he had a feeling he didn't need to be as careful about his hatred of oat milk here in Austria.

"Umm, Kaffee, please." He gestured at the tiny drawing of the so-deliciously-tempting cup filled with dark brown, jet lag-reducing liquid. There was also something called a mélange that looked particularly delicious, and several drawings with whipped cream. The Viennese could breakfast.

The woman running the café smiled and turned. For some tourist-friendly reason, she was dressed in a red-and-white-striped pinafore, which was both charming and confusing to his already befuddled self.

He handed the woman his credit card and exchanged it for a to-go cup of sweet, sweet caffeine bliss. He could do this. He could totally, one hundred percent make this desperate attempt to reboot his life happen.

"*Entschuldigung.*" The voice was feminine with a thick Scottish accent that curled every hair on his body. Something about that voice sliced through his wandering-time-zone brain fog and deep into his chest.

When he turned, his coffee nestled safely in his hands, he stopped breathing.

Not literally, thank Margot Fonteyn, because otherwise he would have dropped his coffee, but it definitely felt like it.

It was Evelyn Zhao, and merciful Zeus, she was even more stunning in person. Her black hair was coiled on her head in an elaborate updo, and even though she hadn't put on her competition makeup, she didn't need it. She had the kind of beauty that launched a thousand bad poems—hopefully not his, but he couldn't rule it out—and dark brown eyes he could drown in.

She was also rubbing her sternum absent-mindedly, and for reasons unknown to himself, he focused on that.

Which was apparently the utter wrong thing to do.

Her expression iced over. She dropped her hand from where it had been stroking her sternum and leveled him with a frosty gaze. *"Entschuldigung,"* she repeated.

Of course she would be a brilliant polyglot too. "Sorry," he stammered. He never used to stammer. *Blame the jet lag.* "I don't speak German."

"It means excuse me." Evelyn crossed her arms over her chest. She was shorter than he was, but her stature more than cowed him. "Do you mind moving so's I can order?"

"Right. Sorry." He shuffled to the side, unable to leave the actual site of this disaster in the making.

He watched, the coffee warming his hands, as she ordered a bottle of water and turned to go. Something in him short-circuited, and he blurted out, "You're Evelyn Zhao."

She unscrewed the cap on the bottle with sure hands. "Ought I to know who you are?"

Her accent really was appealing, possibly the best thing he had ever heard. "Sorry."

"You apologize a lot."

"I suppose. Sorry. Jet lag."

"It can be murder." She lifted the water to her lips, and that was the moment all of the blood in his body gushed southward, leaving him faint and woozy. It was the curve of her throat, that was all. It reminded him of the bend of the Chicago River, in the neighborhood where he'd grown up.

He wanted to kiss that curve.

Maybe he was delirious and should go take a nap. Nope, no time for a nap.

She capped the water and strode past him where he stood like a statue of the idiot he was. "Pardon."

The single word roused him like nothing else had so far. Evelyn Zhao. The *get of all gets* this weekend. Job. He had a job. If he blew this, Noah would never forgive him. DancesportTV would die. He wouldn't be able to pay his rent or buy Topher the limited-edition fully electric Lego set he had been talking about for months. He wouldn't even be able to get a job herding three-year-old wannabe ballerinas.

Willing energy into his lower limbs, he chased across the lobby after her. Thank goodness this hotel believed in rugs or he would have skidded across the parquet like his one ill-advised turn at ice skating. His coffee sloshed over the side of the cup, scalding his wrist.

He slid to a stop beside Evelyn as the elevator doors opened. He fumbled to apply the lid of his coffee, trying to keep the remaining liquid contained.

She looked askance at him as the doors opened, now back to rubbing at the spot on her sternum.

"Ms. Zhao, can I ride with you?"

"I suppose." She stepped inside the elevator and tapped the button for the fourth floor.

He flushed, his heartbeat racing from exhaustion and running like a madman across a crowded hotel lobby. "Oh hey, we're on the same floor."

She didn't respond, her expression closed and inscrutable.

He shifted his coffee to one hand, the unscathed one, as the elevator started its ascent.

"Ms. Zhao, forgive me for earlier. I'm Jackson Alder. I'm a producer at DancesportTV?"

Her brown eyes flicked to him, but he knew full well he was running out of time. They were already on the second floor, and he didn't hold out hope this dance goddess would wait for him once the doors opened again.

"Anyway, I'm here at the waltz championships to interview some of the sport's best and brightest."

The doors opened, and she stepped out first, not waiting for him. He raced to keep up. "I would love to have a chance to sit down and chat with you this weekend. Whenever you have time. I can work around your schedule."

His room was to the left, but hers was to the right, and he followed her. She turned as she neared a door with her key card in hand. "You want to interview me?"

"Yes." He nearly sighed the word. "Yes. Just a few moments of your time. Whatever you want to talk about."

She chewed on her bottom lip, and it was the single most enticing and absorbing movement he had ever seen. "To promote Dancesport?"

"Yes." He had a couple of other interviews with crowd favorites and rising stars set up already, but Evelyn Zhao, fresh off her injury, would be the crown jewel of the weekend.

"I have to get ready for the prelims." She swiped the key card against the lock, and the light flashed green three times. "Find me afterward, and we can talk. But only for a couple of minutes. And I will not be saying anything about my injury."

The door closed in his face, almost hard enough to spray him with coffee again.

His breath caught and a wave of fatigue rolled over him.

How could he turn this interview into the *get of all gets* if she wouldn't talk about the one thing everyone wanted to hear?

three

· · ·

Evelyn

THE ACHE in her chest eased after resting for five minutes with her eyes closed and focusing on her breathing. Meditation had always helped her deal with the pressures of professional competition life. Now she needed it for a more intensive purpose. *If anyone knew…*

Her phone chimed with a reminder that she had only forty-five minutes before the professional open waltz preliminary rounds. Forty-five minutes to apply her makeup and glitter, stretch, hydrate, and eat half a flapjack.

At least she could do the last one on the elevator ride back to the lobby.

She set up her expansive cosmetic case in front of the desk mirror, unrolled the velvet brush case, and opened various pots and creams. This was meditative too. Restorative, even. Swiping on foundation and concealer. Dabbing highlighter and bronzer. Drawing the perfect arcs to accentuate her eyes. Deep muscle memory guided her movements so she had time to think.

She should be using this time to run through the routine in her head, but instead, Jackson Alder's infuriatingly handsome face kept intruding into her reverie.

She had lied when she said she didn't know who he was. She hadn't been living under a rock. Had she been glued to the telly every time *Dance with Me* came on, her mum beside her? Of course. And had Jackson largely been a part of her interest in the show? Definitely. Despite the producers of *Dance with Me* urging him into bad-boy-persona land, he had quietly and subtly remained charming, affable, and undeniably gorgeous when he put on a three-piece suit to judge the dancers, regular people who wanted a chance to learn to dance with the world's best and brightest.

She scoffed and reapplied the glitter to her upper eyebrow. Everyone looked good in a three-piece suit, but Jackson? With that curve of his jaw, the shock of dark, smoky hair?

Smolder territory.

What she had never understood, though, was why he had stopped dancing. He had toured for years with his ballet troupe before judging the two seasons of *Dance with Me*. Maybe he had burned out.

Something in her chest twinged as she carefully painted on her lipstick. She knew how tempting it was to cut back and slip into choreography and teaching. Touring competitively was a grueling, soul-sucking pursuit at times.

Wait, was she pitying Jackson Alder? No. He was a snake, a journalist, intent on finding out her secrets and displaying them for the entire world. She shouldn't be thinking of the ways they were similar.

This was the Evelyn Zhao Reboot in full regalia, here to wow all of Vienna with her skills.

But it would really help if Jackson were less attractive.

Her phone buzzed and she swiped to accept without checking the name.

"Evelyn? That you, darl?" Her mother's voice was tinny from the distance.

"Hello, Mum."

It was tea time back home. Her mother would have set the table with the gingham tablecloth and put out the great brown ceramic teapot with the cozy that a younger and naiver Evelyn had hand-knitted between heats at the Warsaw Dancesport Championships.

"You ready yet? Doesn't the competition start soon?"

Evelyn swallowed the lump of homesickness and checked the time on her phone display. "Yes, but I have time. It's just the gown now."

"Which did you choose? The white or the pink?"

"You pick, Mum. You always choose well." Understatement. Her mother had impeccable taste and had started designing Evelyn's gowns when she was a teenager. It had helped keep the coffers filled after her dad passed away.

"I'd go with the pink. I love the feathers. You look amazing in that one," her mother said. "Are you smiling, lass?" How had her mother known? Evelyn was constantly amazed by the perception of her mum. "Ah, good, I haven't seen enough of that lately."

Evelyn's smile tightened. Thank goodness she was on speakerphone, as her mom could always tell when she was stretching the truth. "I'm all right, Mum."

"Are you? Did you call the doctor? Is your leg all right?"

As if in answer, her heart knocked four times against her breastbone. "No problems. Everything is fine."

Her mother sighed. "I should be there with you."

"No, really, Mum. I'm all right." She inhaled and straightened her shoulders. "I'll call the doctor after the preliminary heat."

"All right. Oh, I heard from a friend that DancesportTV sent someone to Vienna to cover the competition. Maybe they already asked you for an interview?"

A ball of warmth that looked slightly like Jackson settled deep in her stomach. "What do you mean?"

"Hanna and Markus's coach heard through the grapevine that they're interviewing the best and brightest of the sport. Isn't that you, love?"

Evelyn bit the inside of her cheek. Prescient that her mum used the same phrasing as Jackson. A great comeback relied on physical readiness. "I don't know."

Her mother tsked, and behind her, Evelyn could hear the whistle of the kettle on the hob. "Tea's on. You should do the interview, love. Tell everyone who designed your fab gown, and tell them all that you're back and good as new."

"Okay, Mum." She sniffed back the tears that welled in the inner corner of her eyes. "Of course."

"Shine bright, beautiful girl."

"Love you, Mum."

After she hung up, she rubbed at the center of her sternum, erasing the heartache. Good as new. Right. She was good as new.

four

. . .

Jackson

JACKSON BOLTED DOWN THE COFFEE.
The drink had had a chance to cool before he tossed
it back like it was the only thing saving him from
dehydration after a hundred-mile run.

He would've paused to assess that statement if
he'd had the time or bandwidth. Neither of which
he possessed, which was why he was racing
around the empty ballroom space designated for
his interview area. Setting up the lights, chairs,
microphones, and cameras, all while not tripping
over the roughly gazillion wires crisscrossing one
another hurly-burly, was more exercise than he had
done in a month.

Which should hurt. Jackson had always been fit. Even before he took up ballet and expanded into other dance forms, he had been active. *"In the womb!"* His mom would cry. *"He never let me have a moment's rest."*

If she had birthed him as a thirty-two-year-old washed-up dancer and wannabe TV producer, maybe she could have gotten some sleep.

The unexpected thought of his mom stilled his hands from plugging aux cables into the sound setup. His mom had always been his biggest supporter. Kind and funny. The kind of pretty that made everyone around her feel safe, warm, and a little prettier too.

His heart clenched, and he stuffed the thought away for another time when he could dust it off and hold it up to the light for a little longer. There weren't many people in the world like his mom had been.

The overhead speakers chimed four times with a bell-like sound. The first sentences came out in German, but in a lilting, melodious accent that reminded Jackson of rolling, snow-covered hills. Then the atonal voice switched to English. "Contestants, the open professional waltz heats will commence in ten minutes. Everyone to the ball-room, please."

His heartbeat quickened. Ten minutes. He had to get the Steadicam ready to record. Besides inter-views, three of the couples competing today had paid DancesportTV for featuring their perfor-mances. Had to please the paying customers.

He checked the mic on the camera and lifted it to his shoulder.

"*Guten Tag,*" a deep male voice said.

Jackson turned, pasting a smile on his face. He was here by the goodness of the event coordinators. It would be highly unwise to piss anybody off because he had overslept after a too-long flight. "Umm, yes. Guten Tag. I'm Jackson Alder, from DancesportTV."

The man was full-bearded and rotund, with a wide, happy smile and a well-tailored black tuxedo. He shook Jackson's hand, the one not holding a hundred pounds of camera equipment, with vigor. "*Gut! Gut!* I am Herr Schmidtz, from the event staff. We are so pleased you could come and shine light on our little competition. Dancesport needs more engaged followers, *ja*?"

"Yes, absolutely. That's our mission at Dances-portTV." He sounded inane. Maybe he could sneak in one of those mélanges between heats. Whipped cream was a major weakness of his.

"Wonderful. We have such excellent competitors here this weekend. Hanna und Markus, Katina und Dieter...und now Evelyn Zhao is making her big comeback! Make sure to get all that on camera."

"Of course." *Don't think about Evelyn Zhao and whipped cream. Don't do it, Jackson.*

The bells chimed over the loudspeaker again, and Herr Schmidtz investigated the ceiling like tiny birds had brought messages just for him. "Well, we must be going. *Naja?* Cannot miss the first rounds. So exciting, so exciting."

He wandered off, greeting everyone heartily in a mixture of languages, like a jolly Robin Hood doling out greetings instead of stolen treasure.

Jackson desperately needed caffeine. Instead, he hoisted the Steadicam to his shoulder and headed for the ballroom.

five

. . .

Evelyn

ALEXEI LOOPED EVELYN'S hand through his arm as they waited in the on-deck area for their names to be called. Her cheeks already ached from smiling. Was her hair flat? Had she lost too many sparkles on the ride down from her hotel room? She stretched her feet in her dance shoes, her toes scratching against the fabric.

Her heart fluttered, but not in the panic-inducing way. That was good. She would be fine. Her leg had healed. Her heart would hold.

The couples in the first heat completed their round to applause and cheers. They looked like swans twirling around the dance floor, their plumage high and colorful.

She closed her eyes, the lids heavy with mascara and two sets of glittery false lashes. Breathe. She had to breathe and trust her partner.

"All right, then, Evelyn?" Alexei's thickly accented voice was difficult to hear over the clatter of performers leaving the dance floor, the percussive undertone of applause, and her own heavy breathing.

She exhaled, willing her entire body to focus. "All right, then."

With the floor cleared, the announcer approached the microphone. "Our next dancers—"

Evelyn tuned him out. She tuned everything out, everything but Alexei's arm linked with hers, the rise and fall of her chest. If she was to get through these next ninety seconds without falling apart, there really was no other way.

Sway and spin. Her muscle memory kicked into high gear as she followed Alexei to an open spot on the dance floor. It was crowded, but not stifling. The finals would be easier, only six couples sharing the space instead of twelve. She had to rely on Alexei.

Her breathing eased, and for some unknown reason, her mind snagged on Jackson Alder. It wasn't that unusual. Often in the moments directly before a performance or a competition, her mind wandered to unusual things. Had she left the kettle on? Was her mother wearing the gray jumper or the one emblazoned with a giant starfruit?

She didn't really have time to contemplate it, or why the thought of Jackson somewhere nearby simultaneously warmed and cooled her, as the music began and the dance started.

six

. . .

Jackson

THE END of the professional heats was a massive relief, giving the judges time to tally the results before announcing which couples would be entering the semifinals.

Time for Jackson to grab his much-needed caffeine and sugar jolt and set the camera down. His shoulder ached under the strain of holding the device steady while filming the dances.

The "problem" with filming professional dancers was that they knew how to use the floor, how to sweep and ensure that every corner of the room could see their grace and elegance. It was far easier to record amateurs, who tended to stay in the same spot out of lack of floor craft.

Now his problem was the coffee line, which was substantially longer than it had been earlier in the morning when the ballrooms had been less crowded.

His phone buzzed in his pocket as he moved infinitesimally closer to caffeinated bliss.

"Hey, Noah," he said, holding the phone to his ear with one hand and sticking the other in his pocket.

"How's it going, Jackson? Did they announce the semifinalists yet? We should definitely get that on camera."

"Already on it." Why did his friend think he needed to be micromanaged from thousands of miles away? Jackson wasn't that bad at his job, was he? "I scoped out some good angles during the heats, so I'm all set."

"Good. Anyone you think could be a favorite?"

He sighed as two teenagers joined the couple in front of him. All likely wanting their own hot, delicious beverage to keep them awake for the semifinals this afternoon. "The crowd adored Hanna and Markus, to be expected. And, um, Evelyn Zhao and

Alexei Rostov were amazing." Alexei Rostov was also way too attractive, in Jackson's opinion. At least he was happily married.

"Really?" Noah's voice perked up. "Good, that's good. That would make an amazing story, don't you think? Evelyn comes back on top of her game? Partnering with Alexei, too? That Klaus never fully suited her."

Yes, it would, if she had agreed to discuss her injury during the interview, but that was a fish fry for another day. "Yup."

"Jackson." Noah's voice was stern, the tenor enough to make Jackson's spine stand straighter.

"What's wrong? Is Topher okay?"

"Topher's fine. I already checked with Mrs. Carthage. It's you I'm worried about."

"Me? Why?" Thank goodness, only four more people in front of him. "I'm fine."

Noah sighed, so loudly the couple in front of Jackson turned toward him with arched eyebrows. He shook his head and kept his expression banal.

"You think I don't know you've had a thing for Evelyn Zhao for years?"

"It's not a thing." Sputtering. Was he sputtering? *Curse you, jet lag!!!* "I just admire her. That's all. That's normal."

He could almost hear Noah's eyebrows arch in that knowing manner of his that rankled the hell out of Jackson. "Admire her? Jackson, please. She's *exactly* your type. Look, I know you're preoccupied. But don't blow this. Don't go getting all Jackson-doe-eyed and trailing her around like you do. You need to get in, get this job done, then get back here so we can use the footage to make DancesportTV everything we want."

"Right. Absolutely. Coffee first, then wild commercial and financial success."

Noah laughed quietly. "Take care. Upload some of the prelim footage so I can put out a quick reel, okay? Oh, and do one after they announce the semifinalists. Let's post that online today too. Maybe some people will tune in for a live during the finals tomorrow. I can get ad space for that."

Jackson's lip curled into a frown. He hadn't exactly forgotten about the live taping of the finals tomorrow. It just had been something he had dreaded that now required more attention, like a last moving box that sat in the garage unopened for years.

"Sounds good." He attempted to sound chipper. "No worries."

"Great. Interview with Evelyn, killer footage, and we've got this in the bag. Don't screw it up." Noah ended the phone call without even a farewell.

He supposed *Don't screw it up* worked as well as anything.

Jackson inched forward another step. The group with the teenagers in front of him was getting rowdy. He ticked through his mental to-do list instead of focusing on his deep, nearly thwarted desire for coffee.

1. Don't make an ass of yourself in front of Evelyn.
2. Don't go all swoony animated prince in front of Evelyn.
3. Do NOT make ballet puns in front of Evelyn.
4. Don't think about Evelyn and whipped cream. Rats. Not again.

On second thought, maybe he should stop making lists.

He wasn't going to fawn over Evelyn Zhao. Of course not. Just because he thought she was gorgeous and one of the best dancers he had ever met didn't mean he had a crush on her. He was over thirty, not thirteen. He wasn't just going to fall head over heels for some woman who lived on a different continent and traveled the world, when he was bound to Chicago and Topher.

Of course not. He was sensible now, responsible. He had to be.

"Excuse me," a now-familiar, mezzo-soprano Scottish brogue said from at his side. "You look like you could use this."

Like a dream angel complete with halo around her gorgeous head, Evelyn Zhao stood before him, a to-go cup of life-giving coffee in her hand.

Jackson's mouth went dry. *No whipped cream, no ballet puns.* This was going to be more difficult than he had anticipated. "Hi."

"Do you still want to talk?" There was a pleasant expression on her face, but it didn't reach her eyes. Was she nervous?

The warmth in his chest flushed through him from top to toes. He was certain it was because she was agreeing to the Get of All Get Interviews and not because she had brought him much-needed coffee and looked like a goddess.

This was an interview. Nothing more. He would keep his promise to Noah. Absolutely.

seven

· · ·

Jackson

HE DRANK the rich and delicious coffee in a fit of definitely-not-nervous energy as he led Evelyn down the hallway to the small ballroom he had been assigned for interviews and on-site editing.

"Thank you for the coffee."

"Of course." She swallowed a sip of water from a large reusable bottle. "To be honest, I felt a little rough, like I hadn't been polite when we met this morning."

"No, not at all. I barged in on you." He was stammering again.

He needed to focus on his to-do list, not on how clean and floral Evelyn smelled, even though she had just competed. When he had danced, he'd be dripping in sweat after two numbers. He used to have a towel waiting for him behind the wings to wipe off his palms before a pas de deux. Sweaty hands made for challenging partner work.

A wave of nostalgia rippled through him, but it must have been the lingering jet lag.

"Thank you for agreeing to speak with me." Jackson gestured uselessly to the two chairs he had placed opposite one another on his makeshift interview stage. "It's such an honor. I've been watching you dance for years."

She gracefully settled herself in the chair, arranging the flounces of her skirt around her body in a photogenic manner. He bustled behind his camera to check the lighting, then made a few adjustments.

"You've been watching me dance?" She eyed him as he went about his duties. "That's rich, coming from Jackson Alder. I think I first saw you in that gender-swapped *Giselle* at the Royal Ballet. When was that again?"

The blood froze in his veins. Want and memory held him tightly, so fast he could barely breathe.

But he had to. Evelyn was staring at him, her lovely head tilted just so. He had a job to do.

"It was a long time ago. A lifetime ago." Two lifetimes, if he were honest. It was better not to remember. Safer. "But we're here to talk about you." He hid his discomfort by standing behind the camera, zooming in on her and hitting Record.

A hint of a frown furrowed her brows. "Did you hear what I said earlier? About off-limit topics?"

"Yes." Though maybe a selfish part of him had hoped she had forgotten. "I'll respect that."

"Thank you." She played with the folds of her soft pink gown. Jackson had the worst urge to touch it, to run his fingers over the silky fabric. He missed the costumes he used to wear. The way the sparkles and brocade made him feel bigger than himself. Grander. Important. Strong.

She laughed, a small, brittle sound. "I'm rubbish at talking about myself."

"I'll ask questions. It will be a conversation. I can edit everything later."

She still looked nervous. Jackson swallowed, then re-checked the angles, picked up the remote control for the camera as well as his coffee cup, and slid into the seat across from her. "Don't worry. We can hear the announcements from here, so we'll know when they say who the semifinalists are."

Her posture eased, as if his presence were enough to calm her.

No, she is off-limits, the stern Noah-voice inside his brain said.

He sipped his coffee, searching for a neutral topic to start, one that would open her up.

"Tell me about your favorite movie." Inwardly, he cringed. This wasn't a date. He shouldn't even bring anything remotely date-like into this interview. But now it was out there. Smooth, Jackson.

Her brown eyes sparkled in the yellow-bright light. "My favorite movie?"

"Yeah." He scratched the back of his neck, wishing he had thought of something else.

"All right. But you cannot make fun of me for it."

"I wouldn't dream." He liked this Evelyn. She was a little playful, a little brash. Who was he kidding? He liked all the Evelyns he had met so far.

She leaned toward him in a conspiratorial fashion. "It's *The Cutting Edge*."

Unexpected pleasure lifted the corners of his mouth into a grin. *"The Cutting Edge?* The ice-skating movie?"

"The very one." She slipped off her shoes and tucked her feet underneath her skirt. "But you promised not to make fun of me."

"I love that movie." He blushed. This was *not* a date. He did not need to overshare. But something about her invited him to do so, and he was in no state to argue. "I love all ice-skating movies. Hockey, especially. *The Mighty Ducks* ruled my childhood."

Her color heightened. *"Ice Princess."*

He searched his brain but came up empty. *"Mighty Ducks 2."*

She laughed at that, a crisp, clean sound that called to mind heather on a rolling hill. It enchanted him. "Cheap shot, Alder."

"I'm jet-lagged. Forgive me."

"Always." She stopped short suddenly, as though she had said something inappropriate, even though that single word sparked and danced all along his skin. "Fine, since this is a proper interview and all,

I shouldn't take the piss. My favorite movie isn't really *The Cutting Edge*."

Wanting the banter back, he said, "Is it *The Cutting Edge 2*?"

"No." She laughed again, and he had the rising feeling that he would do anything to make this woman laugh. "It's *Blades of Glory*."

For the love of Fred Astaire, this woman was perfect. "With Will Ferrell?"

She nodded. "I love it. It makes me laugh every time."

"It is pretty amazing. The costumes alone are sheer perfection." He had the sense that he was wearing an enormous, lopsided, extra-dorky grin, but he did not particularly care.

She arched a pert eyebrow in his direction. "Something you would wear?"

He had once performed a ballet routine in full peacock costume with feathers on his butt and head. "Absolutely. In a heartbeat." Right, he was supposed to be interviewing her. "Did you ever ice skate?"

She smoothed the folds of her dress. "I tried, but I was complete rubbish at it. I didn't want my parents to waste their money."

He laughed, mostly to himself, and spoke without thinking. "When I was six, I desperately, desperately wanted to play basketball. I was awful at it. My mom still drove me to every practice, though. I didn't have the heart to tell her I was warming the bench at six." His voice caught in his throat, an unexpected lump of grief lodged there, and heat burned the backs of his eyes. He swallowed the emotion and glanced over to her. He needed to salvage this somehow. "Too short." *Poor choice, Jackson.*

She smiled, guileless and kind. "You're certainly tall enough now."

Color rose in his cheeks and he tossed back the rest of the cold coffee. This was way off track. He needed to get back to the grit of the interview, but he had completely befuddled himself.

"Tell me about your gown." That seemed a safe enough topic. It didn't even come close to asking about her injury and subsequent departure from Dancesport.

A light blush rose on her cheeks. "My mum makes all my gowns. She's become quite famous, actually, as a designer."

"And you're her principle model?"

"First and best, so she says." She cast her gaze to the ground, and he followed the gentle curve of her neck.

"You get along well with your mom?"

"Aye. Swimmingly. She's all I have now. My da died, oh, going on six years now."

The lump in Jackson's throat made it impossible to breathe, but he managed to swallow it because she looked upset. "I'm sorry."

She laughed again and looked at everything but him. "That's what everyone says, isn't it? Me too. I'm sorry as well. He was a good da. He took me to my dance lessons and used to sit front row for every competition." Her voice softened. "He'd bring me a dozen yellow roses because he knew I hated red."

Memories of his own mom clouded Jackson's brain. "Parents always know, don't they? They get what matters." If only he could apply that to his relationship with Topher.

She sniffed, as if stifling her own memories. "What about you? Your folks must be very proud of all you've accomplished."

Jackson sipped his coffee, even though it was colder than he preferred. "We're here to talk about you." He cleared his throat. The coffee's bitter aftertaste had singed his tonsils. "So, Evelyn, um, what do you like best about dancing?"

A lightness played across her face. "Everything, really. There's something free inside me when I dance. I know some people say, oh, it's choreography and rules and blah blah, but I've always felt more myself when I'm moving."

"I can relate." Definitively. Jackson shifted in his seat, suddenly regretting the coffee.

She cocked her head toward him again, her gaze assessing but nonjudgmental. "Do you miss it? Dancing."

"This isn't my interview." He was blowing this, wasn't he? Even if this was one of the best conversations he'd had in years and he was smack in hands-off territory.

"You said it would be a conversation. Are you taking it back?"

As if he could deny her anything. "No." He sipped again at his coffee, which was another mistake, as it burned his esophagus. "No, it's okay, I guess. Yes, I do miss it. But…" He thought of Topher on the first day of school, tears streaming down his little brother's face because he hadn't been sure he could get through a day in class without crying about his parents. "…I'm where I need to be. Right now. And that's more important."

She sipped from her bottle of water and shifted slightly, releasing another intoxicating puff of scent. "You're different than I expected."

"Am I?" He had leaned forward without realizing it, so he pulled back a few inches. "I didn't know you expected anything."

"Yes." She glanced between him and the camera. "I know the producers of *Dance with Me* were always trying to give you this bad boy reputation, but it never seemed to take. You were always so kind and constructive to the contestants, and they looked up to you as a mentor. It made me wonder about you. What you were like. If you were as decent to people as it seemed."

"I wondered about you too." He had closed the space between them again, but this time, he didn't particularly care. Why should he care, again? Was there something he was supposed to be doing? It was difficult to focus when Evelyn was beside him.

Her face was a heartbeat from his, and this close, he could see a strand of hair had escaped from her careful, heavily varnished updo. He shouldn't. He absolutely shouldn't. But then her gaze met his, those rich brown eyes filled with warmth and deep-seated joy and understanding.

He couldn't help himself. He had denied his own wants and needs constantly and he was too foggy and jet-lagged and enraptured with her to stop himself now.

With one finger, he brushed the errant hair from her cheek and tucked it behind her ear. He felt more than heard her inhale beneath his touch.

"Jackson—"she breathed.

But he never got to hear what she was about to say, as at that moment, the loudspeaker spat angry, interrupting German.

Evelyn jumped away from him as if he had scalded her. He practically sat on his hands, shame flooding through him.

"I have to go. They're announcing the semifinalists," she said exactly as the voice on the loudspeaker switched to English.

"Sure, okay. I'll be there too. In a moment."

He needed approximately six hundred years to compose himself.

"Thanks." She wrung her water bottle between her hands, then stood, did an awkward sort of curtsy, which of course was not awkward because everything about her was graceful and lithe, and practically ran from the ballroom.

Jackson sank back into his chair and folded his hands over his head. What had he almost done? He had touched an interview subject. This was bad. Very, very bad. Very, very unprofessional.

And he would be more unprofessional if he didn't hurry his butt up and get to the semifinal announcements.

eight

. . .

Evelyn

EVELYN RUSHED BACK into the main ballroom, beelining to where Alexei was sitting.

What, for the love of good porridge, had she been thinking?

Sitting with Jackson Alder, with his good looks and fine posture and utter sincerity. She shouldn't have told him about her father, that was certain. And the way he had evaded her questions about his own parents...wasn't that suspicious? Yes, suspicious. He was an interviewer whose goal was to ferret out her secrets, not some superbly attractive man interested in her as person. He only wanted the gossip, and he was going to do whatever it took to find out what she was hiding.

No, she wasn't hiding anything. She rubbed again at the spot on her sternum, her breath coming in shallow gasps. No one could know.

Alexei stood when she approached, her polished dance heels in his hand. "Everything all right?"

"Yes, of course."

"Good."

She toed off her comfortable warm boots and hurriedly slipped into her ballet-pink dance shoes. There. Transformation to ballroom princess complete. She was a professional. She could do this. "Have they announced anyone yet?"

"Not yet." He fixed his gaze on her face, his blond curls shellacked to his head. "Do you need a moment? You look flushed."

"I'm all right." Hah. Jackson Alder. *Calm down, heart.* She didn't have the capacity to deal with a romantic attraction. That was part of why Alexei had been such a perfect partner. He was already married to the love of his life, Bjorn, who was at home in Scotland with their twin toddlers.

Gebhardt Schmidtz strolled up to the microphone, carrying a tablet in one hand. "Ladies und gentlemen, I have here our semifinals list for this year's Vienna Waltz Championships. We saw some excellent performances in the initial round, but here are the couples who will be advancing. We will have two heats, to commence shortly. Afterward, we will announce the finalists at this evening's Crystal Gala. Don't worry, I asked them to make sure they have plenty of käsespaetzle and schnitzel for all. It is my favorite." He paused for effect and received a light smattering of polite laughter in response. Evelyn clutched the edge of her seat, her knuckles whitening. This was it. She had worked to get back to this part of her life for almost an entire year. "Let me read aloud the names of the couples advancing to our semifinals."

Evelyn suddenly realized she couldn't hear anything. It was as though she was stuck in a wind tunnel and the only sound around her was the buzzing of white noise. She glanced around, unmoored, and then when she saw him. Jackson Alder, at the end of her tunnel. He was staring directly at her, a half smile creasing his face, his dark brown hair unkempt and sexy-glorious.

Warmth and calm spread through her. *Jackson Alder*.

Alexei took her hand, and she followed him as he led her from the table to the on-deck area.

Across the room, Jackson held the camera with one hand and applauded with the other. She could read the word on his lips as plain as day. "Congratulations."

nine

. . .

Jackson

JACKSON SPENT the afternoon the way any man who had almost made a massive, career-ending mistake by almost kissing the girl of his dreams would do.

He threw himself into his work.

He interviewed three couples. He uploaded edited videos from the preliminary and semifinal rounds. To no one's surprise, Evelyn Zhao and Alexei Rostov had been...transcendent. They were guaranteed to go to the final rounds.

Not that he gave himself a moment of brain space to consider that.

Around five o'clock that evening, as the ballrooms emptied so the attendees could prepare for the evening's dinner and gala dance, Jackson found himself with an astonishing thing: free time.

It was disconcerting, to say the least. He hadn't had free time in years. Not since before the accident.

Maybe it was the jet lag or the long day or the unexpected blank block of time staring him in the face, but he was overwhelmed with exhaustion. More than anything, he could use a nap.

He packed up the equipment he didn't want to leave unattended and headed for the elevator. A quick nap, then he would join the dinner and gala and schmooze. Oof.

His phone buzzed in his pocket as he stepped off the elevator on his floor. The sinking feeling in his gut told him it was Topher.

"Hey, bud." Drat, he was being too bright again.

"Jackson, I'm so sorry to bother you," Mrs. Carthage said. Jackson's fatigue deepened to the point he barely managed to slide his hotel key from his pocket.

"It's fine." It wasn't. He loved his brother—he wanted to take care of his brother—but did he absolutely have to do it right then? "What's going on?"

"I know you're far away and all—"

"Really, Mrs. Carthage, it's all right." He let himself into his hotel room, where he stacked the equipment beside the bed before falling face-first into the mattress. Bad idea. It was going to swallow him whole.

"Topher got in trouble at school again."

"Seriously?" The fatigue both settled in his bones and evaporated as he sat up to run his hand through his hair. "What happened this time?"

"Topher won't say." Mrs. Carthage's voice grew softer, as though she were looking away from the phone. "The principal told me to tell you that he needs a specialist."

"What? Why? It's a public school. Aren't they supposed to do assessments and everything? Don't they have resources?" Like Jackson knew. He was winging this whole pseudo-parent thing like the clueless college dropout he was.

Mrs. Carthage sucked her teeth. "I'm sorry, Jackson. Really, I am. Topher is such a lovely boy, and the two of you have both been through so much."

Jackson sat on the edge of the bed, his head between his knees. He drew in a ragged breath. He should have been the one to be called by the principal. He should have been there for Topher. That was his job, even more than DancesportTV. But he wasn't in Chicago. He was in Vienna, having improper thoughts about ballroom dance's darling. "Thank you for being there," he finally said. "I'll call the school Monday morning, and I'll take it from here."

"I know." Her voice softened into an almost flirtatious tone. "I'd do anything for the two of you. I hope everything is going well there so you can come home soon."

"Yup. Absolutely." If her definition of *going well* was derailing his own desperately needed interview by almost kissing his subject. How had things gone south so quickly?

He knew exactly how it had happened. People should never meet their greatest crush. They could turn out to be the most awesome person on the planet and crush dreams of meeting someone else.

Mrs. Carthage brightened over the phone. "Okay, well, we'll see you soon!"

"Of course. Thanks." Jackson turned off the phone, covered his head with a pillow, and screamed into it as loudly as he could.

On second thought, maybe he could finagle his way out of the gala. He was in no mood to schmooze.

ten

· · ·

Evelyn

"I HAVE no interest in the gala," Evelyn said into her phone. She stood before her closet, pondering the two dress options she had brought and despising both of them.

"Look, we did a cracking job this afternoon at the semifinals." Alexei cleared his throat, the sound reverberating through the phone. "It's important we hear the announcements."

"There's no need for me to be at the dinner, that's all." Correction: she didn't want to attend the dinner. Her heart had been palpitating all afternoon and she didn't want to let on anything was amiss.

Alexei sighed again. "All right, love. Look, it's bath time for the twins, so I've got to run to video chat with them before their bedtime. See you tonight, yeah?"

"Okay." She hung up the phone and held it in one hand, still staring into her closet. The two offensive dresses were both black, plain, respectable tea-length with flowing skirts. One had a beaded neckline, and the other a gold-braid belt.

Boring. That's what they were. They certainly wouldn't attract a man like Jackson.

Not that she was trying to attract Jackson.

She showered instead, to cleanse her mind of all its myriad distractions. Scrubbing glitter out of her hair, she refused to remember the way it had dusted Jackson's cuffs. Nor would she recall how when he brushed a hand across the back of his neck or through his sheaf of hair, he left little streaks of sparkles behind.

It was entirely too charming. Jackson was too charming, and he lived on an entirely different continent.

It would never work. Never.

After much deliberation, she chose the dress with the gold-braid belt, paired it with her golden gladiator stilettos, and left her hair down. For no other reason than that she liked it that way.

Alexei texted her as she slipped out the door.

> Announcement not expected until nine-ish *frown emoji*

She tucked the phone into her small purse, turned away, and stopped dead in her tracks. Her blood warmed in her veins, making her feel a little more alive than usual. It was how she felt when she performed.

This time it was for Jackson. Jackson Alder, waiting in front of the elevator bay in a dark suit tailored to his tall, lanky frame. He was doing relevés and whistling the theme song from *Game of Thrones*.

She wanted to laugh. Laugh like she had earlier that afternoon in the interview. Fun. She had missed fun.

She moved to stand beside him, strictly because he was standing by the elevator, and how else was she supposed to go down to the dinner she didn't want to attend?

From her closer vantage point, she could appreciate better the lines of Jackson's muscles through the slim-cut suit. Heat rose to her cheeks.

"It's a fine evening to wait together for a lift," she said.

He whirled toward her, a sheepish and terrified look on his face, but when his gaze found hers, his entire body relaxed like he was sliding into a warm bath. She bit her lip, her skin warming, as the heat in his eyes raked down her body and back up again. It was like he painted her with his gaze, and she liked it. No one had ever looked at her like that before, like she was the nectar of the gods.

He closed his eyes and shook his head, rubbing a hand against the stubble on his jaw, like he was embarrassed. Wanting to reassure him somehow, she stepped closer to him. "I'm sorry," he mumbled, his voice full of sandpaper.

"Whatever for?"

"Staring at you like that."

Want trilled up her spine, coiling deep in her belly. "I didn't mind."

He smiled a little more broadly, the expression lifting into his eyes. How unfortunate—the man had golden flecks in his eyes that sparkled in the harsh hotel lights. "You look gorgeous."

She thrilled a bit and did a small twirl, suddenly feeling better about the despised dress. Maybe the braided belt wasn't so bland. "Thank you. You as well. You look quite dashing in a suit."

"Are you wondering how long it will take me to reference 007?"

Laughing, she shook her head. "That would rather cheapen the moment."

At that moment, the elevator dinged and the doors slid open, revealing an empty car. Evelyn wrung her handbag between her palms. There was no reason to be nervous. She had to attend the dinner and socialize with people and reply blandly whenever anyone asked about her injury.

It sounded exhausting.

Jackson gallantly held one arm against the door, letting her pass first. "Off to the gala?"

"I suppose."

He joined her inside, hit the button for the lobby, and the doors slid closed. She was suddenly very aware of him beside her in the tight space. Heat radiated off his body, and what was that scent? Cedar and fresh linen.

"You sound roughly as excited about it as I am." He shoved his hands back into the pockets of his suit trousers. If she allowed herself more than a quick glance, she would wonder how he fit anything else in there. Though he hadn't danced professionally in quite some time, he'd clearly kept his physique.

She blushed. It was no good wondering about a man who was completely wrong for her. Well, not completely... No, completely. Entirely. He lived on a different continent. They were here together for only a night. She needed to pull it together.

The elevator descended slowly, giving her far too much time for contemplation. Dratted elevator. "You know, this is my first time in Vienna," Jackson said, then rolled his eyes like he second-guessed himself.

It was utterly charming. "Really?"

"Yeah. I had hoped maybe to have a moment or two to explore, but this is a whirlwind weekend." He rolled the toe of his shoe along the ground, as though his feet never could be still after dancing for so long.

She understood. "I've never really been here either. Just once before, with my parents. We drove through on our way to Prague."

He shifted his gaze to her, a shy, hopeful look on his face. "I have a crazy idea."

She bit her lip, then grinned. "Is it to ditch the dinner and go exploring in Vienna?"

"Oh. Well, yes."

"All right, then." The door opened on the lobby, but she hit the button for their floor instead, and the doors closed again. This was fine. She would only miss the dinner, not the finals announcement. Only because she hadn't really seen Vienna. Only because she couldn't handle the questions about her injury. Only because— "Let's do it."

eleven

· · ·

Jackson

HE FELT LIKE A TEENAGER. Running to his room, giggling like he hadn't in ages, meeting Evelyn back in front of the elevators, dashing down the service staircase together. Yup, he had officially reverted to his nineteen-year-old self, sneaking out of rehearsal through the stage door with Avery Potts.

But Evelyn was not Avery Potts.

Evelyn was not like anyone he had ever met.

When she had sidled up beside him in front of the elevators, all the air had left his body. She was his air. No, no, that couldn't be right. She was stunning, that was all. The black dress that wrapped around her body, skimming the middle of her calves.

Now she was buttoned into a thick pink wool coat with a collar that cocooned her neck. Not that she hadn't been gorgeous when he had seen her before, all painted and costumed, but this time, she looked real. Tangible. She could be both goddess and goofy ice-skating-movie connoisseur.

And he liked it. Strauss help him, he liked *her*.

Jackson pushed open the door to the outside and stepped into the fresh air, inhaling deeply. Vienna smelled of wood smoke and cinnamon and spun sugar. It was like a living *Nutcracker* waltz.

The streets weren't busy, but he could see people inside restaurants and bars and cafés, huddled over warm drinks and plates of delicious-looking food. Here there was laughter and warmth and company.

It all felt a world away from his life in Chicago, home of thunder snow.

Evelyn slipped her hand into his as if it were the most natural thing in the entire world. Her color had heightened, making her luminous in the poor light from the alleyway. She closed her eyes and tipped her nose to the sky. "It smells like how I always envisioned *The Nutcracker* would smell."

His breath caught in his chest. "Me too." He wanted to stay there with her, in that moment, but the cold made her shiver and laugh.

"I'm famished. Let's get something to eat."

Jackson obliged, though he had absolutely no idea where they were going. All he knew was that he had her hand, warm in his. Every other worry melted away in the face of that reality. "What are you in the mood for?"

She scrunched up her nose in an adorably pensive gesture that made him want to kiss her. That realization both surprised him and came as zero surprise. Of course he wanted to kiss her. It wasn't like he would act on it. He could be a gentleman.

"I don't rightly know. Something warm."

"Right. Warm." Jackson tore his gaze from her and forced himself to take stock of his surroundings. Pale cobblestones shone blue in the glow from the homes and streetlights. Houses and shops tightly packed along the winding street, all wood and stone, both ancient and modern simultaneously. It looked like a movie set, Old European Grandeur. "Wow. This is not enough, but Vienna is gorgeous."

She nodded, her steps matching his even though she was at least half a foot shorter than him now that she wasn't wearing her heels, but warm, soft, fleece-lined boots. "It is. It looks like a place where magic still exists."

He bumped her playfully with his elbow, if only for another moment of contact. "Aren't you from Scotland? Isn't there magic in the lochs and heather? I've seen *Brigadoon*. I auditioned for it twice."

She arched an eyebrow at him and painted her perfect mouth into a faux frown. "Poor you. Did you not get cast? I'm so pleased you deal with disappointment well."

"I'll have you know, they had nothing to say against my dancing." He cleared his throat and grimaced. "They found my singing lacking."

"You can't carry a tune?" She laughed broadly, squeezing his hand as she did. His heart paused every time she did that. "Well, now you need to prove it."

"Wait, what?"

"Sing for me, Mr. Alder." She batted her actual lashes at him, and he had the sudden, vague urge to buy her a private island.

"Why would you want to hear me sing off key?"

"Because I'd like to." As if it were the simplest request in the world. "Though if you sing 'Surrey with a Fringe on Top,' I'll let the wolves have their way with you."

A smile tugged at his lips. He had the feeling that if she let him, he would do anything and everything she asked. "Is that your favorite song?"

"Long story. Anything else, please."

So he didn't sing "Surrey with a Fringe on Top." He butchered Lady Gaga instead, to the utter and sheer delight of Evelyn and the horror of the group of Hungarian tourists walking beside them.

He didn't care. He sang at the top of his lungs for one thing and one thing only: the sight of Evelyn applauding, wiping tears from beneath her eyes because she was laughing too hard to contain herself.

When he finished, he took a deep bow. An older, impossibly stylish woman carrying a reusable grocery bag and heavily buttoned against the cold, muttered something at them in German, which only made Evelyn laugh harder.

"She cursed you and your poor singing," Evelyn said through her tears. "Said you'd bring bad luck on all performers everywhere."

"That seems a little harsh."

"Sounded better in German. You're right. You really are a terrible singer."

He laughed. "We can't all be Robert Fairchild. My last agent, after we heard *Dance with Me* was going to be canceled, kept trying to sell me on auditioning for *The Masked Singer*. At least until I sang "Happy Birthday" for him. That shut him up quickly."

Her stomach rumbled, reminding him of why they had played hooky from the gala, which was seeming like the best decision he had ever made in his life. "Come on. Let's walk down here. I see people on that street ahead. We can follow them for food."

"All right."

twelve

. . .

Evelyn

BEING with Jackson was too easy. He didn't demand or push. He anticipated her needs. He would have made an excellent dance partner.

They wandered the streets of Vienna, marveling at the artistic sweets displays in the confectionery shops, picking up wurst and chips from a green-and-yellow painted stall to eat as they walked. In one shop was an elaborate sugar and chocolate display of two waltzers in bright colors, wrapped in each other's arms.

She had no idea where they were or what time it was, but for once, she didn't care.

Being with Jackson was fun. Being with Jackson felt like she could be whole again. She didn't need to pretend everything was all right.

Threading her hand in his felt…right. In a way it never had before.

A delicate snow flurried around them, enough to make the evening impossibly magical, but not so much as to cause worry.

Evelyn paused halfway down the pedestrian thoroughfare and stuck out her tongue. The snowflakes swirled on her taste buds, redolent of sugar and spice.

Jackson watched her, a bemused expression on his face. He had a remarkable range of expressions. Not surprising, given how long he had been a performer. "I haven't done that in ages."

"Then why am I doing it alone?" She didn't care if it was coquettish. She cared only that Jackson joined her, opening his mouth wide to catch the falling ice.

Laughing, she reveled in the frosty feeling of the melting snowflakes. "So, Jackson Alder. Tell me something no one else knows about you."

He crossed his arms and grinned broadly. "Are you turning the interview tables, Ms. Zhao?"

"Aye." Her brogue had deepened, an unexpected and delightful occurrence. Usually when she wasn't at home, she found herself hiding it, leaning into more BBC-appropriate tones. Apparently she wasn't worried whether Jackson could understand her. He seemed to do just fine.

He turned, pensive, and she followed him down the cobblestone street toward a pretty park lined with an ironwood fence. Music flowed between the snow-covered trees and hedges. They were playing Mozart, of course.

Jackson sighed, sticking his hands into his pockets. For a man with such a history, he was remarkably soft-spoken about himself. She liked that humility. "I don't talk about myself a lot."

"That's odd. Aren't you famous?"

He laughed a little, more from surprise than delight. "Says the great Evelyn Zhao. No, you know how it is for dancers. We're constantly over-shadowed. We work as hard as any athlete, and we're still relegated to the two a.m. ESPN42 slot. If I hadn't been on that reality TV show, people would never know about me. That's the reason I wanted to start DancesportTV. I wanted to give our athletes their due, showcase them and them alone."

There was an aura of sadness around him, one she understood well. She looped her hand through the crook of his arm as they passed beneath an archway decorated with twinkling crystal fairy lights. "I like the stories and interviews you do. You have a way of talking to people."

"My witty repartee, asking you your favorite movie?"

"I rather liked that."

He glanced over at her before concentrating on the scenery. She couldn't blame him. The park was undeniably…magical. People in heavy winter coats and hats ambled along the flagstone paths between hedges built of snow and ice. Light installations in the shapes of various woodland creatures bounded across what would have been the green were it not winter and covered in snowdrifts. The scent of cinnamon and mulled wine permeated the air. In the far corner of the park, a four-piece string orchestra paid homage to Austrian classical composers.

Anticipation filled her, like she was at the edge of some sort of precipice and only had to step over to find herself somewhere new, like Narnia. She had a sense a lot of it had to do with Jackson, but she had absolutely no idea what to do with that realization.

She also realized she had no idea what to say next. The scenery and music had lulled her into a state of complete brain fog.

Fortunately, Jackson saved her. "Want a glass of something?" He gestured to a stall selling glasses of mulled wine and cider with people crowded around it.

Her cold fingertips warmed to the idea. "Certainly. I don't drink alcohol when I'm competing, but a cider sounds lovely."

She waited in line beside him, but when they got to the front and he started stammering in English, she remembered how terrible his German was and ordered for them. The vendor, a portly man wearing a knit cap pulled low over his voluminous gray hair, handed her two glasses.

Jackson followed her, appearing befuddled. "They give you the glass?"

"You're meant to walk about, drink it, then return the glass before you go. Don't worry, you'll get your coins back." She tapped her cider to his mulled wine. "*Slainte mhath.*"

"Cheers."

They sipped their drinks, her gaze locked on his as sweet, liquid warmth rushed down her throat and into her stomach. It was enough to take her breath away. Her heart thumped against her ribcage, but this wasn't the terrifying arrhythmia of earlier. This was a beat like that of a drum finding its rhythm.

"This is good," he said, swallowing on the last word.

She sipped her cider to hide her smile, the sweet spice warming her. "Why don't you talk about yourself a lot?"

He shivered as a gust of wind blew through the park, and they started walking. "I could ask you the same question."

Even though there was no alcohol in her drink, her tongue felt looser. She felt more limber, less stressed than she had all weekend. Maybe honesty would help. "For me, I suppose it's because I never thought there was too much interesting about me."

He turned, incredulous, taking her elbow between two of his long fingers. "Wait, what? I don't believe that."

She shrugged, though the familiar loneliness stiffened her muscles. "I'm a small-town girl from Scotland. My da was a grocer, and my ma was a seamstress, now gown designer. I found dance early, and it's all I ever really did. If I hadn't made it, or hadn't made a good show of it, I don't know what I'd be doing right now." She scuffed at some fallen snow with the toe of her boot.

"I have a feeling you'd land on your feet."

When she turned to him this time, the heat in his expression held her rapt. She had been wrong before. It wasn't just that he was good-looking. It was that his heart showed when he looked at her. He was guileless and open and honest, things she had always wanted. "Thank you." She shivered, though there was no wind now. "Please, tell me something about yourself so I don't feel so self-conscious. I oughtn't have said that."

"I disagree. You can tell me anything." They had neared the string quartet, both sipping the last few dregs of their drinks. "But fair. This is something I haven't really told anyone. I don't have a lot of friends, so maybe it's that I don't have someone to tell."

She touched his cheek gently with her fingertips. "You can tell me."

His gaze softened. He closed his eyes and his words breathed across her face. "I miss dancing. I miss it so much sometimes it physically hurts."

She recognized that feeling, from as recently as her injury. "Why did you stop?"

A dark expression clouded his features. "It—It's complicated."

He looked like she did, holding the weight of the world on his shoulders. Like her, he needed to unburden himself. "Come on. Let's return our glasses, and then you can tell me. I'm practically a stranger. I'm not going to tell anyone what you say. Maybe it will make you feel better to get it off your chest."

"Maybe." His words were quiet, but he followed her the few meters back to the stall where they returned their glasses. She had the momentary thought of keeping it, as a souvenir, but she wouldn't forget this night.

"After all, after this weekend, we'll likely never see each other again." She stopped, the glib words halting her in her tracks. Why did that idea fill her with such a depth of sorrow? It was true. But still, it made her feel empty to think of not seeing him again.

He looked almost like she felt. "I have to be honest, that makes me a little sad. But I know." He swallowed loudly. "Okay, so me and dance."

Right. She sniffed back the tears that threatened behind her eyes. "You and dance. A tumultuous relationship? Enemies to lovers?" That was better. Humor helped bring out that extremely appealing smile of his.

"Not quite. More friends to lovers, for sure. I told you about my failed attempts at basketball. One night, my mom was working late, and I was in our apartment. This was after my grandpa died, so it was just the two of us. The only movie I could find that wasn't terrifying was *Billy Elliott*."

"I love that film." Evelyn mentally clocked the other, more subtle information. It made her like him more, unfortunately for her sanity.

"Yeah, me too. It shifted a lot for me. I loved the strength and power and rhythm of it. I asked my mom if I could try ballet, and of course she said yes." A small smile of remembrance flitted across his face. "I took to it pretty quickly. That whole thing about boys shouldn't do ballet, but that never rang true to me, and my mom didn't care, so neither did I." He sighed, hands in his pockets, idly watching the string quartet. "I mean, there are some things I don't miss about dance. I don't miss the uncertainty over your next job. I don't miss the grueling practices. I'd like to say I don't miss the awful personalities that sometimes accompany top-end ballet, but I think you run into that in any field."

She laughed slightly in agreement.

"I don't miss worrying constantly about getting injured." His eyes widened and he froze, but she was already ahead of him. "I'm sorry, I shouldn't have said—"

"It's all right." And it was. For the first time in months, it was. "I know you didn't mean anything by it. It is the constant fear, isn't it? The career-ending injury." But that was all she could say for the moment as a lump the size of Jupiter formed in her throat.

He softened beside her, taking her hand in his, and that sensation, of his warm, strong hand holding hers, grounded her. "I'm sorry," he said, his voice soft in the background of the alfresco concerto. "I'm sorry. I know you said you didn't want to talk about it. I wasn't trying to push you."

"You're not." She closed her eyes and reset herself in the senses she could feel and touch and smell. The holiday scents of spice and wine and cold, fresh snow. The violin and cello meeting in tandem on a soaring harmony. Jackson's warm hand in hers, like a cozy fireplace on a chilly evening.

She opened her eyes, not surprised, not resigned. Just ready. "It's really all right, Jackson. I don't mind talking about it with you."

His hand in hers was tentative but supportive. "You don't have to. But if it helps, I'm happy to listen."

She had tried everything else, and none of it had helped. Not bottling it up. Not talking to her therapist—not that she could tell them her biggest secret. Maybe telling Jackson would ease at least some of the burden she carried.

Shaking those thoughts from her head, she focused on the connection between her hand and his. His attention thrummed through his skin and into her palm. It was more than pleasant to feel so seen. "It was an accident. Like all awful things, a random act of fate. I was cycling home from the market and a car backed into me. They couldn't see me past the hedgerow." She felt it all again in a rush of still photographs: singing to herself as she pedaled, the wicker basket hooked to the front handlebars piled with apples and cabbage. The slight crunch of twigs and dirt beneath her tires. The sickening crash, the thud, the pain, lying on the ground in a heap of blood, mixed with crushed apple bits and leaves. "I still remember it smelling sulfurous, like crushed cabbage. That probably sounds ridiculous." Jackson didn't respond, but she knew he was listening. "I was in hospital for a few days, not too long. Long enough for them to operate on my leg and set up the visiting therapy." Long enough to find out about her heart condition, but she kept that part to herself.

"I wasn't sure I'd ever be able to dance again, let alone compete. But I had to try." Tears welled in her eyes, and if it had been cold enough to freeze them on her cheeks, she would have had diamonds sparkling on her face. "My da always sacrificed so much for me. My mum too. I couldn't throw all of their hard work, all of my hard work, away in a moment. I was so terrified of the unknown future that I threw myself into therapy, into getting well. I forced my body to heal itself." Her heart sped as though it remembered that phase of her recovery too.

"Did it work?" He asked, his voice soft and kind.

"No." She wiped the tears from beneath her eyes. "It made it worse. I don't know why I expected anything different. A body cannot push itself past its limits, no matter how fit you think you are. I was too proud. Too arrogant. I could have injured myself more." She closed her eyes, memories of the subsequent hospital trip forefront in her mind. The cardiologist with his packet of papers, the headline in bold print. WOLFF-PARKINSON-WHITE.

"I'm glad you didn't."

It was sudden, unexpected, and so on the nose Evelyn had to laugh. A good, old-fashioned belly laugh that reminded her of her father and ended with her curled up against Jackson, crying into the wool lapel of his coat.

Without speaking, he unbuttoned the coat and tucked her inside, against the heat of his body. The tears stilled as she warmed, as she breathed in the enticing scent of him. It was rare to find someone like this, someone who would hold her without speaking, who would warm her on a cold, perfect night.

She forgot to care that it was temporary. She forgot to worry about her heart condition. She forgot the importance of being back at the hotel for the announcement of the waltz finalists.

She wrapped her arms around Jackson's middle, nestled her head into the soft fabric of his dress shirt, and let herself forget everything besides him.

thirteen

· · ·

Jackson

THERE WAS MORE to her story.

He knew that, just as he knew there was so much he hadn't told her.

But he didn't care. Evelyn curled into him, nestled against him with his arms around her, was the best thing that had ever happened to him. One million percent. No contest.

He didn't want to count the minutes they stayed like that, wrapped together like an actual couple. He would have preferred if time really had stood still.

But because the universe always had other ideas when it came to him, his phone buzzed in his pocket, trilling through the satisfying silence he had been enjoying.

Evelyn pulled away first, sniffling and taking her warmth with her. "Do you have to get that?" Her voice was thick, like she was either about to cry or had a ball of yarn in her throat.

He cupped her cheek, the phone forgotten. Her skin was so soft, and she leaned into his hand like a cat searching for contact. "Evelyn—"

His phone buzzed again, shaking him out of his reverie. What was he doing, musing?

"It must be important," she said, stepping out of his touch.

"It's not." He slipped the now-despised phone from his pocket and shut off the alarm he had set. "It's just a reminder." He hesitated, then decided she would want to hear the rest. "Half an hour until they make the finalist announcements."

"Oh. Right." She crossed her arms around her body. "I suppose we should be getting back then."

"Right. Getting back." But Jackson couldn't make his feet move. Not back toward the hotel, the crowded ballroom full of people who had been gossiping and drinking and eating too-rich food. He wanted to stay there, in the park that wouldn't have been out of place in a snow globe.

She turned away from him, and desperation welled inside him. He had the sudden conviction that if she walked away, he would never see or talk to her again, and that left him completely bereft.

"Evelyn?" What was he doing? He didn't know, but then he realized he also didn't care. He held his hand out to her, bowing slightly. "May I have this dance?"

Her hesitation lasted hours with his hand extended toward her. He was a fool, a total cheese—

She slipped her hand into his and curtsied. "I'd be delighted."

It was as though his entire body lit from the inside, like he was a disco ball rotating from a ceiling. She stepped into his arms, and his limbs lifted into his dance frame. His muscles were molten memory, and his body thrilled at the familiar sensations.

None of this was about dance, though. It was all her.

There was a small area cleared in front of the quartet, and Jackson spun Evelyn toward it, their feet flying over the icy cobblestones.

The music seeped through his bones, and Jackson closed his eyes, leaning into it. This was how he felt best, moving his body in rhythm. Evelyn moved like an extension of himself. He had connected with partners before, out of necessity and attraction and practice. Dancing with Evelyn felt like he had finally found something that had always been just out of reach. She was his lost city of Atlantis, his Ark of the Covenant, his pirate treasure. She was everything he had been working toward his entire life.

He noticed the other people on the floor enough to move around them, to spin her and let her show off her spectacular talents. His heartbeat pulsed with the music, ticking the metronome of three-quarter time in his chest.

Why had he gone so long without this? Why had he pushed it aside and denied that he loved it?

She squeezed his hand as he lifted her in a spin then set her back on the ground, linking her to him through the connection at their hips. Liquid desire warmed through him.

No, it wasn't him. It was her. He had been waiting for her.

As they twirled around the outdoor dance floor, he couldn't take his gaze off her. The soft light of the evening highlighted each one of her features. She was gorgeous, no way around it. And he was… what? Smitten? Besides being archaic, the word also didn't quite express the depth of how he felt. It was like a bottomless pit of want edged in gold braid and marabou. Did she feel it too?

The song wound to a close, and Jackson pulled Evelyn into him, spinning her closer and closer until she was flush against him and he could cup her face in his hands. Her cheeks were bright and warm beneath his fingers. "Thank you," he said, gliding his palm over the curve of her cheek.

She caught his gaze with hers, her brown eyes depthless as a Scottish loch. He wanted to dive in and drown in her.

He should probably not say that aloud.

She leaned against him, molding her body to his, and threaded her hands into the lapels of his coat. "Jackson."

He wasn't sure he could speak without making a tool of himself, so he nodded.

"Kiss me."

What the lady wanted, she should have. He couldn't stand in her way if he tried. Without another thought, he closed the inches between them and pressed his lips to hers.

She was soft and sweet, all apples and spice and every good thing. Long-dormant parts of his brain sparked to life as he massaged her bottom lip between his. It wasn't typical to feel this click, this electricity, thrumming through him. Why had a kiss never felt like this before? Like they were two opposite poles of a magnet, drawn inexorably toward one another.

He ran his hands over the smooth, soft hair at her temples, pulling her deeper into him.

This was too good. This should last forever. He wanted to stay there, Evelyn in his arms, Mozart playing in the background, the soft tickle of snow across the back of his neck.

He was more himself and better than he had ever been. All the usual stresses and strains melted away under Evelyn's touch. Chicago, his flagging business, Topher, his mom. It all seemed easier to manage with her there.

She pulled away from him, breathing heavily, her hand leaving his coat. Cold sank into him. "We have to get back," she panted. "We're going to be late for the announcements."

Whiplash struck cruelly, faster than a gunshot. He did his best to keep the disappointment from his voice but knew he had failed. "Yeah. Okay. Let's head back."

fourteen

. . .

Evelyn

EVELYN RUBBED at the ache behind her sternum as they walked briskly back to the hotel.

She had overdone it. She hadn't planned to, but it had been too easy to slide into the moment. Dancing with Jackson had been more than she had expected. She had danced with a lot of partners over her career, but despite Jackson's difference in experience, everything had just...clicked. It had been far too comfortable to waltz with him, following where he led around the outdoor stage, the music guiding her sway. How could she not have kissed him?

But somewhere in the exertion and exhilaration her heartbeat had taken offense.

Then she had offended Jackson.

The palpitations eased as they entered the brightly lit hotel lobby. Jackson had barely said a word as they made their way through the snowy evening, flurries landing on his shoulders like ice on a mountain ridge.

She wanted to tell him she was sorry. But that would mean explaining about Wolff-Parkinson-White syndrome, and despite his earnest honesty, he was a television producer. Her spine tingled. Wouldn't that be a wonderful story for his channel? Evelyn Zhao—broke her leg in an accident and then found out she has a potentially lethal heart condition. One exacerbated by exercise.

This had all been a test. For herself. To prove to herself that she could still compete without the medications or the radiofrequency ablation procedure. Then she'd never have to tell her mum the truth.

Maybe she had been wrong.

Jackson opened the door to the ballroom where the gala was being held, his expression stony sorrow.

She had to speak to him, now or never. He might not look at her again.

"Jackson—"

"Good luck, Evelyn. Though I don't think you'll need it. You're brilliant."

She deflated, the heat and grief in his gaze weighing on her like an anvil. "I'll see you around. All right, then?"

He nodded as she brushed past him. He was so stiff, so different from moments before.

But to apologize would mean to explain, and she didn't feel ready for that. Her heart wasn't ready for that.

As she strode into the ballroom, squaring her shoulders to project a confidence she did not inwardly feel, Alexei dashed toward her. "Where've you been, love? They're about ready to make the announcements." He took her hand and pulled her toward an empty place setting beside him. A waiter in a frilled white shirt and black trousers appeared and filled her water glass.

"Would you care for something to eat?" the waiter asked in German.

"No, thank you. Just the water, please." She drained the glass in one quaff, suddenly thirsty beyond reason. The waiter refilled it before moving away.

Her entire body reverberated with anxiety. She glanced toward the corner of the ballroom, where Jackson stood with his phone out, recording the festivities. But she could sense the exact moment he turned his gaze to her.

She sipped again at the water. She needed to calm down. If she didn't, she might have a problem. It would help if Jackson weren't still looking at her.

"Everything all right?" Alexei tapped her shoulder, and she whipped her face to him, pasting a smile on her face.

"Perfectly. Why do you ask?"

He arched an eyebrow. Of course he would see straight through her. That was one of Alexei's biggest drawbacks. He understood things without being told.

"Well, I don't know. You disappear and completely miss dinner, then show up with Jackson Alder two minutes before they're meant to make the announcements." He drank from his own water glass in an infuriatingly pointed manner.

"I'm not certain what you're implying."

"He's Jackson Alder, Evelyn. He's even better looking in person than on TV. Like a lanky Hemsworth." Alexei glanced over where Jackson stood, phone in hand and talking animatedly. Evelyn deflated slightly when she realized he wasn't still looking at her. "Doesn't he live in America, though?"

"Chicago," she replied automatically, though her mind was elsewhere. Something was wrong. Jackson's face was pinched, and color had risen along his neck. He cast a quick glance into the ballroom, seemed to notice no announcements were happening, and ducked out the door.

Alexei followed him as well. "I wonder what that's about."

"I don't know." She felt unsettled, like she was about to be nauseated or break into a cold sweat. Neither would be appealing. She needed to be the unflappable Evelyn Zhao. "It must be important, though. You'd think he wouldn't want to miss the announcements."

Maybe he had a girlfriend back home who needed him. Evelyn shivered despite her warm winter coat and the close heat of the ballroom. He didn't seem the type to cheat, but she hadn't exactly asked him either.

"Can I take your coat?" Alexei held out a hand toward her, and she slipped it from her shoulders automatically. Her partner folded it over the back of her chair. "You sure you're all right?"

"Yes. Yes, I'm all right. Nervous, I suppose." Ha. Understatement.

He covered her hand with hers and used the tone she imagined he used to comfort his twin toddlers. "I think we've got this in the bag. Tomorrow will be easy peasy, lemon squeezy."

"Right. Of course." Focus. She needed to focus. Sweat beaded along the back of her neck.

Herr Schmidtz stepped up to the microphone, his cheeks brick red. He had clearly been enjoying the excellent Zweigelt wine that had been served with dinner. "Guten Abend, guten Abend." A smattering of applause greeted him. Evelyn clapped but in a distracted way. "Thank you all for joining us for this lovely dinner and this wonderful event. Vienna and waltz go together like…like schnitzel and spaetzle." More robust applause met this statement. Evelyn couldn't take her eyes off the door where Jackson had exited. Did he know they were making the announcement now? What if he missed it?

She took her phone from her pocket and set it on the table, angling it so it recorded Herr Schmidtz. If she couldn't apologize to Jackson for not explaining why she had broken their kiss, at least she could record this.

"Let's get to our wonderful finalists. First of all, from the beautiful country of Denmark, Hanna und Markus!"

At one of the tables opposite Evelyn and Alexei, Markus helped Hanna stand and they bowed in appreciation. Evelyn picked up the phone to record their reaction. Hanna looked particularly lovely in a tea-length dark green brocade dress and her light yellow hair up in curls.

Alexei took the hand she was not using for filming and squeezed. Five spots left in the final.

Anticipation danced up her spine, but it wasn't entirely due to the finalist announcements.

Herr Schmidtz called the names of three more couples, and Evelyn dutifully recorded all of them, still wondering where Jackson had disappeared to and whether everything was all right with him.

At the microphone, Herr Schmidtz danced a little with his hands in the air. "So exciting! Two spots left. All of the dancers were so beautiful, weren't they? All right. Couple number five in the waltz finals tomorrow will be…Evelyn and Alexei!"

Applause like white noise rang in her ears. She barely registered Alexei pulling her to her feet, bowing, smiling. They had done it. They had made it to the finals. If they finished in the top three, her triumphant comeback would be complete.

Why didn't it feel better?

As she took her seat again, the rictus curve of her lips frozen on her cheeks, she realized Jackson still hadn't come back to the ballroom.

She hoped everything was all right.

fifteen

· · ·

Jackson

JACKSON PACED THE EMPTY
BALLROOM, his phone glued to his ear. It was
going to be all gross and sweaty now, the perfect
cap to his night.

"Topher. Topher, calm down."

His brother sobbed on the other end of the phone.
"It's not okay. Jackson, why aren't you here? You
should be here."

Jackson ran a hand through his hair, still damp
from the snow flurries outside. Why wasn't he
home with his brother, who needed him? Why was
he gallivanting around Vienna with a woman who
hadn't felt what he had? "I'm sorry, buddy. I'm

leaving tomorrow, after the finals. It's the soonest I can get away."

"It's not soon enough." His tears were audible over the phone.

"I'm sorry." At the rate he was going, he should just have it tattooed to his forehead. "Look, I would be there if I could. I know you want me to be there, and I want to be, really I do." He sighed deeply, remembering not his brother's face, but the feel of Evelyn slipping out of his grasp. She was ephemeral; she wasn't real. His brother was real. His business was real. He shouldn't entertain any other ideas. "Just...tell me what happened again?"

Topher sniffed over the phone. He had refused the video chat, which meant he was red-faced and sobbing. "I hate this school, Jackson. I hate Chicago. This place sucks. All I see everywhere are Mom and Dad."

Jackson's stomach plummeted. He wanted to contradict his brother, to tell him of course he didn't hate Chicago, it was just a bad day. At the same time...he got it. Did Jackson even still like it?

He didn't have time for this. He checked the time on his fitness tracker—he was already so late. What if he had missed the announcements? Noah was going to *murder* him. With a spoon or other blunt instrument.

"I know it's hard right now. I know it sucks." Jackson balled the hand not holding his phone into a fist. "But it's not forever. At least we have each other."

"We would if you were here."

Why were kids so good at emotional manipulation? "I am here, Topher. I'm the one who's doing this, for us. You are the most important thing in the world to me." Evelyn's face rose unbidden in his mind, but he pushed it away. Pipe dreams were for other people. He forced the conviction into his voice. "Everything is going to be okay. I promise. I'll be home tomorrow."

"I can't do this anymore, Jackson." Topher was whining, the kind of sound that wormed its way into Jackson's ear and wouldn't let him go. "Please. Please."

He sighed again and sank onto the floor in a heap of washed-up ambition. "We'll talk about it. Okay? I love you, Topher. I gotta go."

Topher said nothing but hung up the phone, leaving only silence in Jackson's ear.

The buzzing of voices in his head was certainly loud enough to distract him from his brother's disappointment. All the *Dance with Me* producers who wanted him to be something he hated. The choreographers who drilled his self-confidence into chalk ash. Evelyn saying she needed to get back, barely acknowledging their kiss. His mom's voice, emblazoned forever on his call log, reminding him to call his stepdad for his birthday, the last time he had heard from her.

His chest felt hollow, a cave of loneliness and grief.

"Are you all right?" A soft Scottish accent burred through the empty ballroom.

Jackson lifted his gaze and saw her. Evelyn. Wringing her hands and so impossibly beautiful it was no wonder she was a fantasy. "I missed it, didn't I?"

She paused, her boots whisper soft along the floor. "I'm sorry. I don't have your number; I wasn't able to text you."

He didn't want to keep looking at all that untouchable beauty so he hung his head between his drawn-up knees. "I'm sure congratulations are in order. You'll be brilliant tomorrow."

It wasn't what he wanted to say. What he wanted to say was that he felt connected to her, like she was a part of him in some indelible way that was difficult to describe. There had always been that crush on his part, the distant adoration, but meeting her in real life had felt like meeting his soulmate. Which was ridiculous because he was in no way prepared for a soulmate. Not that he liked the host of connotations associated with the word mate and he really wasn't that guy and—

She knelt beside him, and her hand brushed against his arm. Warm tingles flooded through him. "Jackson. Are you all right?"

"No." He met her gaze and saw his surprise mirrored in her own dark eyes. "Sorry, I shouldn't have said anything."

Her face softened. "I don't mind. Do you want to talk about what's going on?"

He folded his hands over his head, digging his fingertips into his scalp. He shouldn't want to talk about it. She did not need his drama. "It's okay. You probably need to rest before tomorrow. You are a finalist, aren't you? I'd be stunned if you and Alexei aren't on that list."

Her posture hardened before she folded her legs beneath her and sat beside him. "We are. Thank you for believing we could make it. I wasn't half sure myself."

"It's been a long road back for you, hasn't it?" This was easier, to talk about her.

The corner of her mouth tilted in a smile. "It has. But I didn't come to talk about me. You look upset. It had to be something monumental to keep you from filming the announcements. I'm here if you want to talk."

And he did. The words were cordoned off behind his heart, so tight and looming, like they might consume him if he didn't let them out. He was so tired of holding it all back. "My career is probably over."

"Why?"

"Because I can't pull myself together." He tugged his knees closer to himself. "I got a call from my brother, Topher. He's seven and has some... I don't know. I thought his school would do testing when he started having issues, but it's a public school because it's not like I can afford anything else, and so far they want me to handle it. But I have no idea what I'm doing."

She moved closer to him, her now-familiar scent comforting. She rested her hand on his shoulder. "Why do you have to handle it?"

The question cut through his misery. A simple question with a very complicated answer. One he didn't talk about. Oh well, he was going to crash and burn anyway. He had an interview with Evelyn Zhao where she didn't discuss her injury, and no finals announcement. He would probably botch tomorrow's livestream too. He'd have to buy a souvenir spoon with a picture of St. Stephen's cathedral on it, so Noah could murder him with something reminiscent of the scene of his failure.

Why not tell her? "I have to handle it because there's no one else." Telling her didn't feel the way he had imagined. Opening up to Evelyn was oddly liberating. "It's just me and him now. My neighbor and my business partner help, but it's just been the two of us for the last couple of years." Her grip tightened on his arm, as though she wanted to siphon away his grief. Slowly, he covered her hand with his.

"My mom had me when she was eighteen. For a long time, we lived with my grandpa, before he passed away, and she didn't date much. But after I left for college and then the ballet company, she met Ray. I'd never seen her so happy." He sniffed, the memories flooding through him from where he had buried them so deep. "They got married, and then she found out she was pregnant. I was away a lot, and I tried to come home as often as I could. When I got the job with *Dance with Me*, I thought it would change my life. Our lives. That's a huge understatement." He closed his eyes against the memory of his mom's elation when he had told her the news. "It gave us all a lot more freedom and flexibility and financial security. I had even been looking at buying a house in Chicago, to be near my family." Squeezing her hand, he closed his eyes.

"Then two years ago, when *Dance with Me* shut down, my mom and Ray were driving home from work. They always carpooled together so they could have time to talk. They called it a mini date. I was babysitting Topher, and there was this huge ice storm." Grief heaved within him, but Evelyn was there, grounding him through her light touch on his arm. He couldn't stop now; he had to get this all out. "I thought they'd stay at work or with friends nearby, that they wouldn't dare go out in the storm. But they were both lifelong Chicagoans. A tractor trailer slid on the highway and—"

Evelyn wrapped her arms around his neck and, after a beat of hesitation, he folded his around her. The tears didn't come, not this time, but just holding her, his grief ebbed. The constant tension in his chest eased.

She didn't say anything, but he didn't feel she needed to, not now. He knew she understood. It was so comforting to have someone who understood.

sixteen

. . .

Evelyn

EVELYN'S HEART POUNDED, but she held tighter to Jackson, as if holding on to him would ease her own pain. She couldn't force another person to bear the weight of her own grief.

"Are you all right?" He breathed against her neck, causing her entire spine to tingle.

A half laugh, half sob barked from her throat. "I can't believe you're asking if I'm all right when you told me about your parents."

She felt him blush against her cheek, almost as though it made her flush as well. "I didn't mean to say it."

"Did it help?"

He paused, then squeezed her tighter against him. Something deep in her belly curled and reached for him. "Yes, I think it did. I don't talk about it much."

"Losing a parent isn't an easy thing to discuss."

He pulled away from her then, but only enough to cup her face between his palms. His eyes searched hers, and her mouth went bone dry.

That kiss. The one she had shoved to the bottom of her mind because it was too precious and too frightening to keep at the forefront.

But with him so close to her now, his lips inches from hers, her brain replayed every moment, every stroke, every sensation.

"Evie," he whispered, his gaze holding hers.

The nickname struck through the barriers of her self-control like a saber through a champagne bottle. No one had called her Evie in ages. It felt like Jackson had somehow unearthed an unknown part of her. Evie was the one who loved ice-skating movies. Evie was the one who wore rockabilly dresses when she went out with her friends, many of whom had fallen by the wayside. Evie was the one who would laugh so hard at her da's silly jokes, she would snort lemonade from her nose.

Could Jackson want both of the people within her? Evie and Evelyn?

Klaus hadn't. He had only wanted Evelyn the perfectionist, Evelyn the professional. Wasn't that why he had broken up with her after her accident? She had no longer fit his mold.

Jackson didn't seem to care. He stroked her cheeks with those graceful, long fingers, and when he gazed at her, she felt like he really *saw* her. The Evie/Evelyn she wanted to be again. Not broken. Not ill.

"Evie," he said again, the word more a breath than a verbalization.

Enough, she thought, closing the distance between them and pressing her mouth to his.

Her body sparked and sparkled when they collided, like it knew this was where she was meant to be. And she wanted it, wanted it so badly, wanted *him*, like nothing she ever had before.

The wanting stole her breath, even as her body heated to such a degree she could start fires.

She slid into his lap, pressing her body to his, wanting to feel him against her. He held her like she was the buoy keeping him from drowning and she was one hundred percent there for it. Nothing mattered outside that kiss.

"Evie." Jackson threaded his hands along her temples, his fingertips spreading electricity throughout her body.

"Jackson." The moan rose from somewhere deep in her throat. His name felt too good on her tongue, cinnamon and spice and everything that was right with the world.

And wasn't that the issue? She wasn't ready for this intensity of emotion, this depth of attraction. She had only just started her life anew, and her heart was so fragile.

Though it physically pained her to do it, she placed a hand on his solid chest and pushed him away.

He blinked several times, like waking up from a good dream.

Grief gnawed behind her breastbone. His eyes were full of hurt. "I'm sorry," she said, once she managed to catch her breath.

His hands flexed against her waist, like they were reluctant to release her. She didn't fully want to be released, but she could deal with that later. "Did I—Did I do something wrong?" he asked. His voice sounded battered and hoarse, a man lost at sea for twenty days.

"No. It's me." Tears welled in her eyes. "I didn't come here for this. For you."

"I know. But it's happening, isn't it?" His gaze pleaded with her to accept it, to accept him. "I feel different when I'm around you. Like I can hope again."

The urge to tell him about her Wolff-Parkinson-White rose up her throat and snagged at the back of her mouth. That was her secret to bear, not his. It wasn't as though he could do anything about it. "I'm distracting you," she said, deciding in the moment that it was the right thing to say. "We're distracting each other. I have to focus on finals."

"Right." His gaze didn't leave hers, like he knew she was lying. "Of course. You'll be wonderful, Evelyn."

A pang rocketed through her chest. Not Evie anymore then. "Thank you." Realizing that she was still perched on his lap, her arms dangerously close to him, she stood. Distance was better. Being so close only made her long to lean in again. He tasted of home, and that was perhaps the most difficult thing of all.

Jackson looked bereft, his lean frame humbled and crooked. He stood, awkwardly, shoving his hands into the pockets of his trousers. If Evelyn were allowing herself this attraction, she would admit how well he wore that suit, how it would be stamped forever on her brain.

"I, um, I forgot to tell you." She pulled out her phone, feeling awkward and uncertain and not at all herself. "I recorded the announcements for you. That's why I came, not for—I wanted to send you the video file. It's not very good. I'm not a professional, obviously. Unlike you." She needed to stop rambling, but it was more difficult than she had anticipated. He smelled so good and had felt so good beneath her hands. She didn't want any of that to stop yet knew she couldn't have him.

His posture softened, a hint of a grin tugging at his lips. "You recorded the announcements?"

"Yes. Yes. Again, it's not the best quality. Perhaps you can fix it or something—"

He moved toward her, like he was going to hug her, and in a fit of confusion, she stepped backward. The hurt on his face was enough to bruise. "Thank you." He stiffened again.

Tears rose behind her eyes, and she had the desperate urge to be alone, in her hotel room, so she could have a good and proper sob. "I need your phone number."

He rattled it off, the numbers clipped and staccato. Her own fingers stuttered over the phone screen as she added him to her contacts. Jackson Alder, there in her contacts. "Thank you."

He sniffed loudly and scuffed the toe of his shoe against the floor. "So we're not going to talk about this?"

Her spine stiffened. "What is there to say?"

He barked a wounded laugh. "I don't know. We kissed. Twice. And it was—"

Her body warmed with memory. "Incredible."

"Yeah. And afterward, you pulled away. Did I force this on you?"

"No, of course not."

"So then, what?" He hung his head, no longer meeting her gaze. "You don't like me? My breath is terrible? You don't feel it too? I mean, I'm filling the void here. If this is all me—"

But it wasn't. "Jackson." Tears pooled at the corners of her eyes. "It's not you. But it's complicated, isn't it? You live in Chicago, and I'm in Scotland. You have your brother to take care of, and I'm restarting my career." These were not the words she wanted to say, but she felt the truth of them. "This is just a moment. A brief, magical moment in a foreign country, when you're already stressed out and jet-lagged." She swallowed, tasting the words before she loosed them. "This isn't real."

He shook his head, his luscious hair flying. "I don't think that. I don't know how this is going to work, but I don't want to step away from this. I don't want to close the door on it forever." He stepped toward her but didn't touch her or take her hand. The air between them was charged, ionic, drawing her toward him even though her feet stayed planted.

"I *feel* different when I'm with you. Like I'm me again. I'm not just Jackson, ex-danseur-turned-reality-host or the older-brother-now-terrible-parent. Not a borderline failed TV producer, one low paycheck away from starvation. I can be me when I'm with you." He slid one hand from his pocket and rubbed the stubble on his jaw, the same stubble that had brushed her cheek only minutes before. "You don't know how badly I need that. To be me again. To feel like myself, and not just some strung-out version where I can't do anything right."

Nodding, she let him draw her into his orbit, his hand now sliding around her waist, secure and steady. It was too seductive, this feeling, this one he described. She wanted to wade into it and cast all of her other worries away.

He was so close to her, his face a centimeter from hers. So close she could count the flecks of green in his hazel eyes. She cupped his chin in her hands, letting her fingers play over the stubbled curves. She dipped into the dimple beside his mouth. *Jackson*.

Behind her, she heard a loud and insistent throat-clearing.

Jackson pulled away, leaving his hand on her waist.

Heat flared in her cheeks and she turned to see who had interrupted possibly the most romantic moment of her life.

Alexei stood by the door, left ajar. "Sorry. I didn't mean to interrupt. Everything all right, love?"

Was it? What was she doing, kissing Jackson when she needed to get her head into finals?

She pulled away from him and smoothed the skirt of her dress. "Perfectly. Jackson and I were just—um—"

"Interview," Jackson coughed. "It's part of the interview."

Her stomach sank. This was for the best, even if it hurt. "Exactly." She forced a bit more enthusiasm into her voice but it still felt like ice tripping off her tongue. "All part of the interview."

seventeen

· · ·

Jackson

JACKSON LET himself into his hotel room and promptly fell face-first onto the hotel bed. What in the ever-loving world had just happened?

He groaned, the soft bedding absorbing his misery.

They had connected. He had told her about his mom and Ray, a story he never told anyone. That had been a huge issue in the last few relationships he had tried to establish. "You're too closed off, Jackson." "You're holding back, Jackson." This time he hadn't held back. He had laid it all out for her, and she had still wanted him. For the first time in ages, when Evelyn had kissed him, he had felt like things might actually be okay.

Then she had pushed him away.

He rolled over onto his back, still groaning.

If he weren't drowning in self-loathing, he could admit she had exercised the cool head he was supposed to have. Alexei had clearly needed her for something. This was her big comeback, he shouldn't make it about him. Maybe Evelyn was holding back. They didn't know each other that well, no matter how strong his feelings for her had become. Besides, they lived on completely different continents.

It could never work, no matter how badly he wished it would.

His phone buzzed in his pocket. Great. It would be Noah or Topher, ready to leap down his throat about some other issue he had bungled.

His face softened and his breathing eased when he read the message.

> Evelyn Zhao: I'm sorry about earlier. Here's the video I took. It's probably awful.

A video box popped up on his screen, and he tapped it to download to his phone without really paying attention. She had texted him. She had done something unutterably kind for him. No one had done anything like that in ages. Did she even realize how much this meant to him?

He typed out numerous replies before settling on one.

> Jackson: Thank you. Really. This means so much. I thought my business partner was going to eat me alive.

...

> Evelyn Zhao: Can't have that. He'd starve, you're too stringy.

...

Smiling, Jackson removed his suit jacket and made himself comfortable on the bed, holding the phone in his hands.

> Jackson: Tonight was amazing. Thanks for the dance

> Evelyn Zhao: Eh, my feet were cold, so moving helped lol

He dismissed his immediate thought, that he could warm her up, as probably inappropriate. Probably.

> Jackson: Glad I could help. Next time we should go ice skating

His heart seized when he saw the three dots appear. Maybe he shouldn't have said anything about a next time. Tomorrow was the finals and his flight back to Chicago. "Next time" was a storybook castle in the cold Austrian air.

His hands flew over his phone screen, tapping out his apology for mentioning a second almost-date, when her reply landed with a friendly ping.

> Evelyn Zhao: Grand. Preferably not the day before a comp so I can ice my bum after I fall 7200 times.

...

> Evelyn Zhao: Best get some rest. Night, Jackson.

Jackson cradled his phone, his eyes falling shut even as he typed his response. Jet lag had caught him again.

> Jackson: Night, Evie.

eighteen

. . .

Evelyn

MORNING COMPETITIONS WERE NOT Evelyn's favorite, particularly after she had been up late with Alexei, rehearsing one of their more complicated patterns.

Or, more accurately, deftly avoiding Alexei's pointed and amused references to Jackson.

Still, when her alarm went off in the wee hours— she needed time to stretch, set her hair, and apply the layers of makeup necessary for competition— she thrilled a little at the familiarity of it all. She had missed competing. She had missed dancing. Alexei was, in every sense, a superior partner. Though dancing with Jackson—

She needed to get him out of her head. Evelyn set out her travel yoga mat and slid into the familiar rhythm of sun salutations.

Jackson...complicated things.

She had read and reread his text messages last night before falling asleep, parsing each word, savoring the *Evie*.

But she was not good girlfriend material. All her prior relationships ended the same way. Badly. Full of drama.

Drama she currently could not handle due to her concomitant pressing medical issue.

She exhaled as she extended her leg backward into a deep stretch from downward dog pose.

Yes, the palpitations were getting worse. Yes, she needed to talk to the doctor. But it was fair that she was scared of it all, wasn't it? No medical procedure, no matter how benign the bored doctor made it sound, was completely safe. She knew that as well as anyone. Better than anyone.

She couldn't drag Jackson into any of this. No. It wasn't the right thing to do. He had his own issues to manage, and it didn't sound like he wanted any help from her.

Irritated at herself for getting so distracted while practicing yoga, of all things, she shook her head and focused back on her breathing.

The competition today was what mattered. She and Jackson would be going their separate ways shortly, and maybe that was for the best.

———

Jackson

Jackson woke up earlier than expected, groggy from a combination of jet lag and fatigue over the events of the previous day. A quick shower set him more to rights, clearing his head of at least the travel fog. Reviewing the text messages from the night before, the ones from Noah that he hadn't read because he had been sleeping like the dead, woke him up completely.

> Noah: Where's the footage from the finals announcement?

> Noah: What time is it there?

> Noah: Text me back. I need to go over one of the angles from the semifinals. Do you have more coverage of Hanna and Markus?

> Noah: Did any of the couples who paid us for private videography get into the finals? It better not be all E Zhao and partner, Jackson.

> Noah: Is this the entire interview with Evelyn? You didn't get anything. Come on, Jackson. We need more.

And on and on.

Jackson ran his hands through his wet hair after he threw the phone onto the tangle of bed linens in a fit of pique.

We need more.

Jackson dressed quickly. They all needed more. Topher needed more of him. Noah needed more of him. Jackson needed more of himself.

His heart knocked against his chest, almost as if saying, "But what about Evelyn?"

He packed up his video equipment, shaking the thoughts from his brain. What about her? She was funny and kind and understanding and perfect.

But she lived thousands of miles away and traveled constantly for her work. There was no future here for them, no matter whether he wanted it or not.

Swallowing the grief that rose when he thought of not seeing Evelyn again after today, Jackson hoisted his equipment and set out in search of coffee. He was an adult, and adults had to make difficult decisions.

nineteen

· · ·

Evelyn

THE BALLROOM WAS PACKED ALREADY. Evelyn made the rounds of her acquaintances, other competitors she knew who hadn't made the finals, distant friends, searching over their heads for Alexei.

At least, she told herself she was looking for Alexei.

When she spied Jackson, setting up his camera and mic near the corner of the dance floor, her heart flopped and tumbled.

No. Not today.

She wouldn't let it affect her today, not even when Jackson's gaze found hers in the crowd. She stilled, every muscle suddenly alive and warm and tingling. *Jackson*, her body sang. To the tune of "Surrey with a Fringe on Top," of bloody course.

He straightened slightly and moved one arm as if to wave, which was so old-fashioned and adorable and charming, and then someone grabbed his arm and pulled him away from her.

Flustered and fighting an unpleasant wave of jealousy, she turned away, searching the crowd again. Alexei. She needed to find Alexei.

"There you are," Alexei said, joining her at her side.

She turned to him, her apparent object of desire, even though she kept looking over his shoulder to watch Jackson setting up his camera equipment. His hair flopped over his forehead in a way that made her want to tuck his curls back into place.

Which was completely inappropriate because Alexei was talking to her about their routine.

She needed to get her head back in the game. Jackson was a distraction, but the waltz finals were her actual, real life. The actual, real life on which she depended. What sort of triumphant comeback would it be if she choked during her performance?

Willing every ounce of competitive spirit she had ever possessed into existence, she nodded at Alexei, listening intently and smiling in all the right places. Whisk, sway, spin, contra body movement. Yes, yes, yes. She could do this.

She folded her hands, squeezing her palms to concentrate on her breathing.

Herr Schmidtz sauntered up to the microphone and introduced the opening act before the finals. Vienna's finest child dance troupe, all eight and under, waltzing to classic Mozart.

But she couldn't let herself get swept up in it. No matter how adorable they were, little ones in starched tea-length dresses and block heels, stiff postures except for the few who had succumbed to the beauty of the music and their youth and made up for their technique with enthusiasm.

Before the accident, she would have sat at the table, cooing and awwing like a proud aunty.

Now she could barely look at them. Did they know what they were getting involved in, a lifetime of love for a sport that was overlooked by so many? A sport that would consume their lives and finances, that would make them feel at the top of a mountain and also like they were trolling the Mariana

Trench? A sport that might bring them the most wonderful man, and then carry him thousands of miles away? Loving a sport like this could break their fragile little hearts.

Tears rose, but she forced them back. She couldn't let them ruin the double layer of false eye lashes she had placed.

"We're almost up," Alexei said, taking her elbow gently. "You all set?"

She sniffed and straightened, painting the well-trained smile on her perfect Rockette-red lips. "Of course. Let's go."

twenty

. . .

Jackson

IT WAS impossible for Jackson to ignore Evelyn once she entered the ballroom. It wasn't just her innate presence, the way every light seemed to find her of its own accord. It wasn't only her jaw-droppingly gorgeous cobalt-blue gown, his favorite color—not that she would have known—that reminded him of the ocean off the coast of Hawaii, where he had taken his mom on a vacation with his first real paycheck. It wasn't the way she and Alexei moved around the ballroom, like champions, the same way he used to walk on performance days. "You strut," his mom had said.

"It helps with my confidence," he had replied.

He didn't need a justification for his awareness of Evelyn, he supposed. He only wished she returned his appreciation.

His phone rang. Noah again. "I'm all set up here for the live feed. Are you ready?"

"Good morning to you too, Noah." Jackson adjusted the camera angle. "Everything here is fine. Thanks for the messages."

Noah sighed loudly over the phone. "I know it's a lot. But you're there and I'm here, and I really want this to succeed, Jackson. I have your taped intro all keyed up."

"I've got this. I do." And he would. In a minute. "It's starting. Sending you the feed now." This time, just for the sake of it, he hung up on Noah.

In the on-deck area, a mass of small children assembled, all under eight and in too-fine clothes that would not be suitable for getting muddy. Jackson turned on the recording from his camera, capturing the entire experience.

All right, the little kids' dancing was adorable. Jackson didn't move the camera much to eliminate jerking movements, but he knew this would be a money shot for a live feed. Parents circled the dance floor like anxious moths around a flame, some coaching and coaxing, others tearful and waving.

He remembered his first performance, where he had played a dancing cow in his studio's "Old MacDonald" revue. His mom had left work early, something she had only ever done twice, and she had sat with his grandpa in the second row on the aisle, holding a bouquet with three perfect yellow sunflowers. Just for him. They had never missed a single one of his performances, not until he was grown up and out of the house and his mom couldn't always travel to where he was. She had always been there in spirit.

Grief gnawed at his chest. It wasn't fair that his mom wasn't there anymore. It wasn't fair that Topher was stuck with him. It wasn't fair that he couldn't be with Evelyn Zhao when he wanted nothing more.

Through the raucous applause accompanying the children's finale, he glanced around until he saw Evelyn. She stood beside Alexei in the on-deck area of the ballroom, holding his elbow, looking every inch like gold medalists. She caught Jackson's gaze briefly, her dark eyes widening and a hint of pleasure flashing across her face before she faced forward again.

Jackson flushed and turned back to his camera, adjusting angles, trying to quiet the rush of butter-flies in his stomach. It was time. Time for the finals. Two minutes of waltzing, then half an hour before the judgment was announced. Then he would interview the winning couple, maybe a few others for Noah-pleasing good measure, and finally find a cab to the airport.

His stomach plummeted at the thought of leaving. There wasn't enough time. Not enough time to get to know Vienna, and certainly not enough time with a certain woman in a cobalt-blue dress who captivated his every thought. Not enough time for the things he wanted.

As if on cue, his phone buzzed, and he checked it quickly, ensuring he wouldn't miss a moment of the waltz finals. He would have to capture each couple with close-ups as they were announced.

It was a text message from his brother. Jackson softened.

> Topher: Mrs S told me I had to show this to you.

Jackson glanced up to ensure Herr Schmidtz had not yet ascended the dais to announce the waltz finals. He checked to ensure the live stream was still recording, then opened up the photo Topher had attached.

It was a picture Topher had drawn of him and Jackson, standing in front of an amorphic blob shape his brother had colored in with silver crayon.

He supposed it was the thought that counted, and less the drawing talent, before the real identity of the amorphous blob hit him.

It was the Bean, the metallic sculpture in downtown Chicago. He had taken Topher to the Museum of Art the past summer in a fit of boredom and without any other ideas on how to occupy the kid. Topher had adored it, had spent hours running through the rooms of the museum, asking questions Jackson couldn't answer but wished he could. He had trailed his brother the entire afternoon, and afterward they bought hot dogs with neon-green relish and sport peppers from a street vendor and ate them on benches staring at the Bean.

It had been a good day, memorable in its rarity.

And then it seemed like Topher had completely forgotten about it. For weeks afterward, Jackson offered to take him back to the museum or to explore another Chicago landmark, anything, but Topher had shut down, never acknowledging the previous visit.

But apparently he remembered.

Emotion swelled in Jackson's throat, enough to choke him. He opened the screen on his phone and typed out the only reply he could muster.

Thanks

He hit Send, then stuffed the phone into his pocket, blinking back tears. He couldn't film anything if he couldn't see. He needed to go home.

————

The six couples competing in the finals were some of the best dancers in Dancesport and hailed from all over the world. None of them were surprises, though Jackson heard plenty of mutters about Evelyn and Alexei's readiness to compete. It wasn't justified.

After all six had been announced, each taking a moment to bow and wave to their fans before finding an open spot on the floor, Herr Schmidtz held the microphone with a Santa Claus-style grin on his face. Jackson zoomed in slightly before readjusting to capture the whole floor.

"And here we are, meine Damen und Herren, the Vienna Waltz finals!"

The music started, and couples moved together, swaying with the rhythm of the music.

Jackson did his best not to focus exclusively on Evelyn and Alexei, but it wasn't easy. Though all the couples were technically proficient, Evelyn and Alexei had the spark, the indescribable glow that drew all eyes to them. When they completed a complicated step with effortless grace, the entire audience sighed and clapped. Their dance was poetry in motion, Fred and Ginger reborn in a glittering ballroom in Austria.

His own heart swelled and spun as he recorded all of the dancers, but he had seen enough after only thirty seconds to know they were going to win.

But then, after a minute and a half, with barely ten seconds left, Evelyn fumbled. Not a huge error, and it happened while she was on the opposite side of the floor from the judges, but Jackson saw it through the lens of his camera. He saw the sheen of fatigue slash across her face, a momentary blur in the mask of perfection.

What was that about?

The music ended abruptly, and all the couples broke apart and bowed to the generous and well-deserved applause.

Jackson focused on Evelyn. Color ran up the back of her neck, and even as she held her posture and maintained the illusion, he knew something was wrong. Her hand gripped Alexei's elbow too tightly, her posture was too stiff, too unyielding, her smile too forced.

A text buzzed in his pocket as he turned off the live stream feed.

> Noah: Good job. Adding the tag.
> see you back for the live finals
> announcement.

Jackson didn't bother acknowledging it. Something had happened to Evie and he desperately wanted to know what it was.

As the finalists left the dance floor, Jackson quickly packed his equipment, but the crowd, now released for the time being, swelled and swallowed him like a rising tide.

He abandoned the equipment, pushing through the crowd and searching instead for Evelyn and Alexei. They weren't with the other finalists, being congratulated and interviewed.

Spinning in place, Jackson looked for anything that might indicate where they had gone. She had looked like she was in trouble.

He couldn't see anything in the ballroom. Well-dressed people milled around, completely obstructing his view.

The hallway. She must feel as claustrophobic as he did. Alexei would have removed her to the hallway.

Jackson dashed through the doors, pulling his phone out and typing her a quick message.

Are you okay?

twenty-one

. . .

Evelyn

SHE COULDN'T BREATHE. Steel bands wrapped around her chest, squeezing, not allowing her lungs to open and take in the oxygen they so desperately needed. A black veil shrouded the edges of her vision. She couldn't hear anything. She was at the bottom of a pool, sound and vision muffled.

Her mum was going to kill her, if her heart didn't get to it first.

Then a warm pair of hands slid along her jaw, the touch soft and soothing, the massage easing the passage of air in her body.

Jackson.

It had to be.

"Evie." The word reverberated in her, more felt than heard.

She focused on it, let it bring her out of the depths and closer to the light. One of the hands holding her face released her cheek, and now she felt the soft calluses caressing a spot on her wrist. Her breathing eased and her vision cleared, just enough to make out the now-familiar outline.

"Evie."

Jackson knelt before her, his face etched with concern. It broke her heart to see it, to see the worry she had caused. He massaged the pressure point along her wrist. "What happened?"

She swallowed, dragging her voice from her larynx like a reluctant mule. "Where's Alexei?"

"Calling an ambulance." Jackson nodded behind him, and dimly, she made out Alexei's shape and the distant sound of his voice.

Then Jackson's words cut through her fog. "An ambulance? No, no, I can't—"

Jackson circled her wrists with his long fingers. "Evie, what happened? Alexei said—"

"I'm fine."

"You're not."

"I am!" But even as she tried to assert it, another wave of crushing pain ran through her body, doubling her over.

Jackson wrapped her in his arms, and heaven help her, she leaned into him, grateful for the strength. "Tell me," he whispered.

The weight of carrying her secret alone for so many months cowed her. She was tired of it, tired of ignoring and minimizing it. Exhausted from carrying it alone. It would be a relief to have someone else know.

"I have a heart condition," she whispered into his ear, nestling her head into the crook of his neck. "It's an abnormal heart rhythm. Wolff-Parkinson-White. They found it after my accident, when I was in hospital."

To his credit, he didn't ask her questions or mansplain it. He merely held her more tightly. It made it easier to continue her confession, letting the words flow from her like water.

"It's not always serious. I was fine for a while. After I pushed it in therapy, though, everything got worse." She shivered, remembering those dark months. "The doctors offered medicines, but they made me feel sick, off balance. Then they told me about a procedure, but I didn't want to do it. I thought I'd be all right. I didn't even tell my mum."

His grip on her tightened infinitesimally, but he didn't say anything. She couldn't even begin to tell him how much that meant to her, that nonverbal understanding.

Alexei ran into the room, phone in hand. "The ambulance is on its way. Shall I get some water? Call for a doctor in the ballroom? There's got to be a medical person about."

"No!" That would the worst thing imaginable—to have attention called to her illness when she had tried so hard to hide it. Not because it wasn't important, but because she didn't want it to define her. She had been labeled and placed in so many buckets in her life, and she didn't want this one too. Not when she and Alexei were starting something brilliant. Not when Jackson was looking at her like she was…

"I'll stay with you." Jackson's voice was quiet and not fully directed at her. He was looking at Alexei. "You should go back to the ballroom. For when they make the announcements. I'm sure you won."

"No, I can't go without Evelyn." Alexei pleaded with his eyes, even as another wave of pain ricocheted through her.

She bit her lip to hold in a scream. "I can't. I'm so sorry, Alexei, but I can't. You have to go. Tell them anything you want."

Alexei knelt beside her and kissed her forehead like the brother she had always wanted. "I'll tell them you're a goddess, love."

Tears welled in her eyes, and now, knowing that she wouldn't be able to get back up in front of the crowd, she let them fall and let her mascara run. "Don't tell them that."

"All right. I'll tell them I stepped on your foot as we were leaving the floor and now you can't walk." He winked at her, his face creased with kindness and concern. "You'll have to field all the offers for a new partner."

"No, thanks."

Alexei kissed her temple and left.

Jackson's gaze bored into her, but she couldn't meet it. Not now that he knew.

Fortunately, she was spared the burden of reply, as the paramedics entered the room. The next half hour was a flurry of her failed attempts to explain Wolff-Parkinson-White in German before Jackson pulled up his phone's translation app, examinations, and then finally before the paramedics laid her on a gurney to put her in the ambulance.

"I have to come," Jackson said.

The paramedic shook his head. "Family only," he said in German, his expression apologetic.

With her vision fading, Evelyn reached for Jackson's hand and clasped it tightly. "He's family. Let him come."

The Austrian paramedic shrugged before letting him climb into the ambulance with her.

She clutched his hand, his warmth her lifeline.

———

Two hours later, groggy from the beta blocker they had given her and overwhelmed by the deluge of information and options, Evelyn turned to look at Jackson.

He sat beside her bed, unmoving, his tall, elegant frame hunched.

Doubt and grief coursed through her. She couldn't do this. He had a brother. He had a job. He had missed the finals and the interviews he no doubt desperately needed for his show. All because of her.

She forced herself into a sitting position. Jackson stirred, a sleepy smile creasing the corners of his mouth.

"You're up," he said, his voice cracking. "How are you feeling? That doctor, I think he was the heart guy, but you know my German is awful, he might have been—"

"You should go." The words caught in her throat, but she forced them out, knowing she was doing the right thing.

The light in his eyes evaporated. "What? No. Evie, I can't leave you alone here."

"I'll—I'll call my mum. Or Alexei. I won't be alone." She was lying and hated it. She wouldn't call anyone. Even her mother didn't know the extent of her illness. All she had told her was that she had a *little heart thing, but it's all cleared up.* If she had told her the truth, her mother never would have let her leave Scotland.

"No, please." Jackson's brow furrowed, making him even more impossibly handsome. Which wasn't fair when she was trying to do the right thing. "Evie—"

"It's all right." She squeezed his hand. "You should go. I should have had this done before."

"Why didn't you?"

The lies she had told herself died on her lips. He deserved at least the truth. "I was scared." Her voice was barely above a whisper, barely above a breath. "Terrified, really. I don't fully trust doctors, not the ones at the hospital where they diagnosed me."

"Why not?"

It was a simple question, such a simple question, and yet the answer was too complex. She exhaled a shuddering breath.

"It's—it's because of my da. Those doctors, they misdiagnosed him. He had leg pain, and they told him it was just arthritis. Then he was losing weight and the pain got worse, and we brought him back in to have an injection, but he—he died on the table. Turns out he had metastatic cancer." The memories and buried grief rose in a flood so quickly they engulfed her like a wave of red-hot lava and ash. "Maybe if they'd tested him earlier…"

Jackson squeezed her hand. "I'm so sorry. That sucks."

She closed her eyes and breathed. In, out. In, out. In three-quarter time. "So I ignored it. Well, not ignored. I couldn't take the medicines—they made me lose my focus. Made my balance unsteady. I didn't want to do the ablation the doctors told me I needed. I poured myself into training, into getting fitter, beating my illness at its own game." She laughed, but it was hollow and dark. "I'm a fool."

"No, you're not." Jackson wrapped an arm around her shoulders, and if she didn't know she was supposed to send him away, she would have wanted to stay there forever. "You're not a fool. You're grieving. You're scared. That's all completely normal."

"Is it normal to sign yourself up for a professional waltz competition, knowing your heart might not take it?"

Jackson smiled softly, running one hand from the angle of her jaw down her neck and skimming over her collarbone. "Not for the average person. But you're nowhere near average, Evie."

Her skin thrilled even as her heart sank. She had to do this, even if it was the hardest thing. "Jackson, stop."

"Stop what?"

"Stop…being so wonderful." She covered her face with her hands. She had lost some of her false eyelashes, and no doubt her makeup ran all over her face like a Dali painting. Of course he would be amazing when she was already struggling to do the right thing while she was a mess, literally and metaphorically. "Please. It makes this so much more challenging."

His expression froze, the furrow deepening. "Then don't do this."

"Jackson, you know this can't work."

"Why? What, you don't care for me?"

Didn't he see it? Of course she cared. He had accompanied her to the hospital, absorbed everything she told him, helped without being asked. How could he think she didn't care? She more than cared, she lo—she loved him.

And when you love someone and know that you could be toxic, you need to let that person go.

Even if it broke your already-bruised heart.

She summoned every last bit of strength she possessed and steeled herself. "Jackson, it's not that I don't care about you. I do. Too much. To the point where I know that we don't have a future together."

"Evie—"

"Stop." She held up a hand. A nurse appeared at the doorway to her room but quickly exited when she saw what was transpiring. Evelyn understood. Who would want to be a witness to two people breaking each other's hearts?

"Jackson, stop. We live on separate continents. We have other responsibilities. You have your brother; I need to focus on my health. This was a moment in time, one of those oddly perfect crystalline moments, where two people meet on vacation, but that's all it is." Her body felt hollow and empty, a vessel to be filled with tears. "Look at this. You're here with me, and you're missing everything you need to do to save your business. That isn't right. I can't take you away from everything that matters to you."

Jackson abruptly stood and turned away from her, running his hands through his hair. His posture was that of a marionette whose strings had tangled or gone limp. When he spoke, his deep voice rumbled in the tiny sterile room. "You matter. You matter to me."

You matter to me too, she wanted to say. *I love you.* Even though she had never said those words aloud to someone not related to her by blood. "Then you should go. I need you to go. Please trust I'm telling the truth."

He hesitated for a long moment, so long it stretched into minutes, hours. Whole lifetimes flew by in those instants where she watched him, standing on the precipice. For a moment, she thought he would continue to protest, and was she really strong enough to withstand more?

But he was innately a good man, one who listened and trusted what people said. "Goodbye, Evie."

Without further fanfare, he left.

Evelyn slumped into the uncomfortable hospital bed with the itchy sheets and the cardiac monitor beeping its irritable sounds into the sudden silence.

That was the right thing. Wasn't it?

twenty-two

. . .

Jackson

THOUGH HE HAD THOUGHT it was only something that happened in movies or gory TV shows, Jackson turned into a zombie.

It happened the moment he left Evelyn's hospital room. Everything around him vanished, so he could see only what was in the tunnel directly before him. People said hello or gestured toward him and he passed them all right by. Somehow he made his way back to the hotel, packed up his equipment, and smiled dully at the right place at the right time, but none of it felt real. Jackson was a zombie.

Well, except for the desire to eat brains and whatnot.

He tried not to think about Evelyn while packing his gear into the taxi that took him to the airport.

He tried not to think about her while waiting in the security line, but every person with her color hair made him turn three times to ensure it was not actually her.

He tried not to think about her while buying a cup of bad European coffee, which was still infinitely better than the bad American coffee he would buy at O'Hare, or the truly heinous airplane coffee he would have to endure during the long haul back to Chicago.

While not thinking about Evelyn and vacantly perusing magazines, he impulsively bought three travel-sized bottles of whiskey. Nothing else would improve the airplane coffee.

Somewhere over the Arctic Circle, long legs crammed at awkward angles in his economy seat, he finally passed out. The whiskey had turned out to be a good investment, except that it meant he could no longer pretend he wasn't dreaming of Evelyn.

Until, that is, the moment he woke up from his ill-timed drunken stupor, a line of dried drool congealing in one corner of his mouth, and realized he had completely forgotten to buy a present for Topher.

His brother was going to kill him.

twenty-three

. . .

Evelyn

EVELYN'S MOTHER met her in Vienna, arriving mere hours after the radio frequency ablation she had deferred for far too long.

Apparently, some problems could not be willed away or stuffed into a box deep in her psyche with willpower and copious hours of yoga practice.

Still, when she woke up from the anesthesia and saw her mother standing there at her side, eyes full of tears and holding three hand-tatted lace handkerchiefs, she wondered why she didn't feel immediately better. There was still a hole in her heart, one that could not be burned or sutured.

Her mother recognized fairly quickly that something was off, because apparently mothers could always tell. "It's nothing, Mum," she kept asserting, even while she told herself she wasn't being fair to Jackson. He wasn't nothing.

On the flight home, sitting beside her mother, she rotated her phone in her palms, over and over and over. His number was there, right there in her phone. All she would have to do was text him. Reach out.

But she didn't, and it felt awful.

———

Her mother eyed her even as she lined up the fabric on her sewing machine. "Out with it."

Evelyn bit her bottom lip and ignored her mother's pointed stare. She dabbed more of the extra strength glue onto the back of a crystal and used the adhesive tool to pick it up and place it on the gown precisely where it needed to be. "Is that needle right for that type of fabric?"

Her mother rolled her eyes. Of course it was. Even Evelyn knew that was a flimsy excuse to avoid the conversation. "What happened in Vienna? Don't tell me nothing. And don't say it's about your heart condition that you lied to your wonderful, caring mother about. No more, please."

Evelyn sighed and picked up another crystal, depositing it beside the first one in the whorl pattern her mother had designed. "Nothing happened, Mum."

Lies. She lay awake at night stalking Jackson on social media. Two nights before, she had been up until four in the morning, watching shaky hand-held footage of his old ballet performances. He looked way too good under stage lights, the cosmetics highlighting the shape of his eyes and the strict contours of his jaw. Plus, muscles. So. Many. Muscles.

Her mother clicked her tongue against her teeth and sewed a line of perfect, even stitches on the stretchy fabric. "You look like someone's had her heart broken."

"No."

"Don't tell me it's Klaus. That numpty."

Evelyn snorted in surprised laughter. "Of course not. We broke up ages ago."

"How is everything with Alexei?"

"Fine." Now that she had finally had her procedure and Alexei wasn't scared she might break if he pushed the choreo, things were going swimmingly. At least in that department. "He sent me a picture of his twins on the dance floor. They're so cute, holding hands."

Her mother narrowed her gaze. "You know, I wouldn't mind some grandchildren."

"Mum!" Evelyn threw her decorating tool on the table, nearly upsetting the jar of crystals. Thank goodness she hadn't dropped it. She would have been on her hands and knees cleaning up crystals for the next forty-two years.

"Hmm." Her mother sewed quietly for a moment or two, but Evelyn knew full well she hadn't dropped her train of thought. "So, who is it? Who's got you all up tae high doh?"

"I'm not flustered, Mum." She yawned, an unhelpful reminder of her evening activities falling down the internet Jackson Alder rabbit hole. It wasn't her fault he looked completely amazing in tights.

"Well, whoever it is, tell them to get over here and meet your old mum."

"I'll get right on that."

———

Later that night, after a healthy serving of mulled wine and hours of videos of Jackson from a deep cut performance of *Swan Lake* in Tokyo, Evelyn found her phone in her hand, and the text message exchange with the man himself open on her phone.

"Why not?" She hit Send before falling into a deep sleep full of dreams where strong arms lifted her into the sky like she weighed nothing more than air.

twenty-four

. . .

Jackson

"JACKSON!" Topher called from the living room like it wasn't ten feet from the apartment's kitchen. "I don't want spaghetti again."

"I'm not making spaghetti." Jackson set the box of spaghetti back onto the pantry shelf and cast around for something else quick and relatively foolproof to cook. It would help if his brother ate anything more than the four foods he typically consented to. "Let's have yogurt."

"No."

Jackson sighed and closed the door to the small pantry. Of course nothing would be easy. At least he had finally managed to make Topher an appointment with a school psychologist. That was the only bright spot since returning from Vienna. Otherwise, life had been awful.

Everyone was pissed at him:

1. Noah, for delivering only half of what he had needed
2. Topher, for leaving him and not being a competent parental figure. Oh, and forgetting his souvenir. Bad big brother.
3. Mrs. Carthage, for not lavishing her with praise and attention for completing something he had *paid* her to do—watch said ungrateful brother

It did not help that every night he tortured himself by scrolling through social media and online videos of Evelyn Zhao. If he were honest, he didn't need the videos. He remembered every moment they had been together in perfect clarity. If his memories had been a diamond, they would have been worth a cool million.

Unfortunately, though, he was not with Evelyn. Evelyn had told him to piss off, from her hospital bed no less. And he, like the lovestruck fool he was, had listened.

Because it was clear to him now that he was, in fact, wildly in love with Evelyn Zhao.

Maybe he could be forgiven for falling so hard and so fast, and maybe not. One way or the other, however, all he could think about was her.

His phone chimed as he rummaged through the refrigerator for a Topher-appropriate meal. Lacking any diverse culinary options, he took out his phone to read a text.

Noah: We need to talk.

Jackson slipped the phone back into the pocket of his jeans with a sigh. Yes, they did need to talk. But not right now. Not when he was trying to get his life back together. A life he was no longer sure he wanted.

Topher had been right. Everywhere he turned in Chicago, memories of his mom assaulted him. There she was at the corner of Wabash, holding his hand to ferry him across the street. There in the window of that thrift shop, perusing vintage furniture to replace the rickety TV trays his grandpa had never relinquished.

Not that he didn't love his mom, but it was like the whole city was a ghost of her, and it wouldn't let him go.

And he saw it in Topher too. He saw the daily struggle to get through, to keep his head up. Even to get out of bed in the morning and face a town full of the most important people no longer in their lives.

He pulled some veggie burgers from the freezer and preheated the toaster oven. This would have to do for now.

His phone chimed again as he sliced an apple for a side dish. A fine chef, he was not.

"I don't have time for you, Noah," he sang, removing the phone from his pocket. He almost dropped it into the pile of thinly sliced apples.

Evelyn: I misd yu.

Besides nearly dropping the phone, Jackson suddenly realized he was still holding a sharp knife in one hand and placed it on the safe surface of the cutting board.

So she had likely deactivated her autocorrect, but… she had reached out. Finally.

His heart swelled and jumped. His fingers raced to type out reply after reply, but they were all wrong. Too needy, too wordy, too stalker-y, too clueless.

At last, he settled on a classic.

Jackson: Hey

He debated adding an emoji, but there really wasn't one appropriate to convey the volcano of emotions threatening to erupt inside of him.

"What are you doing?"

Jackson leaped from the chair, not realizing he had been leaning against the island, eyes glued to his phone screen, for the past however long. At least there wasn't smoke rising from the toaster. He hastened to turn it off and transferred the veggie burgers to plates. "Making dinner."

Topher narrowed his eyes at him and crossed his arms, suspicious in the way only younger brothers could be. "Why do you look all weird?"

"I don't look weird." Yes, he did, and yes, he knew it. His face felt flushed and even his hands sweated as he assembled the veggie burgers and arranged the apple slices on the plate in what he hoped looked appetizing instead of the height of ineptitude. It wasn't the worst meal he'd concocted. That had consisted of a spoonful of peanut butter, still on the spoon, and three emaciated grapes he'd found at the bottom of the crisper. "Dinner's ready."

Topher reluctantly stood up from the Lego city he was rebuilding for the hundred-thousandth time and clomped over to the small kitchen table that had once belonged to their mom. Jackson knew if he looked under the wood by his brother's seat that he'd be able to find all the misspelled ballet words he had inscribed there with an empty ballpoint pen years before.

The thought made him unbearably sad and also chased away whatever excuse for an appetite he had.

Topher crunched into an apple slice and brandished a second in his direction. "What happened to you? You've been weird since Vienna."

"Everything is fine." Jackson did not think about Evelyn as he picked at the top of his veggie burger.

Unable to let things rest, and because he was a seven-year-old destined to torture him, Topher bit into his burger and pulled a face. "This is hard."

"It's dinner. Eat. You need fuel." His admonishments were languid.

They ate in silence for a few moments before Topher finished all his apple slices, and Jackson wordlessly slid his own onto his brother's plate.

"Is it a girl?" Topher asked, drawing out the last word until it was at least four syllables.

Jackson was too exhausted to reply. "Why are you asking?"

"Because you're a doofus. And you're acting like Lucas Bendito in my class. He really likes Devi Sittachandra, so he sits around all moony-eyed." Topher rolled his own eyes before polishing off the remainder of his apple. "It's so gross."

"You're at that age," Jackson replied, lacking any better retort. Was his brother at that age? Jackson had absolutely no idea. Apart from having once been a seven-year-old himself eons before, he had zero experience. Compounding the fact that he was a terrible parent substitute.

"So, who is she?"

"Who is who?"

"The girl. The one you met in Vienna who's making you act all weird, like Lucas."

Jackson's mind stopped and started again, like an old car whose battery needed a jump. So he wasn't a picture-perfect parent. His brother was alive, attending school, catching up on first-grader gossip. They might not be thriving, but they were alive. Why shouldn't he talk to his brother like that was exactly who they were—siblings? He thought back to Topher's picture, the one he had sent of the two of them in front of the Bean. Maybe they could even be friends, if that wasn't a weird dynamic.

"Okay." Jackson pushed away his untouched plate of overcooked veggie burger. "Her name is Evelyn."

Topher's eyes widened. "Evelyn Zhao?"

"How do you know who Evelyn Zhao is?"

Topher scoffed. "Please, Jackson. I'm your brother. I've seen how you look at the videos of her dancing whenever you have a free moment and think I'm not looking." He sipped at his glass of water, and when he spoke again, his tone was gentler. "She's really pretty."

"Yeah. She is."

"Soooo…you like her?"

Like her? So much more than like. Jackson ran his hands through his hair and sighed. He wondered if Lucas Bendito had been doing that a lot lately too. "Um, yeah. I do."

Topher leaned backward in his chair, one thousand percent bratty younger brother mode. "Do you *looooove* her?"

Jackson barely had to ask himself. It was like the answer came from every part of his body that wasn't trying to ignore it. "Yeah. Yeah, I think I do."

"Then what's the problem?"

Like it was all so easy. "This isn't second grade. I can't have a friend of a friend pass her a note at recess."

Topher rolled his eyes again, in such a grand gesture it had to have given him a headache. "You have a phone. Why don't you call her?"

"Because she lives in Scotland."

"So?"

Now Jackson rolled his eyes, and it did give him a massive headache. A Topher-sized one. "Scotland is thousands of miles away. We live here."

Topher sipped his water, considering the information, though surely he knew where Scotland was, unless the public school system had neglected basic map-reading skills. "Why do we live here?"

The question struck Jackson like a rogue wave, knocking him flat and stealing his breath. "What? What do you mean?"

"Why do we live here?" Topher gestured around the room. "In Chicago?"

And though he knew exactly what he was supposed to say, Jackson didn't have a reply ready. "I don't know. I grew up here. This is your home."

"It's not anymore." Topher crossed his arms and set his mouth into a grim expression. "I hate Chicago. It's too cold and windy, and the El smells bad, and there are so many people." Topher chewed on his lip, tears rising in his eyes. "Everywhere I turn, something reminds me of Mom and Dad."

Nodding, Jackson leaned forward slightly in his chair, resting his elbows on the table. "I—I know what you mean."

"Right?" Topher wiped the tears away from his eyes. "It's like I can't get past it. It's not that I don't want to remember them."

"I know." Topher didn't reply, as he was chewing his lip and staring down at his empty dinner plate, so Jackson continued. "It's like their ghosts won't let us move on. I want to remember them too. But I feel like we are just running in place here."

"Yeah." Topher looked out the window of the kitchen/living area. Wind gusts screamed past the pane, flurries of ice and snow on their way. "I'm going to play with my city again."

"Sure."

But Topher's words lingered in Jackson's brain. As he washed the dishes and made Topher's lunch for school the next day, the words stewed.

He needed a plan, and he had the perfect, grandest of grand gestures in mind.

twenty-five

· · ·

Evelyn

"MUM! I'm going out for a run, then off to meet Alexei." Evelyn stowed her phone, credit card, and keys into the band around her bicep, and fixed a rucksack carrying her dance clothes onto her back.

"Are you taking water?" Her mother emerged from her shop, holding a handful of embroidered labels. "You need to drink more water."

"I'll get some at the studio." She kissed her mother's cheek. Of course she was grateful for the help and the attention, but she had been a little stifled ever since she had come home from Vienna. She needed a fresh start. A new world. She and Alexei had won the Vienna Waltz Championship, and even if she hadn't been physically present to accept her trophy, it still meant that her great comeback had been exactly that. A triumph. Even if it felt hollow without Jackson there too.

The wintry morning had dawned with a thin layer of frost on the hills, but at least the ground was hard and firm beneath the slap of her trainers.

Running had always helped her to get in shape for dance and vice versa. Even though now, as she ran from her mother's home into the village where the train would take her to Alexei's studio, she still couldn't shake the idea of Jackson.

Hey

That's all he had said. Honestly? He couldn't have mustered anything else?

Panting, she purchased a bottle of water from the station and waited for the train, her plastic rail card in hand.

Granted, she had late-night drunk-texted him two misspelled words, so perhaps that was on her.

Once on the train, cozily ensconced for the next thirty minutes while en route to Alexei's, she ignored the old man with the bulbous red nose who eyed her in her running kit and stuck her headphones into her ears. The universal piss-off gesture.

To her surprise, when she opened her phone, she had several notifications on social media. Friends she hadn't talked to in ages.

> OMG Ev did you see this?

> Tell me he has a brother

> You look stunning, luv

> Congrats on the waltz comp

What on earth were they talking about?

Confused and definitively not making eye contact with Bulbous-Nose-Gawker, she opened one of her social media feeds, and a video popped up on her screen.

The cover image was of her and Jackson, sitting beside one another during the initial interview.

She tapped on the image, mesmerized by the lines of Jackson's face, and then there he was, captivating her entire screen, his warm smile lighting up her face.

"Ballroom dance is an insular world, but it brings people together," Jackson said into the camera. "It's a sport about connection and rhythm. And Evelyn Zhao is the undisputed queen of Dancesport." She flushed, even though she knew he couldn't see. He was thousands of miles away. Jackson was still talking in the video. "Rightfully so. Not only is her technique perfection, but her love of the sport shines through every performance. It motivated her recovery from a traumatic accident." She steeled herself, waiting for him to comment on her heart condition, but to her surprise, he mentioned nothing. "This interview shows a little bit about what it is that makes Evelyn so special. I say a little because I doubt anything can capture how special she is. I only met her for a brief moment in time, but I'm pretty sure even in that short span of time, she changed my life. She's an incredible person and a beautiful dancer, and if you agree, make sure to like, comment, and subscribe."

The video faded into her interview, but she wasn't watching herself. She watched Jackson's reactions to her. His easy smile, the tangible chemistry she could feel even now through her phone screen. Connection and rhythm. That was what they had.

The train slowed and Evelyn looked up, surprised it was her stop already.

She disembarked, her mind back in Vienna, her phone heating her hand. Jackson. Jackson had stayed with her, to his own detriment, in the ambulance and the hospital. Jackson had danced with her in a winter wonderland. Jackson had kissed her like she was the missing piece in his puzzle.

She had held him like he was hers.

On the short walk from the train station to Alexei's dance studio, Evelyn came to an important decision.

She flung open the door, momentarily startled by the rush of heat from inside the studio. "I'm going to Chicago."

Alexei stepped out from behind the check-in desk, stretching his arms over his head. "That's a waste of time, love."

Shaking her head, she toed off her trainers and removed her rucksack, ready to change into her dance shoes. "I have to. I don't know if you saw the video, Alexei, but Jackson—"

"Is here."

Her head snapped up at the deep, friendly tone, the one she had missed so much over the last few weeks.

There he was, standing in the middle of the dance floor, holding a dozen yellow roses, a plaid button-down shirt clinging to his frame. He had a charming expression on his face, somewhere between hang dog and sheepish. He really did resemble a lanky Hemsworth.

Her hands froze, her feet only in stockings. But she wasn't cold.

"I probably should have called," Jackson said, casting an apologetic look toward Alexei before fixing his gaze back on Evelyn.

"Not at all." Alexei raised his eyebrows at her, as if to say, *why aren't you doing anything? The man flew halfway around the world to be here.*

But she couldn't move. Her heart felt so full it might burst.

"Hello." A young boy stepped out from behind Jackson, holding a model train engine in one hand and spinning its wheels with the other. "Are you the girl my brother's in love with?"

Her cheeks flushed as heat and warmth streamed through her body. She dug deep into herself to find her voice again. "I—I'm Evelyn Zhao. You must be Topher."

"Yes," the boy said simply. "Can I play on the chairs?"

Jackson turned to his brother. "If it's okay with Alexei."

Alexei picked up a sheaf of papers. "Come on, Topher. Let's give these two a moment alone. You can play in my office."

Evelyn watched, still stunned into immobility, as Alexei gathered Jackson's brother and they moved away, discussing the intricacies of Scotland's rail system and leaving her and Jackson alone.

Alone. From across the studio, Jackson found her gaze.

"I'm sorry to turn up unannounced. And with my brother too."

What was happening? She was tongue-tied and overwhelmed and so...pleased. Feeling returned to her numb extremities and she stood. "I saw the interview."

"Oh." He flushed bright red, almost to his hairline. "I, um, hope you didn't hate it."

"I love it." Her feet propelled her forward, toward him. Confidence returned. "I missed you, Jackson." It wasn't enough. It didn't fully encompass everything she felt about him, but it would have to suffice for now.

"I missed you too." He moved toward her, his steps larger than her own, covering more ground, which was perfectly all right with her. "I kept watching all these videos of your dance performances and replaying the interview, over and over. But it wasn't enough. It wasn't actually seeing you."

They were almost touching now, her head at the level of his chest without the benefit of her dance shoe height.

And she wanted to touch him. Even from this distance, she could feel heat and electricity pulsing off his skin, ions pulling her closer to him. So she gave in. She reached over and took his hand in hers. Relief coursed through her. The thrill of connection wound between them, and she felt… complete. She couldn't let go of his hand. She ran her fingers over the calluses on his fingers, over the veins running between the bones, and then laced her fingers with his.

"Evie," he whispered.

She couldn't look at his face, not now. "I watched all these videos of you. Deep cuts, from performances when you couldn't have been more than twenty-one."

"That's a bit creepy."

She laughed, the relief now rising in waves of joy. "I suppose it is."

He squeezed her hand in his, and then laced the other one with hers, pulling her closer to him, flush against his body. "I know this is surreal, Evie. But I want to be with you. I want to see where this goes, where it leads. I'll do anything to have a chance with you."

Reality gnawed at the base of her spine. "Jackson, you're in Chicago. Are we going to try the long-distance thing? I travel all the time for competitions and showcases."

"We'll figure it out. How are you feeling?"

With him there? Like she could fly. "All's well. I had the ablation. I should have had it sooner."

"You were frightened, justifiably so." He pressed his forehead to hers. "I'm glad you're okay. But if you're not, you can tell me."

She wanted so badly to stay there with him, to be in this place with him. The cocoon of his arms was everything she wanted, everything she needed. She would do anything to stay there. She tilted her face upward and brushed her lips against his cheek. "Let's figure it out. Please. I want this to work." The words hesitated in her throat, but as she spoke them, she knew they were the truth. "I love you, Jackson. We haven't known each other that long. But this feels right."

She barely got the last word out before Jackson's mouth was on hers, his hands pulling hers around his waist. Leaning into him, she cupped his face, his wonderful face, and let herself be carried away by him.

He broke the kiss, brushing his lips across her cheek and pressing them on the bone just beneath her earlobe. "I love you, too, Evie."

She threw her arms around his neck and aligned her body with his. She fit with him.

He held her tight, supported, like he would never let her go. She hoped he never would.

epilogue—three years later

Jackson

"Clap for Mama." Jackson pressed Mirabelle's chubby palms together in a clapping motion. Some might say eight months was a little early to applaud, but Jackson knew it was never too soon to start. Not when her mother was a world champion.

On the dance floor, Evelyn and Alexei bowed. Their showcase to "Moondance" had been a definite crowd-pleaser, a highlight of the Edinburgh Dancesport Festival, even if Jackson was incredibly biased.

Topher applauded beside them. "Don't you have, like, stuff to organize? I can hold her."

Jackson snuggled his daughter closer to his chest, reluctant to let go of her. He also knew, though, how much Topher loved his niece, so he kissed Mirabelle's soft, sweet-smelling hair and handed her to his brother. The baby cooed and grabbed a chunk of Topher's sweater, balling it up in her tiny hands.

Topher's face softened, and he bounced her just the way she liked.

"Mr. Alder," Maeve MacReady said, tablet in hand. "As organizer of the festival, would you like to say a few words before the waltz championship?"

"Of course." Jackson smoothed the lapels of his suit before tickling behind Mirabelle's knee, earning himself a deep giggle.

Topher rolled his eyes, the full picture of a ten-year-old boy who thought his older brother was full of mush.

Jackson didn't care. The last three years had been the best of his life. Topher was thriving in Scotland. He had made good friends who accepted him for himself, and he had picked up a love of fishing from Alexei's husband, who took them out to the river at least once a month. Moving DancesportTV headquarters from Chicago to the small village where Evelyn and her mom lived could barely be considered a hardship.

And then, there was Evelyn.

She stepped off the dance floor and into his arms. He folded himself around the layers of neon-blue spandex and tulle, pulling her close and kissing the side of her head. "You were brilliant."

She swatted his arm playfully. "Thanks. How's the baby?"

Jackson nodded toward Topher, who was bouncing Mirabelle near a display of rhinestone dance jewelry. "Perfect. Just like you."

Evelyn rolled her eyes and kissed his cheek. "Ah, you big softy, I love you, too. Now go make your announcements."

He squeezed her one last time before ascending the small dais at the front of the ballroom floor. "Thank you so much, Evelyn and Alexei, for that incredible performance!" He clapped, encouraging another round of applause. Evelyn, now holding Mirabelle, curtsied, and his daughter's dark curls bounced like springs. "And thank you to everyone here for supporting the Edinburgh Dance Festival. This is our second year, and its success is due entirely to you." At the back of the room, he spied Noah talking to Maeve, his second-in-command. "And special thanks to our sponsor, DancesportTV. Ballroom is an incredible sport, and it's because of this community of dance lovers." Applause and whoops greeted him. He found Evelyn's gaze across the floor and smiled. "Now, enough of me. Let's dance."

also by natalie cross

———

Want more love and dancing? Check out *Ballroom Blitz* and immerse yourself in a friends to lovers romp where Patrick and Anita fight their rising attraction all while prepping for a ballroom competition and evading a stalker. Can their love survive?

———

Interested in learning more about Natalie Cross? Sign up here for her monthly newsletter, snag your free book, and be the first to hear about new releases and exciting updates.

offense vs defense

T. Thomas

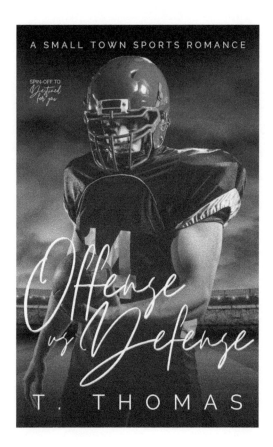

A SMALL TOWN SPORTS ROMANCE

SPIN-OFF TO
*Destined
For you*

*Offense
vs Defense*

T. THOMAS

Formatting: Tiff Writes Romance

Cover Design: Tiff Writes Romance

Editing: Tiff Writes Romance

Proofreading: Kimberly Peterson

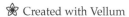 Created with Vellum

one

. . .

Hunter

"HUNTER!" my best friend, Reese, hollered after me as I marched into the locker room. I had to get showered as quickly as possible so I could head home to the ranch. There was always work to be done, and today was no different.

I'd chosen a college as close to home as possible, and I was grateful when they offered me a football scholarship. I'd worked hard to earn my grades and even harder to be one of the best football players the state had seen yet. But despite fans begging me to, I wasn't going pro.

My life began and ended with the Blume Ranch, and I wouldn't have it any other way. I loved my family. I loved the ranch. I lived and breathed the hard labor that surrounded being a cowboy.

And today, like every other day, I had chores to get done, and I wanted to get them done before the cooler air moved in this evening. It was only fall, but winter was going to hit hard this year, which meant the cold was going to move in a lot sooner than any of us wanted it to.

"Yeah?" I called over my shoulder as I stepped into the locker room.

"You headed to the ranch after you leave here, or you got time to chill at my place for a while?" he asked.

Reese had moved out of his parents' house as soon as he graduated high school. They didn't get along at all. His parents were very strict Christians, and though they hadn't disowned Reese when he'd come out as bisexual to them, they certainly hadn't made his life easier. In fact, some of the things they did to him to try to "make him straight again" were disgusting, and I never wanted to repeat them.

The only reason he didn't get sent to a conversion camp is that my dad finally had enough and stepped in.

"Headed to the ranch," I told him as I stripped out of my uniform.

He began stripping out of his clothes as well while I grabbed my towel and soap and headed for the shower. "Doesn't showering defeat the purpose?" He chuckled, following me a minute later.

"Eh," I grunted. "I can't stand the feel of dried sweat."

Reese snorted. "Never understood how you've lived and worked on a ranch all your life, and you can't stand the feel of sweat."

"It's the salt," I told him. I really couldn't stand the feel of the salt on my skin after my body dried. It was...gritty and made me feel like I'd been rolling around in the sand on a beach somewhere, which I wasn't too fond of either.

Reese snorted. I finished my shower and quickly dried off before yanking on a pair of well-worn jeans and a t-shirt, throwing on my flannel shirt on top before grabbing my baseball cap out of my locker. It drove my dad nuts that I wouldn't wear a Stetson; a ball cap just worked better for me. If the bill of the hat was getting in my way, I could just flip it backward and continue on with my day.

Couldn't do that with a regular cowboy hat. The brim was always in my way.

"See you later, Reese!" I called over my shoulder as I headed toward the exit.

"Hit me up later," he replied, his shower shutting off. "We'll grab a beer and fries from the bar."

"Sounds good." And it did. I couldn't remember the last time I'd had a chill moment at the bar. Probably my twenty-first birthday. But being twenty-two in my last year of college, trying to juggle one of the hardest years of my college career along with managing my new job as the foreman and football... yeah, it was harder than I thought it would be.

But it was also a challenge, and if there was one thing I really enjoyed and thrived on, it was a challenge.

I yanked open the door to my truck and slid in before grabbing my phone from my pocket and shooting a text to my dad.

On the way. I'll be there soon.

His response was almost immediate, just as it had always been since I'd gotten a phone. Unless he was on a part of the ranch that cell service didn't reach, he *always* responded to my messages. My dad wasn't the kind of man to show his affection through words, unless he was with my mom. But he was very attentive and always made sure I had what I needed.

That was his love language—taking care of people. And it worked for me since I wasn't keen on having anyone dote on me. It just wasn't my thing. I'd always been an independent kind of person, even as a kid. It drove my mom a little nuts.

And it really frustrated any girl I dated. They wanted affection, to be showered with love and touches, and it just wasn't me. Mom thought I just hadn't met the one for me yet. I figured she was just hoping for something that wasn't ever going to happen.

Because another thing about every girl I'd ever dated—they didn't understand that my first love was this ranch. I would never leave this place. I would never move on. My college degree centered around me being able to take over this ranch one day; I was double majoring in agricultural business and management and animal health.

It was one of Dad's stipulations. I had to hold a degree. I just didn't think he ever expected me to double major like I was. But I also knew he was extremely proud of me. I couldn't go anywhere in town without someone congratulating me on something I'd done because Dad had gone out and bragged about me.

I pulled to a stop in front of the house about thirty minutes later and slid out, my boots thumping on the hard-packed dirt. Dad was leading a girl about my age out of the house. She was a bit skinny, her jeans loose on her legs. She was wearing a worn black ball cap on her head, and she looked tired, a hard look twisting her features into a scowl.

Who in the world was she?

"Dad," I strode up, grabbing both of their attention, "who's this?"

Dad smiled down at the girl, but she didn't return it. She just continued staring at me, not even caring that her stare could be considered rude. Immediately, I didn't like her. And if she was looking for work, I'd run her off if she thought she was going to walk around here with a stick up her butt all the time.

"This is Tess Greenwater," Dad introduced. "She's going to work the horse stalls for a while until I see how she pans out."

I clenched my jaw. "As the head foreman, you didn't think you needed to consult me?" I asked Dad, not liking her attitude. She looked like trouble.

Dad grunted. "Not for this, Hunter. Go on inside. Your mother has food ready for you."

I scowled and then spun on my heel, heading into the house. I heard the girl—Tess—scoff behind me.

It took every bit of my willpower not to turn around and put her in my place.

She'd be gone before the end of the week. I'd make sure of it.

two

. . .

Tess

I HATED MY DAD, and I hated my mom.

Honestly, I probably harbored a lot of hate for only being twenty-one, but life had really screwed me over from a young age.

Most people would tell me that hate was a vile thing. That I shouldn't hate others.

But I *hated* them.

Almost every penny I'd ever earned since I started working at sixteen had gone to paying bills. I'd had no choice if I wanted to keep a roof over my head, water running through the pipes in our house, and electricity humming through the wires.

They were addictive people. I'd been born addicted to drugs. I spent my first three years in foster care. My parents got me back once they got out of jail and rehab, the justice system deeming them fit enough to take care of me.

I would have preferred to stay in foster care. Because they never truly got better. They fell right back into those old habits. I'd been fending for myself for so long, I'd forgotten what it had ever felt like to be able to rely on anyone else.

So, I'd saved up money to buy a bus ticket and savings to help me get started in life once I graduated high school and could leave home. But on my graduation day, I'd gone to grab that stash of money and found the lock broken on the safe and every single coin and bill *gone*.

When I'd confronted them, they'd told me I *owed* them. So, they took everything I'd ever saved and told me I'd never see a penny of it. And when I'd fought them on it, my dad had smacked me so hard, I lost my footing, stumbled, and sliced my forehead open all the way through my eyebrow on the coffee table.

I still had that scar, though I usually kept it covered with my hair.

Fear had settled in my heart after that day, and so when my father demanded my paycheck, I just handed it over without a fight. It wasn't worth getting smacked around.

There was never any food in the house, but I thought they'd been keeping up with the bills, at the very least.

Until two weeks ago when I found out someone had paid the taxes off on the house, and since my parents hadn't paid the money back within the time frame given to them, we no longer owned the house and had to leave.

I'd spent the past few years paying off the mortgage on the house, and just like that, it was *gone*.

Which was why I was now here on Blume Ranch, settling into the tiny bunkhouse the owner, Jackson, had put me in. I'd come to him begging for a job, told him I was a quick learner. I didn't know where else to go that could also offer me room and board with the job. Because without this, I was homeless.

Thankfully, his wife had talked him into letting me stay. Now, I just had to prove my worth, or I was homeless. Again.

I sighed and settled my weight on the bed, staring up at the dark ceiling above me.

Tomorrow was another day. I needed to get some rest. Because I had no idea what awaited me when I woke up and sought out the foreman.

I just hoped I didn't have to deal with that cocky guy I'd gone to school with—Jackson's son. Hunter was rude and a goody-two-shoes. In the eye of everyone in town, he could never do any wrong, and high school hadn't been any different.

And he'd been so *rude* earlier.

I'd seen it in his eyes—he wanted to run me off.

A smirk twisted my lips as I closed my eyes.

He could try. But I wasn't so easily shoved around. If Hunter thought he could run me off, he had another thing coming for him.

I was determined to survive, and that kind of fight… Hunter was no match against it. Not when he'd been handed everything in life and had never gone without.

Not like I had.

When my alarm woke me up the next morning, it was still dark outside, and I felt like I'd barely had a wink of sleep. Grunting, I pushed myself into a sitting position before grabbing my phone and shutting the alarm off. I tossed it back onto the mattress afterward. Wasn't like I needed it. The phone had been shut off for three weeks now. The only thing I used it for was the alarm.

With a tired grunt, I slid off the mattress and padded barefoot to the tiny kitchen, sighing when I remembered I didn't have coffee.

Today was going to *suck*. In fact, every morning until I got my first paycheck and could find a ride into town was going to suck. I *hated* not having caffeine. It made me miserable all day.

I walked into the bathroom and splashed water on my face to wake myself up before I brushed my teeth and threw my hair up into a bun on the top of my head. I frowned when my bangs kept falling into my eyes, but I refused to put my bangs up. If I needed to, I'd borrow a pair of scissors and cut them myself, but not having bangs over my fore-head was *not* an option.

People asking about my scar couldn't happen.

I got dressed in a pair of worn, loose jeans, a long-sleeve plain shirt, and a pair of steel-toed boots. When I stepped out of the tiny bunkhouse, the sky was just beginning to lighten, and cowboys were already pouring out of the main bunkhouse, heading out to do their jobs.

A figure emerged from the shadows, making me jump back in fright, my heart lurching into my throat. Hunter's face eventually became visible to me, though his face was still mostly shadowed beneath his ball cap.

"Can I help you?" I asked him.

"You plan on staring at the scenery all morning, or are you planning to work?" he asked me before he took a sip of the coffee in his hand.

I gritted my teeth and walked off the porch, coming to stand in front of him. "I guess I get to answer to you today?" Yippee. Just what I needed. No coffee and now Mr.-I-Can-Do-No-Wrong ordering me around.

He nodded, scrutinizing me. "I don't know why my dad hired you. You're too skinny for this kind of work."

I ground my teeth together, barely resisting the urge to slap him. He had no idea what I was capable of. Not all of us got three meals a day. "I'm plenty capable, thank you," I snipped. "Are you going to put me to work, or are you just going to insult me all morning?"

He scowled. "I don't like you."

I snorted. "Feeling is very much mutual, I assure you," I retorted, my hackles rising. Then, I turned and stomped off, ignoring him when he called my name.

"Tess!" he called again. "You don't even know what you're supposed to be doing today."

I flipped him the middle finger over my shoulder. "I'm going to find the owner. Maybe he won't be such a prick," I called back, stomping up to the main house.

Someone needed to smack Hunter Blume back into his place, and if that boy wasn't careful, it was going to be me.

three

· · ·

Hunter

I GRUNTED, sweat running down my temples. Coach was pushing us extra hard today, trying to get us prepped for our upcoming first game. And I was exhausted. One look around at the other team members showed I wasn't the only one.

Coach blew his whistle, drawing everyone's attention to him. "Alright, that's a wrap!" he called. "Go shower. You stink."

I snorted. Of course, we stunk. It was hot outside. We were all sweating. What did he expect?

I headed into the locker room and stripped out of my uniform before snatching up my towel and heading to the showers. "You working today?"

Reese asked me as he stepped into the shower beside me.

"Nah. Got today off." I began to lather myself up. "Why? What's on your mind?"

"You feel like heading to Ray's and grabbing a bite to eat? I'm really feeling like a milkshake."

I snorted. Reese had an obsession with milkshakes. I never understood it, and I had no idea where he put all the junk he ingested into his body. "When don't you want milkshakes, Reese?" I asked him. It could be below freezing outside, and if someone offered to get him a milkshake, he'd snag it in a heartbeat. He had an unhealthy obsession with them.

"Ugh. Screw off, Hunter."

I barked out a laugh, shaking my head. "Yeah, I'll join you for burgers and shakes. You coming to the ranch after? We can chill out and play some video games. I'm sure Mom's cooking tonight." She and Dad alternated, and I was pretty sure she would be the one cooking, and then they'd both cook tomorrow for the Sunday ranch meal that all of the ranch hands were invited to. It was their regular routine—had been even before I was born.

"Yes!" he cheered. I laughed. "No offense to your dad, but your mom's cooking is the *best*."

I laughed. "He won't take offense. He tells her himself all the time." It wasn't a lie. Honestly, if I wasn't so jealous of the love they shared, always so happy even when they were arguing, their marriage might've made me sick.

I rinsed off and stepped out of the shower. Once I was dressed, I gathered up my uniform, already thinking of a way I could sweet-talk my mom into washing it for me. I *hated* doing laundry.

Yeah—probably wouldn't happen. Mom and Dad were big on responsibility, which meant I'd end up washing my own uniform. I sighed.

I loved my parents, but man, some leniency would be nice sometimes.

But then again, leniency hadn't made me into the man I was becoming.

———

Reese pointed a fry at me. "Wait—your dad hired a girl? *A girl?*" he asked incredulously, his eyes almost bugging out of my head.

I nodded. I was as surprised as he was. And she was rude and stuck-up on top of that, which wasn't something my parents normally put up with. And the other day, she'd gone to my dad alright. But she didn't get what I was sure she'd been looking for from it. Sure, he put her to work in the barn, but he'd calmly spoken to me about her and told me to be a bit gentle with her.

I hadn't gotten the chewing out she'd been hoping I would get. I'd found her stewing about it later that day. It'd cheered me up a bit because I certainly wasn't happy that Dad was taking it easy on some random girl with an attitude problem.

"She's disgustingly rude," I told him. "The moment she opened her mouth, I knew she was trouble. But my parents don't seem to see it."

"And you said she's around our age?" Reese asked with a frown. "Wonder why we don't know her. Does she sound like she's from around here?"

I nodded. "Definitely. But her face doesn't ring a bell for me. Then again, with how off-putting she is, it makes sense. I tended to avoid the trouble-making crowd. No doubt she was one of them."

Reese grunted. "I don't think you should make assumptions," he told me. "If she's on the ranch, seeking room and board, too, then maybe she's troubled instead of being a troublemaker."

I snorted. "Doubt it," I told him. "You haven't met her yet."

He shrugged. "I'm sure I'll meet her when we go out to the ranch in a bit." He squinted at me. "You know, you can be rude and grumpy, too, Hunter."

I snorted. "Yeah, but at least I know I'm doing it and can own up to it. She can't, and she won't."

He rolled his eyes. "Let me guess, when she got snippy with you, you got snippy right back."

I shot him a disgusted look. "I don't get *snippy*."

He grinned, amused at my irritation with him. "You just got snippy right then."

I threw a fry at him. "Shut up and eat, Reese. I'm done talking about her."

But I couldn't get what he'd said out of my head. What if she really was troubled and not part of any kind of bad crowd at all?

What if I'd been reading her wrong all this time?

I scratched my jaw. That thought didn't settle well with me, and I didn't like the guilty feeling it left in the pit of my stomach.

———

Reese picked up another rock and threw it down the drive. We were laying on our backs on the grass, our bellies full from my mom's amazing cooking, admiring the stars glinting in the clear sky.

I'd never trade this for the city. Never. My soul was *here*. It was fed by nature, by the moon, by the stars, by the sun rising and falling in the sky.

"Dad's been hounding me about going to a better college," Reese suddenly said out of nowhere.

I frowned, not liking where this was going. Reese's dad was a jerk. "Your dad needs to stop shoving his own dreams on you."

Reese shrugged. "I'm used to it. Just a bit tiring to keep having the same conversation over and over."

Boots crunching over the gravel reached my ears, halting our conversation. We both sat up, and Reese frowned at the sight of Tess making her way up the drive, her hands shoved in the pockets of her loose-fitting jeans.

"Jesus. Does she eat?" he whispered.

"You need a lesson in whispering," she said, clearly able to hear him and calling him out on it.

He stood up and held a hand out to her. "Reese Warren. You are?"

She eyed his hand for a moment before tentatively reaching out to shake it. The moment their hands connected, an emotion I had never felt before reared its ugly head.

Jealousy.

I was *jealous* that she was being civil with him.

What was wrong with me?

"Tess Greenwater," she told him.

His eyes widened. "Holy crap. You're the girl who punched Deacon in the face because he was making fun of a freshman."

She shrugged, not the least bit bothered by him knowing her. "That'd be me."

My eyes widened, and I quickly stood from the ground. "That was *you*?" I asked incredulously. Deacon was a bully that liked to pick on those smaller than him. I had never been able to catch him in action before—he was always careful to make sure only those smaller than him were around when he decided to bully someone. And obviously, he'd picked the wrong one to be around when he did it. She broke his nose. It was never the same since.

She scowled at me. "That's what I just said, wasn't it?"

Reese coughed a laugh into his hand. I shot him a dirty look. He just grinned before looking back at Tess. "You got him good, girly. Got the swing of a grown man. I like that."

She rolled her eyes at him, but Reese wasn't deterred. "If you're flirting," she told him bluntly, "I'm not interested."

He grinned at her. "I'm a flirt. Ignore me. It's like my first language."

I gritted my teeth, that jealousy in me turning greener and bigger, and looked at Tess. "Why aren't you in the bunkhouse?"

Reese jabbed his elbow into my side, frowning at me. The calm look that had been gracing her pretty features twisted into a sneer before she turned on her heel and stormed off.

Crap.

I scrubbed a hand down my face.

"What the hell, dude?" Reese asked me, throwing his hands up in the air in exasperation. "What was that for?"

I sighed and laid back in the grass again, choosing not to answer because honestly, I didn't *have* an answer.

Well, I did. But it wasn't one I was willing to speak out loud.

Why in the world was I jealous of Reese getting along with Tess? I didn't even *like* her.

four

. . .

Hunter

I KISSED my mom on the cheek, accepting the cup of coffee she held out to me. It was still dark outside, but within a few minutes, the sky would slowly begin to lighten, turning it beautiful shades of pink, gold, and purple, which meant it was almost time to get started with our morning.

With it being Sunday, we didn't normally do a full day of work. We just did enough to make sure the animals were taken care of. Then, it was a chill-out day until it was time for all of the ranch hands to come up to the big house for a family dinner of sorts.

"Thanks, Mom."

She smiled at me. Dad came down the stairs a moment later, and I headed outside, not wanting to see them together like that. I loved that my parents were so in love with each other, but that didn't mean I wanted to witness what he might be doing to her in that kitchen.

They could be absolutely disgusting sometimes.

I saw Tess make her way out of the tiny bunkhouse she was staying in, heading toward the horse stables. I sighed. I owed her an apology for yesterday...and all the other days that I was rude and harsh to her.

After Reese left last night, all I'd thought about was what he'd said—that maybe she wasn't a troublemaker. Maybe she really was just *troubled*. And that made me feel like a royal jerk. Because who was I to judge her when I didn't know a single thing about her? And who could fault her for judging me when I hadn't given her any reason to think of me in a better light?

I was a foreman, the son of the ranch owner. I should have behaved professionally, and instead, I'd lashed out at her the moment I laid my eyes on her.

And that wasn't okay.

Dad stepped outside, the front door quietly shutting behind him. He easily followed my gaze. He hummed. "Girl like that isn't tamed, Hunter," he told me. "She's not a horse. She's not going to follow your every command just because we're giving her room and board and food in her stomach."

I sighed. "I screwed up."

He chuckled before taking a sip of his coffee. "Oh, yeah, you did. But the good thing is that you can remedy that by apologizing and making an effort with her. Been there, done that. So, I know it's possible. But that doesn't mean it's going to be easy, Hunter. You haven't shown her an ounce of kindness since she's been here."

My frown deepened. Not knowing how to respond to what he said, I finished the rest of my coffee and headed inside to rinse it out and put it in the dishwasher before heading back outside. Dad was already on his way to the barn to grab a tractor, more than likely to drop some hay in the fields for the cows.

I headed in the direction of the horse stables, hoping Tess was in there. She'd been heading that way, but she could have changed course while I was inside.

When I stepped into the stables, she was leading Mercy out of her stable. I silently watched as she petted Mercy's neck before tying her up to make sure she couldn't run off. Mercy wasn't very docile. Only certain people could get close to her. And it spoke volumes that Mercy allowed Tess close. Some days, Mercy didn't even let me near.

I cleared my throat, drawing Tess's eyes to me. She arched a brow at me, her expression immediately closing off from me, not letting me read her. Well, that was my own fault. I'd dug this hole, and now I had to figure out how to climb out of it.

"I, um, I came to apologize," I told her, pushing off the stable wall and slowly making my way to her. I shoved my hands into the pockets of my jeans. Her stare was a bit unnerving, to be honest, and it was making me nervous.

"Apologize?" she asked, her other brow coming up level with the one she'd originally arched. "Do you even know what you're apologizing for, Hunter?" she demanded to know.

I rubbed the back of my neck. I was one hundred percent out of my depths here, but I was trying. I had to. "I'm sorry for being so rude and cold to you when you first showed up on the ranch. I'm sorry for not making you feel more welcome, and I'm sorry for judging you without knowing you first. I'm sorry for my extremely rude behavior last night. I also apologize for how I treated you the other morning when I was coming to show you what your job duties would be."

She hummed and grabbed a shovel to begin mucking the stalls. "I accept your apologies, Hunter, but I don't forgive you. I don't forgive easily—ever."

I nodded. I could understand that. Couldn't fault her for it, either. I'd been a grade-A jerk to her. "Can we start over?" I asked her. "I know that might be bold of me to ask, but I'd like to do that— if you want."

She stood up to her full height, leaning on the shovel. She ran those unnerving eyes of hers over me. I didn't understand how someone my age could be so cold and guarded, and it was only cementing what Reese said. She was definitely troubled, and I didn't like it. I didn't like that someone had made her feel like the world was against her.

"Start over," she finally said, like she was tasting the words on her tongue, mulling it over, trying to decide if she liked them. Finally, she sighed, nodding her head. "Yeah, I guess we can start over." A tentative smile tilted my lips. She narrowed her eyes at me. "But if you screw up again, Hunter, there won't be a second chance, you hear me? I don't give those out."

I quickly nodded. "I understand. One hundred percent," I promised her.

She nodded and turned back to mucking out the stalls. I watched her, not wanting to leave her presence yet. Something about her just drew me in. I was riveted. And though some part of me was telling me that staring this much was rude, I couldn't help myself.

She scowled at me over her shoulder. "My back is going to have holes in it here in a minute," she said. I grinned. She was full of fire, and I was quickly becoming addicted. "Don't you have work to do?"

"Will you come up to the big house today and eat dinner with all of us?" I asked her. She blinked at me. "It's something everyone on the ranch does every Sunday," I quickly added when I saw the scowl on her face deepening.

I needed to tread carefully with her. She read too much into everything, and if I wasn't careful, my big mouth would ruin everything before it'd even started.

She sighed. "Yeah, but if you don't leave me alone so I can work, I'll still be trying to get chores done by the time dinner rolls around."

I grinned and tipped my ball cap in her direction, deciding to leave before I got captivated by her again. "I'll see you at five then, Tess."

Then, I left the stables, unable to get the huge grin off my face. Couldn't have even if I tried.

And honestly, I wasn't all that sure I wanted to wipe it off anyway.

five

. . .

Tess

WHAT DID a girl wear to a dinner like this?

I frowned at my stained jeans and my faded flannel. It would have to do because I didn't have anything better. I sure didn't own a dress—wasn't my style. And every other piece of clothing I owned, I worked in.

I pulled my hair up into a ponytail, sighing when I realized I had to pull my bangs back. They were too long, and I didn't have scissors to cut them myself.

Hopefully, my hat would cover it enough until I could get into town to get my hair cut or get my hands on a pair of scissors.

I fitted my ball cap on my head and then shoved my feet into my boots before walking out of the small bunkhouse, heading up to the big house. All of the other ranch hands were already sitting themselves at the table when I got there.

"Hat off and then go wash up," Jackson commanded, pointing to a door. I was assuming it was the bathroom.

But I was stuck on the hat off order. Fear of everyone staring and piecing together what happened left me frozen.

"I, um—"

"Hat off," he sternly said. "Wife's rules, and everyone will follow them if I have to."

I'd have found what he said funny in any other situation, but my scar was about to be visible. There was nothing amusing about that.

I swallowed thickly and slowly tugged my hat off. His eyes zeroed in on the scar on my forehead, his jaw clenching. But thankfully, he didn't ask any questions—just nodded once and walked into the kitchen. Hunter walked out, smiling when he laid his on me.

That smile faltered when he saw the scar slicing through my eyebrow.

"What happened?" he softly asked me, concern leaking into his tone.

"Nothing," I mumbled. Then, I quickly retreated into the bathroom to wash my hands. I avoided Hunter on my way to the table, though I could feel his eyes on me. Reese grinned at me, his eyes flickering over my scar. But he didn't linger. I relaxed a little. Maybe everyone else would pretend my scar didn't exist, too.

"First big family feast?" he asked me.

I nodded as Jackson and his wife, Ashley, sat down. Ashley smiled kindly at me, and I forced a smile to my lips in return. She didn't even flick a look toward my scar.

"Alright, ladies first," Jackson announced.

Ashley stood and began to make her plate, gesturing for me to follow her. When we were by the buffet table, she leaned in close to me. "If you want, I can cut your bangs before you leave tonight," she whispered.

I looked up at her. So, she *had* noticed. She was just more discreet than the men. "Really?"

She nodded, beginning to make her plate. I did the same. "Want to know a secret?" she asked. I looked over at her, half curious and half suspicious. She nodded her head toward her leg. "Half of my leg comes off at night." My jaw almost dropped open, but I had the decency to catch myself. "So, I know all about scars, Tess. I like to keep mine covered, too."

I swallowed thickly, suddenly overcome with emotion. She got it, and she didn't ask questions. I was more thankful for that than she would ever know.

"I'd love to have my bangs cut," I told her quietly.

She nodded. "Good. Stick around and help clean up, and you've got yourself a deal."

I smiled and returned to the table with my full plate of food. Chatter filled the large dining room once everyone had plates piled high in front of them. I stayed quiet, just listening to Hunter and Reese banter back and forth and Hunter talk about football and how school was going.

And I realized I really liked it here.

Before I even realized it, I found myself wishing I would never have to leave.

And those were dangerous wishes to be having. Because all good things eventually came to an end. That was just the way of life.

"Tess, wait!" I heard Hunter call from behind me as I began making my way back to the bunkhouse. My bangs were cut and now hanging over my forehead again, covering my scar. Now that the ugly, visual part of my past was hidden, I felt like I could breathe normally again.

Which was why I turned around and arched a brow at him in the dimming light. "What?" I asked, watching as he fit his hat on his head.

He scratched the back of his neck, a nervous tick of his that I'd picked up on. "Will you go on a ride with me? I need to check the, um, fences real quick on the river side to make sure nothing got missed. Won't take long," he assured me.

I shrugged. "Sure. I'll ride."

He grinned, and I realized I *really* liked his smile. Sure, Hunter was extremely handsome, but when he smiled, he was *gorgeous*. It was unfair, really. It made it harder for me to keep my guard up around him now that we weren't fighting constantly and he was making an effort to be friends with me.

"I want to apologize for staring at your scar and prying into your business," he said softly as we led Mercy and his horse, Q, out of the stables. I quickly mounted Mercy, patting her neck and crooning to her for giving me no problems.

"It's fine," I told him. "I'm not stupid enough to think people won't wonder why I've got a scar."

He sighed. "I don't like that you were ever in a situation to get one like that," he confessed, glancing over at me as he grabbed Q's reins. "Because it didn't come from a stupid accident, did it, Tess?"

I stared at him, my heart racing in my chest. My hands shook, and I tightened my hold on Mercy's reins. Finally ripping my gaze from his, I looked out over the field. "No," I whispered. "It wasn't a stupid accident."

Hunter sighed. "I wish it had been, Tess."

I swallowed thickly. "I do, too, Hunter."

He brought Q closer to me as we made our way over to the fence. Surprising me, he grabbed Mercy's reins, bringing us to a stop. I swung my head over to look at him, surprised to find his face so close to mine.

Now, my heart was racing for an entirely different reason.

"I know we barely know each other," he said softly, his voice husky, "but I really want to kiss you. Can I kiss you, Tess?"

I licked my lips, my chest tightening with anxiety. Blowing out a very slow, soft breath, I finally nodded, closing my eyes. Softly groaning, he leaned closer and pressed his lips to mine in a soft, quick kiss. And though our kiss was nothing more than a mere peck on the lips, my heart was on the verge of pounding right out of my chest and into his hands.

"I've got one more question," he said, making me open my eyes. He hadn't really moved back—only enough to make sure our lips weren't touching anymore. "Will you come to my game this Saturday?"

I smirked at him. "Give me a better kiss," I teased, feeling pretty bold, "and we'll see."

His eyes darkened, and he gripped the side of my neck, covering my lips with his in a hotter, deeper kiss that had me gasping into his mouth in surprise.

Oh, I *definitely* got a better kiss.

Good freaking Lord.

He pulled back a minute later. My lips were swollen, and I knew my face was flushed red. He wasn't in much of a better state than me. "So, that game?" he asked, sounding a little winded.

I just dumbly nodded my head, at a loss for words.

six
. . .

Tess

I STEPPED out of the bunkhouse, breathing in the cool morning air, loving the way it sort of chilled my lungs. It was cool enough to need a sweatshirt but not so cold yet that I needed an actual jacket. Fall was my favorite time of year, and it was finally beginning to feel like it here. Before long, snow would be falling, coating the world in white.

I readjusted the hat on my head before clomping down the stairs and heading toward the barn to begin my morning chores. Yesterday, Jackson told me he'd need me in the fields, checking fence lines at nine. So, I had three hours to get the horse stalls cleaned and get the horses fed and groomed. If I worked fast and stayed focused, I'd have it all done in just enough time.

We had a storm rolling in around midnight, and it might be a nasty one. So, I understood the need for all hands on deck, especially since everyone on the ranch normally headed to the college on Saturday nights for the football game when they were playing at home.

My cheeks burned when I remembered Hunter wanted me there. He'd specifically asked me to come. And every day since then, he'd been going out of his way to spend time with me—bringing me dinner to the bunkhouse and eating with me, asking me to go riding with him, or even just talking to me early in the mornings while I worked before he had to head to school for his morning classes.

He was completely different from the jerk I'd met the day I'd been hired, and I still wasn't sure how I felt about it. I didn't trust easily anymore—not after my parents had let me down so easily. And while I knew actions spoke a lot louder than words, I was still a little wary of Hunter. I knew he could sense it, but he never let it deter him.

"Morning," Hunter gruffly greeted me when he stepped into the barn around seven A.M. It was a little later than I was used to seeing him. I looked at him over my shoulder, laughing a little. He looked ready to dunk his face in the thermos of coffee he was holding. Reese was standing next to him and didn't look much better.

"Well, what are you waiting for?" Jackson boomed, surprising me and making me jump, my hand tightening around the shovel. Even a couple of the horses stamped their feet in irritation. Hunter and Reese both winced. "Help her out. Your mom's still upset that you two drank her favorite whiskey."

I snickered, turning back to do my job. Jackson leaned over the stall I was working in, nodding his head, a pleased gleam in his eyes. "Girly, you do a better job than half these men around here. Don't forget about nine. And grab whatever horse you're comfortable riding."

I nodded. "Will do."

He tipped his hat at me and walked off, but then he stopped at the entrance of the stables, looking at me over his shoulder. "If these two dimwits slack off, go get Ashley," he ordered. "They're both on punishment."

Unable to hold back my laugh, I nodded, snickering. He walked out. I looked at Hunter and Reese. "Party too hard?"

Hunter nodded, looking a little green. "Normally they don't care, but we drank Mom's brand new whiskey she had specially imported." He groaned. "I think I'm going to throw up."

"Don't you dare," I hissed. "If you throw up, I'm going to."

Reese chuckled and then groaned, reaching up to clutch his head. "God, I'm never drinking again."

I smirked and turned back to what I was doing. "Well, don't stand there all day," I said. "Grab a shovel and get to work. Stalls won't clean themselves."

"Bossy. I like it," Hunter teased. And then, a moment later, I heard him run outside. I plugged my ears so I wouldn't hear him throw up.

———

Football here was *wild*. And it was even wilder with every member of the Blume ranch and their families in the stands, yelling for Hunter and Reese. Cowbells were clanging around me, and someone even had a stupid bullhorn that I was ready to break. I was sitting beside Ashley, and I was pretty sure she was the most enthusiastic out of the entire small crowd surrounding us.

"Go!" Ashley yelled, lurching from her seat. I looked out at the field. Hunter had the ball, and he was rushing toward the touchdown line. The clock was quickly counting down, and he was running for all he was worth.

I stood up, screaming for him at the top of my lungs, my heart in my throat. Ashley grabbed my hand tightly in hers, bouncing on her feet as Hunter drew nearer and nearer to the touchdown line.

Right before the clock buzzed, Hunter crossed the line, scoring the touchdown that was needed to win the game. We all screamed, and for the first time that night, I didn't care about the cowbells or that stupid bullhorn.

Hunter's family and the ranch hands stormed the field. I hung back near the fence, smiling at Hunter and Reese as they got swarmed in hugs and congratulations. It felt like a moment I shouldn't intrude on. I had to admit though, they'd played their hearts out tonight. That game hadn't been easy by any means.

I watched as Hunter scanned the crowd surrounding him, a frown pulling at his lips a moment later. I frowned as well. What had him so upset? He should be ecstatic. He just scored an unbelievable touchdown. He was the reason his team won the football game.

Then, his eyes landed on me, and he separated himself from the crowd, making his way in my direction. I stood a little straighter, nervous now that his attention was solely focused on me and his family was watching us. His hair was a matted, sweaty mess on his head, and sweat was running down his temples. "You came," he breathed.

I shrugged. "You asked me to."

He chuckled. "Didn't mean you were going to. You do whatever you want without a care for how anyone else feels about it, Tess. It's one of the things I really like about you."

I shrugged, ignoring the blush staining my cheeks. "If you don't do what makes you happy, what's the point of living?"

He grinned and then stepped closer. I gasped when he clasped my upper arms, tugging me forward until I fell against him.

"Yeah, what's the point?" he whispered.

Then, his lips covered mine.

seven

· · ·

Hunter

I *STILL* COULDN'T BELIEVE I'd kissed Tess *twice.*

Both times had been a spur-of-the-moment thing, yet it was one of the best kisses I'd ever had in my life, especially the one after my game. I hadn't even cared that everyone was watching. I selfishly staked a claim on her.

A day later with the sun shining down on my face and the cool wind beating against my hoodie, I still couldn't get it out of my head.

I was so done for. So hooked on her. Reese had been giving me crap since it happened, and I couldn't even bring myself to care.

I was practically floating.

I took a sip of my coffee and headed toward the stables. I'd gotten a late start this morning, but it was allowed on Sundays. Now that I was up and a little caffeinated, I couldn't wait a second longer to see Tess. And knowing her, she'd already be in the stables, mucking stalls and brushing the horses.

She didn't slack off for anything. Dad was right; she was one of the hardest-working people we had on this ranch—a valuable asset. And one of these days, I was going to be lucky enough to vocally announce her as mine.

When I stepped into the stables, I was surprised to see Tess angrily shoveling out one of the stalls. Her face was twisted into a snarl. She was so preoccupied with her anger and trying to work it out of herself that she hadn't even bothered making sure her hat and hair covered her entire scar.

I hated that scar. Not because it made her ugly. In fact, it added a beautiful ruggedness to her that was riveting.

No, I hated it because it meant someone had hurt her. And I didn't like that.

"Tess," I called softly. I felt like I was dealing with a wild horse, like one wrong move or sound might make it kick me in the face or rear back. And though Tess was definitely not an animal, she related to these horses more than I'm sure she'd like to admit. Even my mom did. There was a wildness inside of Tess that would never be tamed.

"What?" she bit out, standing up straight to face me, an angry snarl twisting her lips. "I'm not in the mood for your crap today, Hunter."

I set my coffee down. She was trying to drive me away, but I wasn't going to let her. Something was wrong, and I couldn't fix it until she opened up to me.

"You want to tell me what's going on?" I asked, bravely taking a step closer, though there was still numerous feet of space between us.

"No," she sneered before turning back to shoveling. "Now go away."

I shook my head though she wasn't looking at me. "Not happening, sweetheart." The term of endearment just slipped from my lips, but I knew it was the right thing to say when her hands tightened around the shovel, a conflicted look passing over her pretty features. "What's going on, Tess? I can't help you if I don't know what's going on."

"You can't help with this," she snapped. "You've always had perfect parents. The perfect life. People who care about you. Just screw off, Hunter. There's nothing someone like you can do."

Any other person probably would have taken offense to her words, but not me. Not after I'd seen how she could smile when someone stuck around and proved they cared. Not when I'd seen her come to my game, looking uncomfortable most of the time, but still staying because I'd asked her, because I'd *wanted* her there.

Tess was starved for attention, for affection, for love. And I wasn't letting her shove me away when she needed me the most. I wasn't letting her self-destruct and destroy everything I was trying to build with her.

"Try me," I told her.

She stood up straight again and narrowed her eyes at me. "Hunter—"

I hadn't even realized I'd been slowly walking closer to her until I leaned my arms on the top of the stable. From my position, I could smell the sweat clinging to her skin, as well as the scent of lavender. On anyone else, it might've smelled a bit disgusting. But on her, it was just...addicting.

"Don't," I calmly warned her. "Just talk to me, sweetheart." Her eyes flickered away from me when I called her that name again. "I'm not walking away. Just let me help. And if it's not something I can fix, I guarantee you, I know people who can."

She shook her head. "My problems aren't anyone else's."

I snatched the shovel from her hands when she tried to get back to work. I tossed it behind me, watching as she planted her hands on her hips, anger simmering in her eyes. The shovel clanged when it hit the ground, spooking the horses. "You're a part of this ranch now, Tess. That means you're family. And *no one* here turns their back on family. You can try to be secretive all you want, sweetheart, but I promise, someone will find out what's going on with you sooner rather than later."

She gnawed on her bottom lip, her eyes running over my face. I saw the moment she made her decision. Her shoulders drooped, and her mask fell away, revealing so much hurt, it felt like she'd ripped a hole inside of my chest.

"My dad came by the ranch early this morning." I frowned at her, not understanding why that was a bad thing but figuring I'd understand in a moment. "He wanted money."

I clenched my jaw. She'd *just* gotten her first paycheck, and since she didn't even work a full week yet, I knew she hadn't earned much.

"Does he have money problems?" I asked her.

She sighed, looking so much older than just twenty-one. Leaning against the other wall, she crossed her arms over her chest, like it might protect her from some memories. "It's a long story, Hunter."

"I've got time, sweetheart."

She sighed, kicking at the straw with her boot. "My parents are addicts." She looked around her, pausing for a moment. "I was born addicted to drugs. Got thrown into foster care. And I would have preferred to stay there, but the state eventually deemed them fit to be parents again and forgot all about me."

I stayed silent, letting her slowly get it all off her chest. "When I was sixteen and old enough to get a job, all of my money went to paying bills. My parents threw both of their disability checks at beer, liquor, cigarettes, drugs—nothing to help me keep a roof over our heads, water running through the pipes, or electricity in the house."

Christ.

"I finally got smart, realized my parents weren't going to get any better, and began saving up every extra penny I had so I could get out on my graduation night. I was going to buy a bus ticket and just go somewhere. Didn't know where but anywhere felt better than there."

"What happened?" I prompted her when she didn't continue. *What happened to make her end up back here?*

She blew out a soft breath. "I came home on grad night to find the lock on my safe busted and every penny I'd managed to save gone. I got the scar on my forehead from my dad." Rage burned through me—hot like lava. Potent. "They said I *owed* them. And when I fought them on it, he smacked me so hard, I lost my footing and hit the corner of the coffee table."

My hands tightened into fists on top of the stable wall.

She looked up at me. "I left as soon as I could get away, as soon as I felt like I could get somewhere they couldn't find me. I had no money to my name, and I'd seen an ad while grocery shopping that your dad needed some help. And I figured the last place my dad would expect me to be was here."

"Yet he found you anyway," I said quietly.

She nodded. "Yeah." A tired sigh slipped past her lips. "He found me. And he's threatening me if I don't give him what I have."

I growled. "No. Not happening."

She looked at me. "What are you going to do to stop him, Hunter? Trap me on this ranch forever?"

I shook my head, pushing off the wooden wall. "I can't fix this, Tess—not by myself. But everyone on this ranch is family," I reminded her.

"Hunter—"

I was already leaving the stables, pretending not to hear her shouting my name. She wasn't talking me out of this. She may be family to everyone else, but she was *mine*. My future. And I wasn't letting *anyone* harm her ever again.

eight

. . .

Hunter

I WAS FURIOUS. Who could do that to a girl, much less their own daughter? I knew it bothered Tess. She tried to put up a strong, angry front about it, but there was a deep sadness in her eyes that she couldn't hide.

I *hated* that someone touched her. I was vibrating with it. What had she ever done in this world to deserve such hateful, cruel parents?

I stormed up the steps of the house. I knew Tess would be furious with me about this. She'd trusted me enough to tell me, and right away, I was going to tell someone else. But I was falling in love with her, and if her dad was bothering her, I was going to make sure he couldn't do it ever again.

She could be furious with me all she wanted. I'd gladly accept her rage if it meant she was safe.

Her safety was paramount—the only priority in my mind.

"Hunter?" Mom asked. She set down her book, her frown deepening when she saw the fury in my eyes. Quickly, she stood to her feet. "Son, what's going on?"

"Where's Dad?" I asked her.

"In his office—"

I stormed off in that direction, not even bothering to knock before I swung open his office door. He looked up from his computer with a scowl before the look softened when he realized it was just me.

"Ever heard of knocking?" he asked me in a patient tone.

"This is too important," his eyebrows arched onto his forehead. "We have a problem. It's Tess."

Dad sighed and leaned back in his chair, rubbing at his temple. "Hunter, if you're in here because you two had a fight—"

"Her dad came to see her."

Mom shut the office door at that, crossing her arms over her chest. Dad sat forward in his chair, his eyes narrowed at me. "The way you just said that doesn't sound like a good thing," Mom finally said, breaking the tense silence.

"It's not," I growled. "That scar on her forehead? It's because of him. He took all the money she had saved so she could leave after graduation, and when she confronted him about it, he smacked her so hard, she fell, hitting her head on the coffee table."

Dad jerked up from his chair, his jaw tightening. "And you said he came to visit her?"

I nodded once.

"Why?" Mom asked. "Did Tess say why?"

I tore my hat off my head and shoved my fingers through my hair. "He wants money. And Tess said if she doesn't give it to him, there's a real possibility he's going to hurt her."

Dad snatched up his jacket from the back of his chair, shrugging it on. "He won't touch her," he promised me. "Let's go." He grabbed his phone from his pocket. "I'm getting Axel to come with us." I watched as his thumbs quickly moved over the screen. To Mom, he said, "Can you make sure Tess stays on the property?"

"Of course," Mom quickly answered. "I'll keep her distracted."

He nodded once. "Good. Hunter, let's go. He's not touching her ever again."

"You know where he lives?" I asked him.

Dad nodded. "Only place he could live at is her last address. Despite you're previous thinking that I allow just anyone to work on this ranch, I do background checks."

I colored a little, remembering how horrible I'd been to Tess when she first got here. Mom scoffed behind us. "You didn't do one on me."

Dad grinned and stopped in front of the front door, turning to face her. I rolled my eyes and looked away when he gripped the back of her neck and pulled her into a kiss. "Any woman stupid enough to get near that crazy horse like you did didn't need one," he teased.

Mom lightly smacked his chest. "Be careful. Both of you," she added, looking between us. "Do I make myself clear?"

"Yes, ma'am," we both quickly responded.

She hugged me and pressed a kiss to my cheek before stepping back. "I'll have food ready when you get back."

Dad tipped his hat at her before we walked out of the house to go deal with Tess's piece of crap father.

———

Dad banged on the front door. The house reeked of beer and cigarettes. The scent of weed also clung to the air. The yard was overgrown, the weeds knee-high. Glass littered the rotting porch we were standing on, and beer cans decorated the weeds, providing little pops of blue and silver colors.

I couldn't believe Tess had ever lived like this, and I hadn't even seen the inside yet. God, she deserved so much better. Every time I'd been inside her bunk house, it was always sparkling clean, and now it made sense why she kept it that way.

The door swung inward, and a balding man wearing a stained white t-shirt and sweat pants that looked crusted from a lack of washing stared out at us, looking disgruntled and a bit angry. "Who are you?" he sneered.

"I'm Tess's employer," Dad said calmly, his hands in his pockets. "I heard you came onto my ranch unwelcome and bothered one of my employees. I'm just here to warn you that if it happens again, I won't be just bringing a warning." The man's face colored with anger. "I'd advise you to find a job instead of hassling your daughter for money, am I clear? If you *ever* bother her again, instead of me standing here on your porch, it'll be police officers."

The man blanched at the mention of officers. One look around and I knew he wouldn't get off scot-free. The man scowled. "Tell that wh—"

"Finish that sentence," I growled, stepping forward. Uncle Axel put a hand on my shoulder, holding me back from doing something stupid. "I *dare* you."

I had about fifty pounds on Tess's dad and I was quite a few years younger. I could've easily taken him. One look at me and he took a step back. "Girl owes me," he sneered, but it wasn't as strong as the hateful words he'd been ready to spew before I interrupted him.

Dad shook his head. "She owes you nothing. Don't let me get wind of you bothering her again, clear?"

He nodded his head and slammed the door shut. Dad hummed and turned, carefully walking down the rotted steps. We followed behind him.

"Well, that went well," Uncle Axel remarked once we were going down the road, heading back to the ranch.

Dad snickered. "Between us and the mention of cops, I doubt Tess will ever have another problem with him."

I leaned my head back against the headrest, shutting my eyes for a moment, the adrenaline beginning to wear off. "I sure hope not. He messes her up. She was ready to end everything between us because of him."

Uncle Axel squeezed my shoulder from the backseat. "You're a good man for not letting her push you away, Hunter. Woman like her needs that kind of support."

I nodded. I knew that, too. It was why I didn't back down from her. She needed to know there were people in her corner.

The people on Blume Ranch may now be her family, but I was determined to be her man.

———

"What did you do?" Tess yelled as soon as I got out of the truck. She stormed off the porch. Mom was still sitting in the rocker, sipping on a cup of coffee, not at all bothered by Tess's rage.

I caught Tess's arms when she plowed into me, worry and concern etched onto her features. She gripped my jacket, running her eyes over me. "Did he hurt you?"

"Sweetheart," I crooned, drawing her into my arms, "he didn't touch me. I'm okay."

She shuddered in my arms, and I tightened my hold on her. "I've been so worried," she whispered. "You were so *stupid* to go see him like that."

I pressed my lips to the top of her head. "He won't bother you again, sweetheart. We all made sure of that," I promised her.

She shook her head. "I don't care about that. I care about *you*. I'm so *angry* with you right now."

I chuckled, squeezing her a little bit tighter. "Be angry all you want, Tess. I'll take all your anger if it means you're safe."

She huffed. "Stop being sweet. It makes it hard to remain mad."

I barked out a laugh. God, I was addicted to this girl. Lord help me a few years down the line. She already had me wrapped around her little finger.

epilogue

· · ·

Tess

FOUR MONTHS LATER

I WAS on the edge of my seat. It was the last quarter of the game with only a minute left on the clock and a tie on the scoreboard. The guys had made it to the playoffs, and I knew Hunter really wanted this. Heck, I wanted it for him.

It was the first down *again*, and they were so close to the end zone. Ashley was gripping my arm like it was a lifeline, and Jackson hadn't sat down since the fourth quarter started. All of the ranch hands had gathered at the top of the stands to be out of everyone else's view since they couldn't sit down either.

It was nerve-wracking.

"Come on, Hunter," I whispered. He was *so* close. He literally could run the ball if he wanted, but I knew it wasn't that simple. The other team was playing extremely good defense. I knew it could go into overtime, but I wasn't sure if my anxiety could handle even more time being added to the clock.

The clock started again. The ball got hiked to Hunter.

And Hunter ran for it.

Immediately, I was on my feet, screaming at the top of my lungs, my heart in my throat. He plowed through the defensive line, and I winced. I *knew* he was going to be hurting later at the hotel, but I also knew that if he crossed that line and got into the end zone, all of the pain would one hundred percent be worth it.

His foot crossed the line. Then, his other foot.

"Oh, my God!" I yelled, jumping up and down and throwing my arms around Ashley's neck. We were screaming and crying together, both of us so happy for both Hunter and Reese, though mostly Hunter. "They did it! They won!" I screeched.

Hunter and Reese were embracing in the end zone. The entire team was celebrating. Even the rival team was congratulating them on their win, grinning with them.

It was the first time in the school's history that they'd won the championship game. Heck, it was the first time they'd ever even made it to playoffs.

All because two boys decided to stick close to home, to their roots. I knew Hunter and Reese had both gotten huge, major offers from big-name schools, but the ranch meant too much to them both, even if Reese wasn't blood-related to the family.

The big screen above the field suddenly zoomed in on Hunter, drawing my eyes to it since I couldn't make out what he was doing too well. Both teams were sort of swarmed around him.

Then, I saw him opening a small, velvet ring box. Reese was standing behind him, holding up a sign.

Will you marry me, Tess?

"Oh, my God," I sobbed, tears rushing down my cheeks like a waterfall. "He—he—*yes!*" I screamed, running down the stands to the field. I had no doubt those cameras were now on me, focused on the girl running like a crazy woman to her now-fiancé, but I couldn't even care.

"A hundred times yes!" I yelled again as I neared the fence line. Hunter met me there and clasped my face in his hands, pressing his lips to mine in a hard, soul-seeking kiss. My tears were salty on our lips, but neither of us cared. "Yes, I'll marry you," I cried when he finally let me go enough to breathe.

Hunter had taken all of my mood swings in stride. He had never made me feel like crap for having horrible parents. He didn't breathe down my neck, and he let me have my space.

He was everything I could have asked for and more. Sure, we didn't always see eye-to-eye, but at the end of every day, Hunter made sure we never parted on bad terms. He was my soul mate, and I could never ask for anyone better in the world to eventually be my husband.

"I love you," he rasped.

I sniffled. "I love you, too, cowboy. Now, put that ring on my finger."

He huskily laughed and then pulled the small, diamond ring out of its slot before sliding it onto my finger—a perfect fit.

"You're mine now, Tess Greenwater."

I scoffed. "I'm pretty sure I've always been yours, Hunter."

He just grinned and kissed me again while everyone cheered and screamed around us.

Want more of Hunter and Tess?

https://dl.bookfunnel.com/wonbb4mgcx

about the author

If you're looking for happily ever after, you'll find it here.

T. Thomas is a sweet, clean romance author of emotionally gripping books that always end in love and happiness.

She has been writing since she was thirteen years old. She enjoys spending all of her spare time writing, but she absolutely detests editing and proofreading.

T. Thomas can normally be found in her little room of her own that she calls her "woman cave" writing her next book and putting off editing and proofreading for as long as possible.

also by t. thomas

Facebook Group

Facebook Page

Instagram

Twitter

Pinterest

TikTok

Patreon

Keep up to date with new releases, sales, freebies, and preorders by signing up for my newsletter!

Join my newsletter here.

https://thomastbooks.webador.com

Merch store.

Milton Keynes UK
Ingram Content Group UK Ltd.
UKHW041820211123
432980UK00001BB/76

9 798223 094418